I0690374

Secrets to Die For

by

Linda Hope Lee

The Nina Foster Mystery Series,
Book Two

Secrets to Die For

Cover Art by *Kim Mendoza*

The Wild Rose Press, Inc.
PO Box 708
Adams Basin, NY 14410-0708
Visit us at www.thewildrosepress.com

Publishing History
First Crimson Rose Edition, 2020
Print ISBN 978-1-5092-2795-2
Digital ISBN 978-1-5092-2989-5

The Nina Foster Mystery Series, Book Two
Published in the United States of America

Outside, under the canopied entryway, the cold air made Nina shiver. She pulled up her raincoat hood and tied the strings under her chin. Her car was in the south parking lot. The path bordering the lake provided the shortest route. Ducking her head against the onslaught of wind and rain, Nina stepped onto the sidewalk, hurrying past wrought iron chairs and benches and round umbrella tables, their closed umbrellas pointing skyward like miniature spires.

Leaving the building behind, she soon reached the lake path. Underneath tall yard lights, the wet asphalt resembled a silver ribbon. Wisps of fog rose from the water and drifted toward the shore. A cold mist enveloped her, and raindrops collected on her cheeks, her nose, her eyelashes, and her chin. Nina shivered and bent her head against the wind.

Her thoughts turned to Stephen and their upcoming dinner date. What should she wear? Something romantic, Jessica said. Her black dress? No, too fancy. Her blue silk slacks outfit? No, the pant legs would get soaked in the rain—unless she wrapped herself completely in plastic. Hmm, not a bad idea...

A dog's sharp "yip" interrupted her musings. Nina looked up to see Ellie Larkin and Nigel heading toward her. Heavens, why were they still outside? Hadn't she and Jessica watched them return to Marley?

The dog barked again, but his bushy tail, sticking up from behind the yellow coat, wagged cheerily.

"Hello, Ellie." Nina greeted the woman when they were within speaking distance.

Ellie stared blankly from the depths of her hood.

A chill skittered down Nina's spine. Was Ellie having one of the spells Jessica mentioned?

Praise for Linda Hope Lee

"A modern western, packed with secrets, intrigue, and old-fashioned romance, *FINDING SARA* is a story that won't be forgotten."

~*Joanne Hall, Writers and Readers of Distinctive Fiction*

~*~

"*LOVING ROSE* is a sweet, heartwarming read that will tug at your heartstrings."

~*Melissa, Sizzlinghotbookreviews.net*

~*~

"Lee provides readers with emotional drama and puzzling suspense. *DARK MEMORIES* churns with guilt, passion, and intrigue."

~*Romantic Times*

~*~

"A mystery with a slew of suspects and a saucy, fun romance made MURDER BETWEEN THE PAGES a delightful read."

~*Laura, FUONLY KNEW Blog*

Dedication

To Pearl

Chapter One

"Do you think the rain will ever stop?" Nina Foster gazed out the first floor window of the soon-to-be created library at Marley Manor, Richmond, Washington's exclusive retirement community.

"We live in the Northwest, my dear." Jessica Bingham, Nina's grandmother and a Marley resident, looked up from unpacking a box of books. "And it's January. You know what we always say around here— better rain than snow."

As the town's managing librarian, Nina was using her expertise to establish Marley's library. Today, in the initial stages of the project, she and Jessica sorted the donated books, stacking them on several long tables in the center of the room.

Nina was about to turn away from the window and continue her work when something caught her eye. Leaning closer, she made out a person in a yellow hooded slicker trudging along the path bordering Lake Mead, which provided much of the home's setting. Alongside the figure trotted a small white dog wearing a matching yellow raincoat. "Someone is out walking a dog in this storm."

Jessica came to stand beside her. "That's Ellie Larkin and her Pomeranian, Nigel. You've met her, Nina. She and I are good friends."

"I remember Ellie." The image of a tall, bony

woman with iron-gray hair popped into Nina's mind. "Why are she and Nigel walking in this miserable weather?" She hugged her arms. "Couldn't she put him outside for a couple minutes if he had to go?"

"Ellie walks her dog every day around this time, rain or shine." Jessica looked at her wristwatch. "Yep, four-thirty. You could set your watch by them." She frowned. "I've been worried about Ellie lately."

"Why?" She turned to Jessica, neatly dressed, as usual, in brown slacks and a rust-colored sweater that complemented her strawberry blonde hair.

"Because she's often confused and forgetful. A certain amount of memory loss is to be expected at our age. But yesterday, she couldn't remember which mailbox was hers, even though the boxes are marked with apartment numbers. Plus, she often mumbles about secrets."

"Secrets? Do you know what she's talking about?" Anything that suggested a mystery intrigued Nina.

Jessica shrugged. "I haven't a clue, but she becomes very agitated."

Nina folded her arms and leaned against the window frame. "Hmmm, do you think she has Alzheimer's? Or some other kind of dementia?"

"I hope not." Jessica wrinkled her brow. "If she does, she'll have to move into a memory care facility. I'd really miss her."

"Does she have relatives to look out for her?"

"Only her nephew, Roger Blanton, and he hangs around hoping to get some of her money."

Nina nodded. "Okay, now I recall more about Ellie. She won the lottery a couple of years ago, didn't she?"

"Right. Sixteen million." Jessica grinned. "After

taxes."

"Wow." Nina widened her eyes at the thought of winning so much money. "I think I've met Roger, too."

Jessica nodded. "I'm sure we've all been together at least once when you've come for Sunday dinner. I never cared much for Roger." Jessica pursed her lips. "He's a weasly, whiny guy, always complaining he needs money."

"Doesn't he have a job?"

"He calls himself an 'entrepreneur.'" Jessica harrumphed. "I call him a bum."

Again, Nina turned to the window, pushing aside the curtain. Ellie was bent into the wind, her yellow slicker billowing out behind her. Nigel's bushy tail drooped, displaying his lack of enthusiasm for the outing. She propped both hands on her hips. "Someone should go and bring Ellie and Nigel inside."

Jessica shook her head. "She wouldn't come until she was ready. She can be stubborn, especially if she's having one of her spells." She leaned closer to the window and pointed a forefinger. "Oh, look, not to worry; they're turning and heading back."

Sure enough, as Jessica spoke, Ellie wheeled around to head in the opposite direction. Nigel, his tail wagging, scampered after her.

"She'll be okay now." Jessica smiled. "We'd better get back to work."

As she turned from the window, Nina caught her reflection. Strands of her shoulder-length, brown hair escaped the loosely-tied ponytail and hung like exaggerated commas around her face. On some women that might look chic, but on her, the tendrils looked messy. But, then, who could keep a hairdo in this wild weather?

She caught her grandmother's reflection. Jessica could. Her curls were never out of place. The only variation with her hair was the shade, which changed from reddish blonde to red, depending on her whim.

But Jessica was right—they'd better get back to work. Around the room's perimeter, newly constructed, floor-to-ceiling shelves stood ready and waiting to be filled. The smell of recently applied oak stain lingered in the air. Several groupings of comfortable chairs and reading lamps completed the furnishings. "This space will make a lovely library." Nina crossed to the table where she'd been working.

"You are so nice to organize it." Jessica made a sweeping gesture that included the entire room.

"You know books and libraries are my passion." Nina reached into a box and pulled out several hardcover books. "I hope we get enough donations to fill the shelves."

"Not to worry, dear." Jessica picked up a knife and slit open a box. "Director Marshall applied for a government grant. Plus, he's set up a Library Fund, and residents are already contributing. You'll have a budget to buy new books to your heart's content."

Nina looked up and grinned. "Really? That's good news. Current titles will round out the collection."

"I put a sign-up sheet on our bulletin board downstairs asking for volunteers. The next time you come, we should have a crew to help us...Oh, look, here's an Agatha Christie I haven't read." She held up a book. "I'll be the first to check it out."

The muffled ring of her phone grabbed Nina's attention, and she hurried to the chair where she'd left her shoulder bag. Digging into its voluminous depths, she pulled out the phone.

"Hey, Nina."

Stephen Kraslow's deep voice resonated pleasantly in her ear. Stephen was from New York City, having left his job as a journalist to assume ownership of Richmond's weekly newspaper, *The Richmond Review*. "Hello, Stephen. What's up?" She hoped he wasn't canceling their evening together. She looked forward to being with him.

"About dinner tonight—"

Oh oh, he *was* canceling. Her shoulders slumped. "You don't want to get together," she blurted. "You have something else to do—"

"Nina, stop jumping to conclusions. No, instead of eating at your place, I thought we could go out."

"Why? I know I'm not the best cook in the world, but—"

"Going out has nothing to do with your cooking. I have something I want to discuss with you."

Something to discuss that required neutral territory. What could that subject be? Nina's stomach tensed. "Do you have a restaurant in mind?"

"How about Henry's, at the harbor?"

Henry's was one of their favorite places. "Okay, but what do you want to talk about?"

"Uh uh, not until dinner. Can you meet me at seven? I can get away by then."

"All right. I'll be there." Nina hung up, biting her lip. Noticing her grandmother's gaze, she forced a smile. "That was Stephen."

"So I gathered. You two still playing 'your place or mine'?"

5

Nina tucked her cell phone into her purse. "Come on, Gran, we've been seeing each other for only six months."

"I married Tyler after three months and—"

"I know; you lived happily ever after." Nina finished a sentence she had heard often enough to know by heart. "A short-term courtship worked for you and Granddad, but I'm too cautious to jump into a committed relationship after only a few months."

Jessica placed the box she'd emptied under the table and picked up another one. "I didn't think you would commit to a relationship, period."

Hearing her grandmother's dry tone, Nina shrugged. "Okay, so I admit to being a little scared of commitment. Stephen hasn't proposed marriage, anyway."

"Maybe tonight's the night." Jessica smiled and slit open the new box.

Nina shook her head. "I don't think so. He's not ready."

"How long since his wife passed away?" Jessica stacked books on the table.

"Two years." Dating a widower was a new experience.

Jessica pulled another handful of books from the box. "That length of time seems long enough to adjust. If I were you, I'd be prepared. Wear something romantic and fix your hair nice."

Her grandmother's suggestion lingered uneasily in Nina's mind. What if Stephen planned to propose tonight? What would her answer be? Did she love him? She certainly admired him and enjoyed his company.

But her mother's marriage ended in abandonment,

and Nina's few relationships all failed, leaving her more than a little afraid of commitment. The truth was, the idea of marriage scared her to death.

****

Half an hour later, Nina and Jessica left the library—Jessica to join her friends in the dining room for dinner, and Nina to return to her condo and prepare for her date with Stephen

After bidding Jessica good-bye, Nina passed through the reception area, which included comfortable chairs and sofas as well as dining tables and a snack bar where residents could visit with one another and entertain guests.

Marley Manor was the most expensive and exclusive retirement community in the area. The residents of the six-story building lived in the luxury of beautifully landscaped grounds, gourmet meals, a fully furnished spa, a hobby room, a chapel, and an auditorium. The only amenity lacking was a library, and Nina would soon supply that addition.

Near the front door, the middle-aged receptionist, Hilda Stern, sat behind a semi-circular desk. "The weather is awful tonight." She absently patted her upswept hairdo with the tips of her red-nailed fingers. "Drive carefully, Nina."

"I will," Nina promised. "Good-night, Hilda."

Outside, under the canopied entryway, the cold air made Nina shiver. She pulled up her raincoat hood and tied the strings under her chin. Her car was in the south parking lot. The path bordering the lake provided the shortest route. Ducking her head against the onslaught of wind and rain, Nina stepped onto the sidewalk, hurrying past wrought iron chairs and benches and round umbrella tables, their closed umbrellas pointing skyward like miniature spires.

Leaving the building behind, she soon reached the lake path. Underneath tall yard lights, the wet asphalt resembled a silver ribbon. Wisps of fog rose from the water and drifted toward the shore. A cold mist enveloped her, and raindrops collected on her cheeks, her nose, her eyelashes, and her chin. Nina shivered and bent her head against the wind.

Her thoughts turned to Stephen and their upcoming dinner date. What should she wear? Something romantic, Jessica said. Her black dress? No, too fancy. Her blue silk slacks outfit? No, the pant legs would get soaked in the rain—unless she wrapped herself completely in plastic. Hmm, not a bad idea…

A dog's sharp "yip" interrupted her musings. Nina looked up to see Ellie Larkin and Nigel heading toward her. Heavens, why were they still outside? Hadn't she and Jessica watched them return to Marley?

The dog barked again, but his bushy tail, sticking up from behind the yellow coat, wagged cheerily.

"Hello, Ellie." Nina greeted the woman when they were within speaking distance.

Ellie stared blankly from the depths of her hood.

A chill skittered down Nina's spine. Was Ellie having one of the spells Jessica mentioned? "I'm Nina Foster." She pointed to her chest. "Jessica Bingham's granddaughter?"

The woman continued to stare at Nina.

Nina took a step forward. "Ellie?"

Ellie jutted out her chin. "Did you call me?"

"Call you? You mean just now?" Nina wasn't sure whether Ellie meant had Nina hailed her from a distance or called her on the phone.

"Is someone behind me?" Ellie jerked her head to look over her shoulder.

Nina peered through the gloom. All she saw were the boathouse and a dock that stretched into the lake like a long, ghostly finger. "I don't see anyone, Ellie. Do you?"

Nodding, Ellie widened her eyes. "I know their secrets. They might be after me."

"Whose secrets, Ellie?" Nina stepped closer to the woman, lest she miss her reply.

"Them."

Ellie barely whispered while staring into space. Although Nina was curious about Ellie's secrets, a rainstorm was not the time to press for more information. "You shouldn't be out in this bad weather. You'll catch cold. You want to go home, don't you, Nigel?" Nina leaned to pat the dog's saturated head.

The animal stood on his hind legs, stuck out his pink tongue, and pawed the air.

"Do you have a secret?" Ellie narrowed her eyes.

"Come on, Ellie, let's go home. I'll walk with you." Nina laid a hand on the woman's arm.

"No!" Ellie jerked away. Reaching out with both hands, she gave Nina a hard shove.

"Ellie!" Nina struggled to maintain her balance.

Ellie lumbered past her and continued down the path.

Unperturbed by his mistress's erratic behavior, Nigel bounced along beside her.

Open-mouthed, Nina stared after the retreating figures. What had possessed Ellie? Whatever, she was strong. Her attack knocked the wind out of Nina. She pressed a hand to her chest and struggled for breath.

Should she catch up? Obviously having one of her spells, Ellie was in no condition to wander around the lake, especially in this miserable weather. Nina should make sure she returned to the building where someone could look after her.

But Nina had a limited amount of time. She needed to go home, shower, dress, and style her hair. She wanted to look her best for Stephen.

What to do? Nina clenched her hands, struggling with a decision. Then she saw Ellie veer onto the cutoff leading to the apartments. She exhaled a sigh of relief. *Good.* Ellie returned home on her own. Still, she'd thought the woman and her dog had come back earlier, and they hadn't.

Seeking shelter under a nearby pine tree, Nina dug her cell phone from her shoulder bag. Her fingers were stiff from the cold, but she punched in the home's main number. Receiving a busy signal, she left a message informing Hilda of the situation, confident she would send the security guard, or, if he wasn't available, someone else to take care of Ellie and Nigel.

Nina next called her grandmother. The ringing phone went unanswered. She left a message there, too.

Peering down the path Ellie and Nigel had taken, Nina discerned two faint blobs of yellow headed for the building. Although relieved, she had the urge to follow them and make sure they reached their destination safely. She tucked away her cell phone and retraced her steps to the path.

Then she thought about meeting Stephen. She didn't want to be late. What if he *were* proposing tonight? She needed to plan her response. Ellie and

Nigel would be safe. Someone would spot the two wanderers and take care of them. Still, Nina hesitated, wrestling with her concern for Ellie and her obligation to herself and Stephen.

Finally, telling herself she would check later on the two, she turned her steps toward the south parking lot and her car. Still, guilt niggled her. Would she come to regret her decision?

Chapter Two

"You look great tonight." Stephen gazed at Nina through the glow of candlelight at Henry's restaurant.

"Thank you." Pleased with his compliment, Nina absently smoothed the neckline of her emerald green wool dress. "You're looking sharp yourself."

Stephen's blue dress shirt matched the color of his eyes. The candlelight picked up the hints of silver in his brown hair and emphasized the angular planes of his face. He was not handsome in the classic, film star style, but his looks appealed to Nina. His eyes reflected depth and intelligence, his firm jaw defined masculine strength, and his smile lit up his entire face.

After placing their orders, they sipped Cabernet Savignon and admired the view of Puget Sound. A green-and-white ferry left the dock bound for the Olympic Peninsula. With a boisterous horn blast, the boat glided away like a swan setting off across a pond. On a clear night, lights on the opposite shore were visible, but in tonight's rain and fog, the ferry sailed into oblivion.

Nina finally tore her gaze from the view and turned to Stephen. Anticipating the special discussion he wanted to have kept her on edge. She waited for him to bring up the subject—whatever the topic was—but he talked instead about a city council meeting he'd attended.

"The proposed downtown mini-mall, Sixth North, dominated the meeting." Stephen sipped his wine. "The proponents want to build four stories, which would exceed the currently allowed building height restriction. A guy in the audience interrupted whenever someone else had the floor. I've seen him around. His name's Roger Blanton."

The name alerted Nina, and she straightened. "Jessica mentioned Roger today. What's his interest in the project?"

"I'm not sure. He calls himself an entrepreneur, which could mean a lot—or nothing. Judging from his performance at the meeting, I'd be inclined to say the latter." He frowned. "How does Jessica know him?"

"He's a friend's nephew." Nina related seeing Ellie Larkin and Nigel walking in the rain. "Ellie was in one of her confused states. I hope she got home okay."

"Maybe medication causes her confusion. If she's taking more than one, they might not mix well."

Nina raised her eyebrows. "I hadn't thought of drugs. I'll mention the possibility to Gran. But I am worried about Ellie. I should have made sure she and Nigel reached home. I'll call Gran later tonight."

The server arrived with their meals. Nina inhaled the enticing aroma of her baked halibut with hazelnut sauce, at the same time catching a whiff of Stephen's barbecued salmon. For several minutes, absorbed in eating, they were silent. Nina thoroughly enjoyed her fish, with its rich sauce and flaky texture. When conversation resumed, the topics skipped from the editorial Stephen planned to write on the downtown building project to Nina's work on the Marley Manor library.

At last, dinner was over, and their empty plates had been removed. They both declined dessert, and only their refilled coffee cups sat in front of them. Nina took a sip and put down the cup just as Stephen reached for her hand. His touch usually pleased her, but tonight, with their important discussion looming, she kept her fingers rigid.

A few seconds slid by while he held her hand. Outside, rain hammered the windowpane, while inside, the sounds of conversation, like muted music, drifted from nearby tables. Finally, she could no longer bear the suspense. "So, you, ah, wanted to talk about something?"

"I do." Stephen leaned closer and gazed into her eyes. "You know I love you."

She nodded and swallowed. "You've told me so."

He squeezed her hand. "And you love me."

"I do." *I think I do.*

"And you know I want a home and family."

Nina's heart skipped a beat. *Oh, oh, here comes the proposal, and I still don't know how I will respond.*

Stephen let go her hand and reached into his jacket pocket. But, instead of the small, square box she expected, he pulled out a small card. "Before we take the big step, I'd like you to see Becky."

"Becky?" At the unfamiliar name, Nina wrinkled her brow.

"Yes, Becky Young." He slid the card to her side of the table.

Recognizing a business card, Nina leaned to read the printing. "Rebecca Young, PhD." Under the name was the word "Counseling," and then an address, phone, and fax numbers. She dropped her jaw. "You want me to see a shrink?" Her voice squeaked.

Stephen frowned. "'Shrink' sounds disrespectful. Becky is a very qualified counselor."

"You know her personally?"

"I met her and her husband when we all lived in New York. Rich and I belonged to the same health club. He's an engineer. When he took a job with Boeing, they moved here. But we're getting off the track. Look, honey, you have some troublesome issues."

Nina folded her arms. "Issues? What issues?"

"Why, your father abandoning you and your mother when you were so young, for one."

Irritation tightened her stomach. "I've never thought of his leaving as an *issue*. Abandonment was just something that happened."

He raised his eyebrows. "What about your nightmares?"

She shifted in her seat. "Sometimes, my dreams are kind of scary, but—"

"Problems get buried inside a person where they fester like an untreated wound." Stephen laced his fingers together and leaned forward. "I don't want that situation to happen to you. I care about you, Nina. I want you to be happy."

Nina frowned. "Who says I'm not?"

"All right, happ*ier*." Stephen straightened his shoulders. "I know you'll like Becky. She's a very good therapist."

A response sprang to her lips, but Nina bit back the words. She and Stephen were close to arguing, and she did not want to create a scene in public. However, her pulse quickened, and she felt like a pot on the stove about to boil over. Any second now, the lid would blow. Only one course of action would prevent an explosion. She grabbed her purse, scooted back her chair, and jumped up.

Stephen straightened and stared. "What are you doing?"

"I am leaving." Nina ground out between clenched teeth. "Don't make a scene by trying to stop me. Richmond is a small town, and I'm sure people are here tonight who know both of us."

"You can't just walk out." Stephen gestured to the door. "Where are you going?"

"I am going home."

"I'll follow you in my car, then. We were to stay at my place this weekend, but we could do yours two in a row—"

She raised a hand. How could he think she still wanted to spend the weekend with him? "I'm going home alone. I need to be by myself."

Leaving him sitting there with his jaw hanging, she marched to the restaurant's entrance. Numbly, she took her raincoat from the coat rack, pulled it on, and then stumbled outside. The rain for a change was welcome, and the drops cooled her burning face. She headed for her car. People passed her on their way into the establishment, voices drifting from under bobbing umbrellas—people out for an evening, anticipating a good dinner and the company of companions. Just a short hour ago, Nina had been one of them. How quickly her situation changed.

At her car, she pressed the remote control, yanked open the door, and fell into the driver's seat. She couldn't wait to get home. She seethed all the way to her condominium in Viewmont Estates, located on a hillside above the town. However, once inside her apartment, she was at a loss what to do. Finally, she made a cup of tea and took it into the living room. She sat in the dark and sipped the hot brew. The single light from the rooftop outside beamed through the picture window, casting a glow over the room.

Her gaze fell on the fireplace and the empty grate. On any other cold, rainy, Friday night, Stephen would have a fire blazing. They'd be snuggled up in front of the flames, sipping brandy and sharing talk. Talk would lead to kisses and caresses—and lovemaking.

Sick at heart, Nina squeezed shut her eyes, but the images crowded her mind. She stood and took her cup and saucer into the kitchen. She rinsed the dishes and put them in the dishwasher. Resolutely, she marched into the bedroom. Sleep was her best escape.

She was proud of herself for not breaking down in front of Stephen. Crying showed weakness. Crying was a waste of time, her mother, Ivy, always said. As a child, Nina had not been allowed to cry, not in the presence of her mother, anyway.

Later, as she lay in bed, she whispered, "Nothing is wrong with me. Nothing is wrong with me."

****

The following morning, the ringing phone awakened Nina. *Stephen.* What would she say? She sat up, pushed the hair from her eyes, and reached for the phone.

"Nina," said her grandmother's voice, "I'm sorry to disturb you and Stephen, but something terrible has happened."

"What?" Nina's heartbeat quickened.

"Ellie Larkin. You remember, we saw her walking

in the rain yesterday with her dog, Nigel?"

"Yes, yes—what happened to Ellie?"

"She's dead!"

"Dead!" Wide-awake now, shock rippled through her. "How? Where? What—"

"Jake Motti, the gardener...you know him, used to work for the city, in public works?"

Nina gripped the telephone. "Yes, I know Jake. Please, Gran, what happened to Ellie?"

"I'm getting to that. He found her floating in the lake this morning. He tried CPR, but she didn't respond. An ambulance came and took her away."

Regret filled her. She should have made sure Ellie and Nigel returned to the manor. "How did she die? Did she drown?"

"Apparently. I suppose the police will investigate and let us know."

"What about Nigel?"

"Jake found him hiding under a bush, all wet and bedraggled. Don't know what will happen to him now. We're all in shock here, as you can imagine. But, are you still coming over?"

Nina struggled to focus on Jessica's change of subject. "I planned to. I have some free time to work on the library." She glanced at the clock. Eight, already. Time to get up.

"What are you and Stephen doing for the rest of the weekend? Anything special?"

Nina bit her lip. "We, ah, haven't decided yet." Her statement was true—in a way.

"I almost forgot to ask, are you engaged?"

"No...we're not. I'll tell you about last night when I see you."

"All right, dear. I'll look for you."

Nina hung up. A shiver coursed down her spine, and she hugged her arms. She'd meant to call Jessica last night and check on Ellie, but the scene with Stephen had chased all thoughts of the woman from her mind. What could have happened to cause her death?

****

When Nina arrived at Marley Manor, she spotted Jessica in the reception area talking to her friend, Lily Ciliano. The two women sat on a green brocade sofa underneath a large, gold-framed mirror. Lily's walker, with its perky, pink wicker basket, stood nearby. Concerned about her grandmother's reaction to the news of Ellie's death, Nina hurried to Jessica's side.

Her eyes tear-shiny, Jessica rose and enveloped Nina in a hug. "Oh, honey, I'm so glad you're here. What happened to Ellie is so awful."

Nina returned her hug. "I'm sorry, Gran. You've lost a good friend, haven't you?"

Jessica nodded. "I liked Ellie, even though she was a little crazy sometimes."

Nina released Jessica and turned to Lily. "You were Ellie's friend, too, weren't you, Lily?"

The woman peered at Nina through her thick glasses. "I was. But her death wasn't an accident! She was murdered!"

Lily often exclaimed her opinions, as though she wanted to be sure her listeners got the point. Nina, too, had thought perhaps Ellie met with foul play, but she wanted to hear more from Lily before voicing her thoughts. "What makes you think someone killed her?" She sank into a wing chair and gave the woman her full attention.

"Jake said the police think Ellie fell off the dock and drowned." Lily's eyes widened. "But Ellie wouldn't walk on the dock. She was afraid of water. She never went boating or fishing with the rest of us. She wouldn't be on the dock. No, sir."

"Not even in one of her crazy spells?" Switching into amateur sleuth mode, Nina made a mental note.

Lily pursed her lips. "I hadn't thought of her spells."

Nina recalled Ellie's blank stare and the violent shove she had given her. She turned to Jessica. "What do you think, Gran?"

"I agree with Lily. Ellie hated boats. I wanted her to go fishing once when I went with Ardis Morton." Jessica patted Lily's veined hand. "You know her, Lily, lives on four, with the collection of cuckoo clocks that drove her neighbors crazy until she taped all the doors shut?"

Lily nodded. "Those clocks made a racket, all right."

"Anyway, Ellie wouldn't fish with us or go near the dock." Jessica leaned back in her chair. "She'd walk along the lake, but the path was as close to the water as she would get. But, to be honest, I don't know what she would do in one of her spells. She wasn't herself then."

"I may have been the last person to talk to Ellie." Lily adjusted her eyeglasses. "I saw her yesterday afternoon in the laundry room."

A wave of guilt rolled over Nina, and she shook her head. "No, I think I was the last."

"You?" Lily and Jessica said in unison and stared at Nina.

Nina told them about her encounter with Ellie and

Nigel when she left Marley Manor the night before.

Jessica nodded. "I got your message. I told Hilda, and she said she'd send Mike, our security guard, to take care of Ellie and Nigel. But I don't know whether or not she did."

"I should have made sure they got back okay." Nina pressed a hand to her queasy stomach. "If I had, maybe Ellie would still be alive."

Jessica patted Nina's arm. "What happened to Ellie isn't your fault, dear. Even if you made sure she returned, she could have wandered out again. The police will investigate and find out what happened."

Lily harrumphed and shook her forefinger. "Don't count on the police. They didn't find Wildeen Bergman's murderer, did they? Nina solved that crime."

Lily's comment brought to Nina's mind the murder last summer of her friend who owned a local bookstore. Another mutual friend convinced her to look into the crime. She had, in fact, been the one to discover the killer's identity.

"Be a detective again!" Behind her thick glasses, Lily's eyes shone.

"Oh, no." Nina leaned back and raised her hands. Although she'd been successful in solving Wildeen's murder, she'd lost another good friend in the process. No, she'd best leave the mystery of Ellie's death to the professionals.

"Why? You just said you felt responsible."

"Yes, but—" Nina wrinkled her brow and glanced at her grandmother.

"I think we're all jumping to conclusions." Jessica shook her head and folded her arms.

Lily frowned. "By the time the police figure out the

mystery, the killer will be long gone."

"I'd better stay out of their investigation." Nina shook her head. "Lieutenant Russell didn't appreciate my involvement, even if I did help to discover Wildeen's murderer." Eager to change the subject, she turned to Jessica. "Any luck getting together a committee to help us set up the library?"

Jessica's eyes sparkled. "I have three volunteers." She ticked them off on her fingers. "Mabel Whiteside, Selma Ballari, and Lily." She pointed to her friend. "They're ready to work this morning."

"Great." Nina smiled at Lily. Volunteers would certainly help, especially with unpacking the boxes. Although eager to begin work on her project, Nina couldn't purge Ellie's tragic death from her thoughts. "Before we begin, I do need to tell the police what I know about Ellie. Are they still here?" She leaned forward and gazed around the room.

"They were at the lake awhile ago." Jessica pointed toward the front door.

"I'll see if they're still in the area." Nina stood. "How about I meet our new committee in the library in half an hour?"

"Perfect." Jessica nodded. "Lily and I will contact Mabel and Selma."

"See you then." Nina waved and headed for the door.

"Tell the cops you'll help in their investigation!" Lily called after her.

Lily's advice tempted Nina, but she was at Marley for a different purpose. She would tell the police what she knew and then concentrate on establishing the new library.

Chapter Three

Nina exited the building and headed for the lake. Last night's storm left the sky clear, but dark clouds rimmed the horizon, forecasting more rain.

Yellow police tape cordoned off the dock and boathouse. A uniformed officer knelt on the dock, examining the surface, while another wearing hip boots stood in shallow water, poking at the dock's underside. A third man, with curly, salt-and-pepper hair and dressed in slacks and a Richmond Police Department parka, took notes on a clipboard while speaking to a group of onlookers.

Nina recognized him as Pete Russell, the detective who investigated her friend, Wildeen's, murder. She waited until he broke away from the group and then approached him. "Detective Russell."

He looked up, and his lips broke into a smile. "Well, if it isn't Nina Foster. Don't tell me you're involved in what happened here."

His friendly tone put her at ease. "Involved enough to have something to tell you about Ellie."

"Sure. Just give me a minute." He pulled a clean sheet of paper from underneath the stack on the clipboard and fastened it on top. "Okay. Whatcha got?"

Nina told him how she and Jessica watched Ellie and Nigel from the library window. "Then, when I met her later, here at the lake, she acted confused. She looked over her shoulder and asked if someone followed her."

Russell paused in his note taking. "Was anyone in sight?"

"Not that I could see, but visibility was really bad last night. A person could have been hiding by the dock or in the trees. Ellie mentioned knowing someone's secrets. But when I asked her whose secrets, she didn't answer." She expected a reaction to that bit of news, but his expression remained bland.

He wrote awhile and then looked up again. "Anything else?"

Tilting her head, Nina thought a moment. "No, that's all."

"Thanks, Nina." He tucked his clipboard under his arm and stepped away.

Disappointed by his abrupt dismissal, Nina followed him, holding out a hand. "Wait a minute. Do you think someone murdered Ellie? Is that why you're here?"

Russell stopped and turned. A frown creased his brow. "I'm here because I help out where I'm needed, not because I'm investigating a crime. The autopsy will tell us how she died."

"But her fear seemed so real." Nina shook her head. "What about the secrets she said she knew?"

"You think she was murdered, don't you?"

"Murder is possible, isn't it? Your men are searching as though the area is a crime scene." She nodded to the two officers who were still at the lake.

Russell waved a hand. "What they're doing is routine."

Nina doubted the police activity was only routine,

but she wouldn't argue. "Well, anyway, I've told you what I know. I did my duty."

"You did, Nina, and I thank you." He gave a salute. "Now, if you'll excuse me, I gotta talk to some more folks."

Nina was tempted to hang around, but she had other business to take care of. Still, thoughts of what had happened to Ellie lingered. Was her death accidental? Or the result of foul play?

****

Back in the building, Nina walked down the hall to the new library. Jessica, Lily, and two other women sat in the overstuffed chairs, their heads together in conversation.

Lily looked up as Nina approached. "Here's our leader!"

"Hello, ladies." Smiling at Lily's exuberant greeting, Nina shed her parka and hung it over the back of a chair. "I hope I didn't keep you waiting too long."

"Not at all." Jessica gestured to the woman sitting beside her. "Nina, meet Mabel Whiteside."

Nina smiled and nodded. "Welcome, Mabel." Mabel's silver-blonde hair formed a pale halo around a face with eyes and mouth dramatically outlined with cosmetics. Her frilly pink blouse, matching cashmere shawl, mauve skirt, and high-heeled shoes were more suited to a social gathering than a work party.

"Mabel lives on six." Jessica smiled at the woman. "You're our Southern belle, aren't you, Mabel?"

The woman laughed. "Ah guess ah am. Ah moved heah from Texas to be close to mah son. Sam works for MicroTechno."

"Lots of our people have moved here from out of

state to be near their kids," Jessica said.

"I'd like to get away from mine." Lily rolled her eyes.

"This is Selma Bellari." Jessica leaned around Mabel to nod at Selma. "She lives next door to me and is our resident Scrabble champion."

Nina turned to Selma. In contrast to Mabel, she was plainly dressed in a white blouse, a red cardigan sweater, and navy slacks. Her dark, gray-streaked hair was gathered into a loose bun on top of her head. "Nice to meet you."

Selma waved at Nina. "We've heard so much about you from Jessica."

Nina laughed. "All good, I hope. But thanks for coming, ladies. I appreciate your interest in your new library. This room will be—"

"Tell us what you found out about Ellie." Lily sat forward.

"Not much." Nina gave Lily an indulgent smile. "I talked to Detective Pete Russell and told him about meeting Ellie and Nigel last night."

"I bet he said she'd been murdered."

Nina shook her head. As much as she might've wanted him to share information, he hadn't. "The police have to wait for the autopsy before announcing the cause of death."

Selma's nod set her topknot dancing. "I won't sleep a wink if a murderer's on the loose."

"We have good security." Jessica leaned back in her chair. "Mike or one of his crew is always on duty, and all outsiders must sign in and out."

Selma sniffed. "Security didn't save Ellie, did it?"

"Don't worry, ladies." Lily spread her hands.

"Nina will find out who murdered Ellie. Won't you, Nina?" She regarded Nina over the top of the glasses. "You do agree that someone killed her."

Lily's confidence in her abilities brought a smile to Nina's lips. "I must admit her death looks suspicious."

"See. Told ya." Lily sat back and folded her arms.

"Ah know where ah would look." Mabel fingered the frilly collar of her blouse.

"Where?" Jessica's eyes widened and she leaned toward Mabel.

"Dr. Ravensbarger. He was givin' her those pills that made her so crazy. And, my, he is a Mr. Smoothie. Ah went to him for mah backache, and why, he liked to charmed mah stockings off." Mabel fluttered her eyelashes.

Mabel's flirtatious attitude made Nina wonder just who was charming whom.

"He wanted to give me all sorts of tests." Mabel pressed fingers to her cheek. "Said they were free. Can you imagine a doctor doin' anythin' for free?"

Her pink lips twisted into a disdainful grimace. Nina agreed with Mabel's doubts about a doctor offering free services.

"My friend, Georgia, goes to him." Selma shrugged and turned up both hands. "She loves him."

"A lot of our residents see Dr. Ravensbarger." Jessica smoothed a wrinkle from her skirt. "And Sheryl, our part-time nurse, works for him."

"Does anyone know who inherits Ellie's money?" Selma looked around the group.

Reminded of Ellie's fortune, Nina hoped someone knew the answer to Selma's query.

"Her slimy nephew, Roger, gets some of the

money." Lily wrinkled her nose. "But the biggest chunk goes to—" Her eyes wide, she looked around the group.

Everyone leaned toward her.

"Who, who?" Selma grimaced.

"Come on, Lily, give." Mabel clapped her hands.

"The daughter of Ellie's former boyfriend." Lily turned to Jessica. "Isn't that right, Jess?"

Jessica nodded. "The situation is strange. Ellie's best friend stole the man she was once engaged to. The two ran off and got married. Why Ellie would leave most of her sixteen million to their only daughter is beyond me."

"Was the bequest part of her craziness?" Selma wrinkled her brow and looked around the group.

Jessica folded her arms. "I don't think so. She set up the inheritance right after she won the lottery a couple years ago."

"The daughter gets ever'thing? Except the chunk for Roger?" Mabel pursed her lips and shook her head.

"Some goes to Ellie's favorite charities," Jessica said. "But the daughter inherits the biggest part."

"Lucky her." Lily raised her eyebrows.

Nina stood and held up her hands. "Ladies, this conversation is interesting, and we're all concerned and sorry about what happened to Ellie, but we'd better get to work on our project."

"Just tell us what to do." Selma scooted to the edge of her seat.

"First, have any of you ever worked in a library?" Nina looked around the group.

Selma and Mabel shook their heads.

"I was librarian's helper in grade school." Lily raised her hand. "I stamped books with the due date.

The librarian had a pencil with a rubber stamp attached to the end, so you could either write or stamp."

"Are we stampin' due dates on the books?" Mabel picked up a book from a nearby table and held it up. "Using a stamp would sure help me. Ah have a terrible time remembering dates."

"You should join our Word Games Club." Selma patted her topknot. "Making words helps keep the brain active."

Mabel smoothed her skirt. "Thank y'all, Selma, but ah cain't spell past 'cat' and 'dog.'"

"We won't use a date due stamp." Nina picked up a clipboard. "This clipboard will serve as our check-out. People will be on the honor system to record the books they borrow and cross them off when they are returned. A computer with a list of the books will be available, but we'll keep lending as simple as possible."

"I like simple!" Lily bounced up and down.

The woman's enthusiasm brought a smile to Nina's lips. "Me, too, Lily. Now, first of all, we need to finish sorting our donated books. Jessica and Mabel, you can unload the boxes stacked on the floor and put the books on the table. Selma and Lily will sort the books into two piles, fiction and nonfiction."

Everyone set to work.

Nina inspected the books Selma and Lily sorted, choosing those to include in the collection and those to discard. Despite her resolve not to interfere with the police investigation, her thoughts strayed to Ellie's death. Had the woman suffered an accident? Or had she met with foul play?

A woman with an armload of books arrived. She had reddish hair and a sprinkling of freckles across a pug nose. Faded jeans hugged hips that appeared too narrow for the size of her upper body. "I hoped I'd find someone here."

Nina winced at the strident voice.

"Hello, Harriet." Jessica smiled at the newcomer and then turned to Nina. "Harriet Hambly lives on two, home economist, and had a TV program."

"Indeed, I was on TV." Harriet shifted her load of books to display a red sweatshirt emblazoned with 'In the Kitchen With Harriet Hambly.' "Mine was the longest running program ever on Channel Fifty-Four. We were such a smash."

"Harriet loves to talk about herself," Lily whispered behind her hand to Nina.

Nina nodded and smiled. She'd met Harriet and had noticed her self-centeredness.

"I brought copies of my books to donate." Harriet looked around the room. "Where shall I put them?"

"On that table, please." Nina pointed to an empty table.

Harriet crossed the room and deposited her books.

Nina followed, counted twelve volumes, and then looked up. "Did you write all these?"

"I did." Harriet stuck out her chest. "Five cookbooks, four on crafts, two on flower arranging, and one on home decorating. Could my donations have a shelf all their own? They are all autographed."

"We'll see." Nina straightened the stack. She'd had such requests at the library and, not wanting to discourage donations, always gave a vague reply. "I'm not sure how our spacing will work out. But, thank you for your donation. I know the books will be appreciated."

"No one who lives here cooks much anymore." Lily wrinkled her nose. "Why should we when dinner is included in our rent?"

Harriet propped her hands on her slim hips. "A lot of residents use their kitchens." She went to stand beside Jessica. "You cook sometimes, don't you, Jessica?"

Jessica looked up from her sorting. "I do like to bake cookies."

"I'm sure your books will be of interest." Nina used a soothing tone, hoping to avoid an argument between Harriet and Lily. She had the feeling that, for an unknown reason, Lily did not like Harriet.

Harriet gazed around the room. "How are you doing so far?"

"We barely started when you interrupted." Lily picked up a book and studied the cover. "Selma and I are sorting fiction and nonfiction, so don't disturb our piles."

Harriet strolled along the table, picking up books and perusing them.

Nina noticed a birthmark on the back of Harriet's right hand. The shape reminded her of a butterfly with its wings spread.

"I felt terrible when I heard about Ellie." Harriet put down a book she'd been paging through and faced the group.

Everyone nodded and murmured agreement.

"You were a good friend of hers, weren't you?" Jessica reached into a box and pulled out a handful of books.

"We were friends." Harriet turned to Nina. "I saw you at the lake talking to the policeman. What did he have to say?"

Why was Harriet so curious? Out of concern for Ellie? Or for another reason? "Nothing much. I told him about my encounter with Ellie last night at the lake."

Harriet's eyes widened. "You talked to her at the lake? What did she say?"

Nina gave Harriet an abbreviated version of her conversation with Ellie.

"Poor Ellie." Harriet shook her head. "She was really mixed up. What a terrible accident."

"Her death was no accident." Lily pushed out her lower lip. "Someone killed her!"

"Why, that idea is ridiculous." Harriet pursed her lips. "Who would want to harm poor Ellie?"

"Nina will find out who." Lily lifted her chin.

Harriet frowned at Nina. "What is she talking about?"

"Haven't you heard how Nina solved a murder last summer?" Lily waved a hand in the air. "Well, now she'll solve this crime."

Nina felt her stomach clench, but she managed a smile in Lily's direction. "I do enjoy mysteries, but I'll let the police deal with Ellie's death."

Harriet approached the boxes of books sitting on the floor. "Ellie told me she was donating books to the library. Did she?"

"I don't know." Nina shrugged. "We haven't opened all the boxes yet. Why do you ask?"

"She had a book of mine she intended to return but never did. I thought maybe my book got mixed up with her donations."

"What was the title?" Nina picked up her clipboard and pen, ready to record the information.

"Never mind." Harriet waved a hand. "The book's not important."

After Harriet finally left, the room was quiet.

"I wonder if Harriet's unreturned book is what she and Ellie argued about the other day?" Selma broke the silence.

"Tell us about their argument." Mabel sank into a chair.

Everyone, including Nina, stopped working and leaned toward Selma.

Selma's gaze roved over the group. "I was on my way downstairs to check my mailbox, and I heard voices coming from inside Ellie's apartment. As I passed by, the door flew open, and Harriet rushed out. Her face was as red as her hair. She was really mad."

"Ah saw them fightin' in the laundry room last week." Mabel nodded. "Ah don't know what about, though, because they quit talkin' when Ah came in."

Selma added a book to her stack. "Maybe Harriet was mad 'cause Ellie didn't want to give back the book."

"Or maybe Ellie couldn't return the book because she lost it." Jessica propped her elbows on the table.

"Maybe." Selma shrugged. "But I got the feeling those two weren't the good friends everyone thought them to be."

With growing interest, Nina followed the women's conversation. Despite her resolve to keep her distance, Ellie's mysterious death intrigued her, especially since she felt at least partly responsible. Should she follow her inclinations and become involved? Or leave the investigation to the police?

Chapter Four

Half an hour later, Lily looked at her wristwatch. "Oh oh, gotta go. Wally and I have a date to play checkers."

Jessica shook her head. "Haven't you two progressed beyond checkers?"

Noticing Jessica's eyes twinkled with teasing, Nina hid a smile.

"None of your beeswax, Jessica!" Lily reached for her walker.

"Ah saw you two at the movie in the auditorium last Friday." Mabel winked at Selma.

"Didn't I see Wally come out of your apartment the other night?" Selma hid a chuckle behind her hand.

"Nina, tell them to stop picking on me!" Lily pushed her lips into a pout. Reaching into the pink basket attached to her walker, she pulled out a tabloid-size magazine. "I almost forgot the donation I brought." She held out the magazine.

When Nina saw Lily's contribution was a copy of *The Eye*, the most lurid of all the tabloids, she stilled, her smile fading. Emblazoned on the cover were the huge, staring eye logo and the rather alarming declaration, "The Eye Sees All!" She groped for a polite refusal. "Thank you, Lily, but—"

"I saved this issue 'specially for the library." Lily's eyes shone behind her glasses.

"I don't think we have any copies of this magazine yet." Forcing a smile, Nina reached for the magazine.

"I'll donate all my copies. I buy 'em every week at the market."

"How...generous of you." Nina choked out the words.

Shortly after Lily left, Mabel stepped away from the table. "Ah better leave, too. My daughter-in-law's taking me to the mall. Ah need a new dress for the play we're goin' to tomorrow night." She picked up her cashmere shawl and wrapped it around her bony shoulders.

"I must run, too." Selma scooted to the edge of her chair. "I'm hosting today's board games in the rec room."

Nina accompanied them to the door. "Thanks for coming."

"When do y'all want us to meet again?" Mabel paused with her hand on the doorknob.

"I'll check my schedule and let Gran know, and she can contact you ladies."

After they left, Nina placed her hands on her hips and surveyed the room. "Well, we got a few boxes unloaded and sorted, anyway."

Jessica wrinkled her nose as she picked up *The Eye* and waved the magazine at Nina. "What will you do with this? Line the wastebasket?"

Nina grinned. "No, as tempting as that solution might be, we'll put it with the other magazines. Maybe someone will check it out and forget to return it."

"Good idea." Jessica added the tabloid to a stack of magazines on the table. "You were going to tell me about your dinner with Stephen."

Last night's scene in the restaurant, which had been lurking in the back of her mind, now set Nina's stomach churning. She sank into a chair. "Instead of proposing, he wants me to see a shrink and work out all my so-called problems. He even has someone picked out, a woman doctor he knew in New York, who lives here now."

Jessica perched on the chair beside Nina. "What was your response?"

Nina lifted her chin. "I walked out."

Jessica gave her a long look. "You might give his suggestion some thought."

Nina stared. She hadn't expected Jessica to take Stephen's side. "Why?"

"Your nightmares, for one reason."

Nina waved a dismissive hand. "Everyone has bad dreams, sometimes."

"Maybe, but you had a rough time growing up, with your dad walking out when you were so young and your mother wrapped up in her real estate career. I don't imagine you had much parenting. With Tyler and me clear across the country, we certainly weren't any help." She lowered her gaze. "I'll always regret not being there for you."

Jessica's reminder of Nina's troubled childhood brought a wave of sadness. "You and Mom were estranged in those days, weren't you?"

Jessica nodded. "Ivy and I didn't speak for years. Being alienated from your own daughter is hard to excuse, but Ivy was always difficult to get along with. Sometimes, I had trouble believing she was my child. But I should have tried harder. Then I wouldn't have missed your growing up."

Hearing the regret in Jessica's voice, Nina took her hand. "I'm glad you're here now."

Jessica squeezed Nina's fingers. "Me, too, darling. But I hate to see you and Stephen having problems. He's been such a good companion and friend."

A sinking sensation invaded Nina's stomach. "He has, but I just can't agree with him on this issue."

****

Nina arrived home at five o'clock. For the first time in six months, she would be alone on a Saturday night. Since last summer, after Wildeen Bergman's murder was solved, she and Stephen had spent every weekend together, from Friday night to Monday morning.

Well, almost every weekend. A couple of times, he traveled out of town on newspaper business, and once she attended a librarians' conference. Still, their being together had become a habit.

Nina squared her shoulders. She'd survive. She'd gotten along before he came into her life, and she'd get along now. Tonight, she'd go to a movie. She picked up *The Richmond Review*, which unfortunately reminded her of Stephen, and turned to the Entertainment page to check the film playing at the local theater. *Saying Good-bye* was the movie's title. The caption read, "If you liked *An Affair to Remember*, you'll love this movie."

Oh, great, all she needed was a movie about a broken love affair. She was about to check the listings in *The Seattle Times* when the doorbell rang. Since the front gate was locked to outsiders, the person must be one of her neighbors.

Nina went to the door and looked through the

peephole. A gasp escaped her lips. Stephen stood in the hallway, a bouquet of red roses in one hand and a grocery bag in the other.

Her heartbeat quickened. Did she want to let him in? Yes. No. She wavered back and forth. Finally, she took a deep breath and opened the door. Stephen looked as solemn as she'd ever seen him.

"I came to apologize. I know you're angry, but you're too polite to not hear me out."

Gripping the doorknob, Nina held herself rigid. "Did you think I was polite last night when I left you sitting in the restaurant?"

"You were justifiably upset. I handled the situation badly. Are you inviting me in?" He peered over her shoulder.

Nina chewed her bottom lip. Yet, Stephen was right. If he came to apologize, she would at least hear him. "All right." She opened the door wider and stood aside.

Stephen strode in, turned and held out the bouquet. "Your favorite flower, if I recall correctly."

She took the flowers and buried her nose in the cool, silky blooms. The flowers *were* pretty and, yes, she loved roses. "Thank you."

"Here's dinner." He gestured to the grocery sack.

The bag was from The Ming Tree, her favorite Chinese restaurant. He did know her well.

"I'll put the food in the fridge until later." He headed toward the kitchen.

Nina trailed in his wake, still not certain how she wanted to handle this unexpected situation. "You're awfully sure of yourself, aren't you?"

He tossed a grin over his shoulder. "You're a fair

person, Nina. You'll hear my apology." He opened the refrigerator and placed the grocery bag inside.

She took a clear glass vase from under the sink, filled it with water, and arranged the flowers. She turned from the sink just as he shut the refrigerator door. In the small kitchen, they were only an arm's length apart. Their gazes met, and the air crackled with electricity. She grabbed the vase and hurried to the living room where she placed the flowers on a black lacquer end table. The red blossoms reflected softly on the ebony surface, and their fragrance filled the air.

Stephen followed her into the room.

Cautioning herself to remain strong, she turned and faced him. "Your apology?"

He took a step closer. "I'm sorry for upsetting you. I wanted only to help."

She backed up, keeping a distance between them. "Where no help was requested."

He shrugged. "I'm a problem solver. I see a problem, and I jump in with a solution."

"Even if you're the only one who perceives a problem." Oh oh, not quite true. Jessica also thought Nina needed help.

He spread his hands. "My suggestion to see Becky was only because I'm concerned. I want you to be happy."

Was this discussion solving their dilemma? Nina gritted her teeth. They both were firm in their opinions. "Can't you believe me when I say I am?"

Stephen raised an eyebrow. "No, and for the reasons I gave you last night."

She narrowed her eyes. "You're always right?"

"You're picking a fight." He raised his hands.

"Look, I came here in peace."

She didn't want to fight, and yet, she had a right to her opinion, too, didn't she? Could they possibly find a peaceful solution? "What do you suggest we do about 'my problem'?"

"I suggest we go on with our lives—together."

His suggestion intrigued her. "You think your perception of me will change?"

A soft smile crossed his lips. "Or yours might. Time will tell."

Nina idly fingered one of the rose petals. "We can return to the way we were?"

"Of course."

She heaved a sigh and met his gaze. "You're more resilient than I am."

"I don't think so." Holding out his arms, he approached. "Meet me halfway?"

Nina let a couple seconds elapse, still debating. Then, matching his steps, she went to meet him.

Stephen put both arms around her and pulled her close. "I missed you," he whispered.

His breath was warm against her hair. "I missed you, too." The twenty-four hours they'd been apart felt more like weeks.

He tipped up her chin and kissed her.

The touch of his lips sent warmth spiraling through her veins. Nina wound her arms around his neck and returned his kiss. Being in his embrace again filled her with joy.

They stood for long moments kissing and murmuring endearments. Then he pulled away and pressed his lips close to her ear. "We need to go where we can get serious." He walked her backward toward the stairs leading to her bedroom.

Nina stiffened, torn between wanting him and yet knowing their problem hadn't really been solved. But with another kiss, deeper and more fervent, the last traces of resistance melted away. When he finally drew away and led her to the stairs, she went willingly. What else mattered, other than this moment?

Chapter Five

The following morning, Nina awoke deliciously relaxed and happy. She and Stephen were together again. She slid her hand to the other side of the bed, expecting to connect with his warm body.

Instead, she found the bed empty. A sudden panic jerked her to her senses. Had Stephen left? If so, why hadn't he awakened her to say good-bye? Maybe he'd decided reconciling was a mistake.

Then she heard the sounds of pans clanging and cupboard doors opening and closing. No, as usual, she'd jumped to conclusions. Stephen hadn't left. He was in the kitchen making breakfast. She took a deep breath and settled back against the pillows.

Still, anxiety knotted her stomach. They had done nothing, really, to solve the problem between them. Stephen thought she needed professional counseling. She disagreed. Although he had backed off, she knew him well enough to realize he wouldn't give up his mission.

Stephen appeared carrying a mug of coffee. "Good morning."

Wearing jeans from the night before and a clean shirt he'd pulled from his stash in her closet, he looked happy and relaxed. "Morning." Lingering insecurity kept Nina's lips stiff as she returned his smile.

He handed her the mug. "Want breakfast in bed?"

He always cooked breakfast for them, as well as most other meals, too. He carried recipes in his head the way she harbored Dewey Decimal numbers. Nina sipped the coffee, savoring the rich flavor. "No, I'll get up. I want to shower."

"Okay. I'll fix us an omelet."

"If you can find enough ingredients. I didn't shop yesterday. I didn't think—" She shrugged.

"—I'd be here today." He grinned. "Well, I am. You can't get rid of me so easily. I'll find something to use."

Stephen made good on his promise. The omelet was delicious, filled with canned crab, mushrooms, grated cheese, and sour cream that miraculously survived a refrigerator stay of undetermined length.

"I heard on my police scanner that a woman died at Marley Manor," Stephen said after he'd spent a few minutes eating. "What do you know about the incident?"

The reminder of Ellie's death filled Nina with sadness—and guilt. "She was Ellie Larkin, the woman I told you about at dinner before I—well, never mind that now." She waved a hand. "The gardener found her body in the lake."

Stephen touched his napkin to his lips. "Did she drown?"

"I don't know. Her death is the talk of the manor, though." She put down her fork. "Some of Jessica's friends think Ellie was murdered. Lily Ciliano, especially, wants me to investigate. Helping to solve Wildeen's murder last summer earned me a reputation."

"Are you getting involved?" Stephen's brows knit.

Nina rubbed her forehead. "I do feel some

responsibility for what happened. If I'd made sure she returned to the building, and that someone took care of her and Nigel from there—"

He shook his head. "You could have done all that and still she might have wandered out later and met with her accident."

Nina sipped her coffee and put down the cup. "I know, but I can't shake the feeling that her death is at least partly my fault."

Stephen studied her. "What do you plan to do?"

"I might snoop a bit...to see what I can find out." Fearing his disapproval, Nina kept her tone casual.

He put down his fork, sat back, and folded his arms. "Are you sure you want to get involved? If her death was foul play, you might put yourself in danger."

Nina was about to remind Stephen of his days as an investigative reporter when he'd sometimes been in danger, but just then, the phone rang. Caller ID indicated Jessica on the line. "Checking to see if you and Stephen are coming over today, as usual."

Nina and Stephen spent most Sunday afternoons with Jessica, joining her and the other Marley residents for the evening meal. But, since Nina had told Jessica of her falling out with Stephen, she was surprised her grandmother assumed he would accompany her. "Why, how'd you know we—"

"—Are back together?" Jessica laughed. "I'm psychic. I was also young once and in love. Love is pretty stubborn, once you fall into it. Anyway, why don't you come about three? I'll bake cookies to have with our tea."

One eyebrow raised, Nina looked at Stephen. "Jessica's today, as usual?"

He grinned. "You bet."

She turned again to the phone. "Okay, Gran, we'll see you this afternoon."

A few minutes later, as she helped Stephen clean the kitchen, Nina thought about their relationship. They were back together and resuming their established habits, such as today's visit to Marley Manor. But she knew the problem between them hadn't been solved and would undoubtedly appear again in the future. What would happen then?

****

When they arrived at Jessica's apartment, Nina noticed the gray circles rimming her grandmother's eyes. "Gran, are you okay?" She placed a hand on Jessica's shoulder.

"I didn't sleep well last night." Jessica rubbed her eyes. "I can't stop thinking about Ellie's horrible death."

"Any word from the police?" Stephen hung his and Nina's coats in the hall closet.

Jessica led them into the living room. "Not that I've heard."

Nina took a moment to experience the comfort she always felt upon visiting her grandmother's apartment. The cheerful décor brightened even a drab day such as today. The semi-circular, cream-colored sofa displayed cushions in vibrant colors of red, yellow, and orange. Side chairs were covered in harmonizing beige and burnt sienna. A round, glass top coffee table sat in the center.

"Make yourselves comfortable, you two." Jessica gestured to the sofa. "I'll get the tea and cookies."

"I'll help you." Nina followed her grandmother

into the kitchen. The air was warm from the oven and smelled of recently baked cookies. "I'm worried about you." She took cups and saucers from a cupboard and placed them on a tray.

Jessica loaded a plate with oatmeal cookies. "Don't worry, honey. I'll be okay. But I wish we knew for sure what happened to Ellie."

"I've decided to investigate." Nina added a pot of fragrant Earl Grey tea to the tray.

Jessica wrinkled her brow. "Your involvement seemed like a good idea yesterday when we were in the library, but, after my sleepless night, I might have changed my mind. Poking into her death might be dangerous."

"I'll be careful. I'll just look around—nothing drastic."

Carrying the tea tray, Nina followed Jessica into the living room. She smiled at how Stephen had made himself at home, settled in a chair with his feet propped on the matching footstool.

They barely started the refreshments when Jessica's phone rang. She put down her teacup and picked up the receiver. "Hello? Who? Oh, Roger. So sorry about your aunt... Sure, come on up. Three-twelve, at the opposite end from the elevator." She hung up and looked from Nina to Stephen. "Roger Blanton, Ellie's nephew."

"So I gathered." Nina nodded. "What does he want to see you about?"

"He didn't say. But he's on his way up, so I guess we'll find out."

A few minutes later, Jessica led Roger into the living room.

In his fifties, he had close-set, dark eyes, a hooked nose, and thin, down-turned lips. His olive green parka stretched tightly over his barrel chest, and scuffed leather boots peeked from under baggy jeans.

"Roger, you've met my granddaughter, Nina Foster." Jessica gestured toward Nina.

Roger leaned forward and squinted. "Yeah, I remember you."

"And this is Stephen Kraslow." Jessica nodded toward Stephen.

Stephen stood, and the two men shook hands. Stephen was the taller of the two, but Nina judged Roger was at least a hundred pounds heavier.

"Your name's familiar." Roger studied Stephen.

Stephen nodded. "I'm owner and editor of *The Richmond Review*."

Roger planted his thick hands on his hips. "You're the one wrote the editorial that dumped on the Planning Commission for wanting to develop Sixth North."

"'Fraid so." Stephen smiled.

Nina admired Stephen for keeping his good-natured tone despite Roger's obvious disapproval.

"People like you keep this town from reaching its full potential." Roger stuck out his chin.

"I'm sorry about your aunt, Roger." Nina jumped in, hoping to change the subject before an argument developed. Stephen would be polite, but he would defend his viewpoint. On more than one occasion, she'd seen him refuse to back down when challenged. She didn't want to turn Jessica's living room into a debate arena.

Roger acknowledged Nina's condolence with a curt nod. "She was a pathetic case."

"Have a seat, Roger," Jessica invited.

After looking around, Roger squeezed his bulk into an overstuffed chair.

"Would you like some tea?" Jessica gestured at the coffee table.

"Got any coffee?"

"I could make you a cup of instant."

Roger sniffed. "If instant's all you got, I guess that'll do."

"Back in a minute." Jessica rose and left the room.

Roger turned to Nina. "Good you're here. I wanted to talk to you."

His sudden interest took her by surprise. "Really? What about?"

"What's this nonsense I hear from Auntie's friends that you'll solve her murder? Who said she was murdered?" Roger's eyebrows folded into a frown.

My, word had spread quickly. She'd decided to investigate only a short time ago. Still, she might as well start now and see what she could learn from him. "Several of us doubt your aunt's death was an accident."

His lips thinned. "Yeah, well, cause of death is for the police to decide, now, isn't it?"

"They can hand down the official verdict, yes."

Roger leaned forward. "If I were you, I'd keep my nose out of their investigation."

"Fortunately, you are not me." Nina glanced at Stephen and saw his amused smile. She turned back to Roger. "Do you know of anyone who might want to harm Ellie?"

"No, I do not, because no such person exists." He made a fist and pounded his knee.

Jessica returned with a mug of steaming coffee, which she set on the coffee table in front of Roger. Then she held out the plate of cookies.

Roger grabbed a cookie and munched. He picked up his coffee and took a sip, glaring at Nina over the mug's rim.

Ignoring Roger's blatant hostility, Nina considered her next question. "When I met Ellie on the lake path the night she died, she mumbled about secrets. Do you know what she was talking about?"

"Secrets?" Roger's small eyes narrowed to slits. "Like she, maybe, knew something bad about someone?"

Nina shrugged. "I don't know, which is why I'm asking you."

Roger tilted his head. "Yeah, well, maybe I did hear her talking about secrets from time to time. I never thought…hmmm…" He put down his mug and leveled a forefinger at Nina. "You find out any more about Auntie's secrets, you tell me right away, you hear?"

Stephen shook his head. "The first place Nina will go with any new knowledge of Ellie's death will be to the police. Right, Nina?" He shifted his gaze to her.

Noting Roger's admission he knew about Ellie's secrets, Nina nodded. "Reporting to the police is my duty." She meant what she said, even though she would risk a lecture from Pete Russell about meddling in their investigation.

Jessica placed her hands in her lap and crossed her ankles. "Have you decided on a service for Ellie?"

"She's being cremated." Roger reached for another cookie. "Soon as the police release the body."

"Really?" Jessica raised her eyebrows.

"Hey, don't look at me," Roger said through a mouthful of cookie. "Cremation was Auntie's wish. But, yeah, we'll have a memorial next Sunday, here at Marley. We have to wait until Dorleen Longman arrives. She lives in Florida."

"You mean Ellie's heir?" Jessica shot Nina and Stephen a wide-eyed glance.

"Yep. Dor-leen. A dopey name, if you ask me. She inherits some of Auntie's stash, along with me and about a hundred charities." Roger shook his head.

Nina was eager to know how the will was divided but didn't dare ask. Hopefully, she would learn the exact details from another source.

"Dorleen is flying up from Florida?" Jessica took a cookie from the plate.

Roger pursed his lips. "She'll show up to collect her money, but I doubt she'll hang around."

"Let me know if I can do anything for the memorial service, will you?" Jessica picked up the teapot and refilled Stephen's and Nina's teacups.

He waved a hand. "The memorial is all taken care of. Your director recommended a minister. The dining room is catering. Harriet Hambly insists on planning the food. Says she knows what Ellie would want."

"Harriet was a home economist." Jessica added tea to her cup. "On television."

"Whatever," Roger mumbled.

They sipped their drinks in silence.

Nina searched her mind for something to say that wouldn't raise Roger's ire.

Jessica put down her cup and leaned toward him. "Did you want to talk to me about something in particular?"

Roger lifted his chin and straightened his rounded shoulders. "About the development on Sixth North. I've got this really good deal, see, and I could get you in on the ground floor. You'd make a bundle, Jessica, a real bundle. But maybe now is not the best time." He aimed a frown at Stephen.

Stephen waved a hand. "Don't let me stop you from making your pitch. If you've read my newspaper, you know we present both sides. My recent editorial was negative, but next week, Joshua Billings will present the pro viewpoint."

"You can forget about me, Roger." Jessica shook her head. "I don't have any money available for investments."

"Ah, come on, Jessica, you live in a swell place here." He made a gesture to include the entire room. "Don't tell me you don't have a stash you could invest."

"What assets I have are all tied up." Jessica folded her arms.

Roger poked a finger in Jessica's direction. "Okay, but keep my deal in mind, you hear?"

"Sure, Roger. I'll keep your deal in mind."

Knowing Jessica inwardly rolled her eyes, Nina hid a smile. Roger was so obnoxious, she didn't know how he could convince anyone to invest in his projects.

Roger made a couple more efforts to interest Jessica in his investment opportunity and, failing, turned toward Nina. "You find out anything about Ellie's secrets, you better let me know."

"Why do you suppose Roger is so interested in Ellie's secrets?" Nina asked after the door shut on the unpleasant man.

"He doesn't want anything to threaten his inheritance." Jessica placed Roger's mug and cookie-crumb-infested napkin on the tea tray.

Nina tilted her head. "I wonder if he talked Ellie into contributing?"

"I doubt she'd agree." Jessica shook her head. "I think she saw through him." She tapped her wristwatch. "Say, dinnertime is almost here."

Nina added her and Stephen's teacups to the tray and then glanced toward the window. "All right, but before we lose daylight, I'd like to look at the area where Ellie was found. Do you know if the police have finished searching the scene, Gran?"

"I believe so. I didn't see any of their yellow tape when I stepped outside this morning."

Nina turned toward Stephen. "Do you want to go with me?" She tensed, expecting him to discourage her.

Stephen stood. "Of course, I do."

She relaxed and then addressed Jessica. "Do you have a pair of high-top boots I could borrow? I might want to do a little wading."

Fifteen minutes later, Nina and Stephen left the building and headed toward Lake Mead.

Nina stepped gingerly along the path in Jessica's calf-high, green gardening boots. They pinched her toes but would do for the short time she planned to wear them. "I appreciate your coming with me, but I can't help wondering why you're so agreeable. I thought you didn't approve of my investigating."

Stephen gripped her elbow. "I'll worry, all right. But I doubt anything bad will happen in broad daylight, especially if I'm along."

Despite his sincere tone, she couldn't help

wondering if he had an ulterior motive. Perhaps he accommodated her in the hope she would weaken and agree to see Dr. Rebecca Young. If that reason were the case, he had another think coming. No point in arguing now, though. She gazed at the sky and held out her hand, palm up. "Hey, the rain stopped."

Stephen turned his face skyward. "We've been granted a reprieve. Now, our walk will be more pleasant."

Pleasant until they reached their destination. Then, as Nina gazed at the water and thought about poor Ellie, a shiver coursed through her. "I hate to think of someone drowning, no matter how it happened—accident or murder."

Stephen put an arm around her waist. "Death by drowning would be horrible."

"Look at the gouges in the ground at the water's edge." She pointed to the shoreline.

"I see them. The marks might have been made when the police pulled her body from the lake."

Nina nodded. "I'll search the water near the shore. I don't suppose the police missed anything, but you never know."

"While you check the water, I'll take shore patrol."

Nina left Stephen's side and waded into the lake. She took a moment to let her gaze sweep the expanse, including the opposite shore populated with homes set amid towering pine and fir trees. Bringing her attention to her immediate surroundings, she studied the lake's bottom. Rolling back her jacket's sleeves, she fingered objects that looked interesting. However, her findings turned out to be only sticks or rocks.

Then she spotted a dark object half-hidden amid a

plant's long green fronds. Reaching under the surface, she pulled out her find and held it up, letting the water drip off.

"Got something?" Stephen called from the shore.

Nina joined him and held out the object in her palm, so they both might study it. What she found was a rectangular piece of black rubber, about an inch wide. One end was round and the other jagged, as though once attached to something else.

Stephen took the piece between thumb and forefinger. "Looks like the end of a strap, maybe belonging to a boot, but does it have anything to do with Ellie?"

"I don't know, but I'll hang onto it, just in case." Nina took the piece of rubber and slipped it into her jacket pocket. Next, she explored the area under the dock but found nothing of interest. She waded to shore and caught up with Stephen, who had searched the path and the surrounding grass. "Let's look at the boathouse." She pointed to the wooden structure several yards away.

"Good idea." Stephen nodded. "I've covered everything here without finding anything of interest."

They walked across the grass and up the ramp leading to the building's double doors. Surprise rippled through her when the doorknob twisted easily under her fingers.

"You'd think this place would be kept locked." Stephen pushed open the door.

"I agree. Why didn't the groundskeeper secure the door after the police finished?"

They went inside, the boards under their feet creaking and groaning. The air smelled like wet wood and moldy earth. Gray light filtered through several small, dirty windows set high in the walls. On either side of the room rowboats were stacked two or three high. In between, oars hung vertically on the walls.

Nina squinted as she and Stephen made their way down the aisle separating the rows of boats. "I should have brought a flashlight."

Stephen grinned. "You should make a sleuthing kit to carry around—flashlight, lock picks, magnifying glass…"

"Good idea. For now, though, we'll have to make do. I'll take the back of the building while you search the front."

Nina walked along the rows of stacked boats until she came to the building's back wall. The last two boats shielded a third boat. That boat's middle seat was missing, and a jagged hole gaped in one side. Leaning down to inspect the boat's interior, she glimpsed a bit of green cloth crammed underneath the end seat. She tugged on the cloth and pulled it free. "Found something," she called to Stephen.

"What?" He hurried to her side.

"A sleeping bag," she declared when they had the cloth spread on the floor.

Stephen knelt and turned over the flap to expose the bag's zipper. "Do you suppose someone's been staying here?"

"Could be. Not the warmest or the most comfortable place a person could find."

"But the boathouse would do if you needed to hide."

Finding nothing else under the seat, Nina joined Stephen and turned her attention to the sleeping bag.

Something made of metal was caught on the cord. Nina freed the object. "Look, an earring shaped like a bee. How cute."

The bee's body and wings were of a gold metal. Zircons, or maybe even diamonds—Nina couldn't tell which—shone as the eyes. She turned over the bee. "This earring is for pierced ears. The piece that holds it onto the ear is gone, which is probably why the person lost it."

"Okay, but like the scrap of rubber, the earring might have nothing to do with Ellie."

"I know, but I'll take the earring with me, anyway." Nina slipped the bee into her jacket pocket.

"The sleeping bag, too?" Stephen gestured to the bag.

"No, we'll replace the bag where I found it. Until we know more, I don't want the owner to know we've been snooping."

They rolled up the bag and stuffed it under the seat in the rowboat. After looking around awhile longer and finding nothing of interest, they left the building. Dark clouds filled the late afternoon sky, threatening rain, and a cool breeze blew off the water.

"I'd appreciate your not mentioning to anyone what we found today," Nina told Stephen once they were on the path leading to the home.

Stephen frowned. "You're not turning in the rubber fragment and the earring to the police?"

"I am not." Nina needed more time to consider the items and their possible significance. "They had their chance to search. Besides, I don't want a lecture from Pete Russell. If what I've found turns out to be significant, then, and only then, will I contact him. For now, today's find is our little secret, okay?"

"You're not telling Jessica, either?" Grasping her elbow, Stephen guided them around a curve in the path.

"No. She might slip and tell one of her friends, and soon the news would be all over Marley."

Stephen's lips thinned. "Okay, I'll keep my mouth shut. But Ellie's secrets might have landed her in big trouble. I sure hope yours don't do the same."

Nina appreciated the concern she knew lay behind his grim warning. Still, she'd made her decision to look into Ellie's death. Today's search turned up several interesting finds. True, the bit of rubber, the earring, and the sleeping bag might have nothing to do with Ellie. Then again, maybe the items were related to the events of that fateful night. If so, she might have discovered valuable clues that would lead to the mystery's solution.

Chapter Six

Half an hour later, Jessica led Nina and Stephen to the dining room for the evening meal. Stepping into the room always made Nina feel as though she'd entered an elegant restaurant. Fresh flowers decorated the white-cloth-covered tables. Planters filled with greenery functioned as attractive dividers, and paintings of Northwest landscapes decorated the walls. Large windows afforded views of a courtyard featuring a stone fountain surrounded by flowerbeds and wrought iron benches.

Sunday dinner was considered a special occasion, and everyone dressed up. Some of the men wore suit jackets and ties, a rare sight in the casual climate of the Northwest. Probably, Marley residents' affluence had something to do with their choice of attire. Or maybe the reason was because they came from a generation in which dress and appearance were more important than now. Whatever, Nina found the custom refreshing and she, as well as Stephen, always dressed to blend in. Tonight, she'd added a colorful print jacket to her plain blue slacks and blouse, and Stephen wore a brown-and-red striped tie with his tan dress shirt.

The meal was served buffet style. Nina had a difficult time deciding among chicken cordon bleu, stuffed pork chops, and prime rib. Everything looked and smelled delicious. "If I lived here, I'd really have to watch my weight," she commented to Stephen as, along with Jessica, they moved through the buffet line.

"So would I." Stephen grinned as he scooped a generous helping of mashed potatoes.

Nina finally opted for the chicken, to which she added rice pilaf and braised carrots. "I don't even want to look at the dessert tray." She averted her head as they passed a table loaded with pies, cakes, and cookies.

"We're sitting with Lily and Wally." Jessica craned her neck to survey the room. "I see them at a table by the window."

When she reached the table, Nina saw that Harriet Hambly, the erstwhile home economist, was also there, as were two other women she didn't know.

Jessica gestured to the women. "Meet Sue Starrett and Clara Miller."

Nina studied the two as they greeted one another. Sue's gray hair curved around her chin liked giant commas. Clara's sharp-featured face was softened by a generous smile.

Wally Anders, Lily's friend, rose to greet them. "Well, well, our young folk are here."

Wally's black turtleneck sweater worn under a plaid jacket gave him a sporty look. Nina had met him previously and found him to be friendly and personable.

"Does that include me?" Jessica gave him a sly smile.

"Ha ha. Of course, Jessica." He extended a gnarly hand to Stephen. "Nice to see you again."

Stephen put down his plate and shook the other man's hand. "Good to be here, Wally."

"We were talking about Ellie," Lily said, when everyone was seated.

"Everyone's discussing her." Jessica spread her napkin on her lap. "Do you know anything new?"

Nina focused on Lily, not wanting to miss anything to add to her growing file of information.

"No. We're just hashing over old stuff. How's your investigation coming, Nina?"

Lily's magnified eyes studied Nina. Oh, oh, Lily had put her on the spot.

"We heard you're on the case." Sue sliced a piece of chicken and popped it into her mouth.

Clara leaned toward Nina. "Jessica said you looked over the scene at the lake just now."

Harriet sipped her water. "Find anything?"

Avoiding their intent gazes, Nina buttered her roll. "Nothing we could relate to Ellie." True enough. "Right, Stephen?" She looked to him sitting on her right, for confirmation.

Stephen cleared his throat. "Ah, no, nothing we could say belonged to Ellie."

A teenaged server carrying a water pitcher approached. Her short blonde hair was cut at different lengths, and she wore the green skirt and white blouse uniform of all the Marley servers, most of whom attended Westwood High, a private school nearby. Although Nina didn't know the girl personally, she had seen her working in the dining room. She always had a smile and a friendly greeting, but tonight, her eyes were red-rimmed, as though she'd been crying.

Sue wrinkled her forehead as she looked up at the girl. "Kimmie, dear, what's wrong?"

Kimmie swiped her eyes with the back of her free hand. "Oh, I feel so sad about Miss Larkin."

"We all do." Clara nodded. "You were Ellie's

special friend, too, weren't you?"

"She was so nice to me." Kimmie's lips wobbled into a smile. "She always asked how I was doing in school and did I need help with my homework, especially math, because she was an accountant and that subject was her specialty."

"Don't you worry, honey," Lily said, "because our Nina here will find out who killed Ellie." She gestured toward Nina.

Nina wasn't sure she appreciated Lily's blatant expectation of her sleuthing skill, but perhaps Kimmie did know something she could add to her suspect list.

A frown replaced the teen's smile. "I thought her death was an accident." She glanced around the table.

"Some of us think differently." Jessica picked up her glass and sipped her water.

"Will the police be back, then?"

Nina had been studying Kimmie and now saw something akin to fear shining in the girl's brown eyes. Also, her voice had raised a notch. Perhaps she did know something about Ellie's death.

"Depends on what their verdict is." Wally sliced a bite of his prime rib.

Kimmie pushed a stray lock of hair from her forehead, and the charm bracelet on her arm jingled.

"Oh, what a lovely bracelet." Sue pointed toward Kimmie's arm.

"Didn't Ellie give you the bracelet?" Harriet peered around Lily and Wally to stare at the jewelry.

Setting the pitcher on the table, Kimmie fingered the bracelet's silver charms. "Yes, she did. I really love it. I love all kinds of jewelry."

"So did Ellie." Sue nodded. "She had boxes of

bracelets, necklaces, and earrings, every piece of jewelry you could imagine."

Nina mentally filed away that bit of knowledge.

"I'd better get to work." Kimmie picked up the water pitcher and refilled everyone's glass. "Can I get you anything else to drink?"

"Yes, dear, bring me some tea." Clara turned over her empty cup and set it on the saucer. "And not that herbal stuff. I want caffeine. I need to stay awake. My brother's visiting tonight and he's boring. All he talks about is his job." She wrinkled her long nose.

"I'll have milk." Sue held up a hand. "But no glass, just the carton. I want to take it with me."

"Apple juice," Lily requested. "In a small glass, like those we get orange juice in at breakfast."

"Do you have any cranapple?" Harriet asked. "The brand has to be Delmonica. I once did a commercial for them, you know. Wouldn't drink any other kind."

The rest opted for coffee, which made Kimmie's job a little easier. Still, Nina hoped the girl had a good memory for all the group's particular requests.

As soon as Kimmie was out of earshot, Clara leaned forward and looked around the group. "She might be sad about Ellie, but something else bothers her, too."

"What?" Jessica wrinkled her brow.

While Nina ate her chicken, which tasted delicious, she joined the others in focusing on Clara. She had always liked Kimmie, and now, after learning of her special relationship with Ellie, she especially wanted to know more about the teen.

"Boyfriend trouble." Clara raised her eyebrows.

"How do you know?" Harriet picked up her water

glass.

Nina caught a glimpse of a butterfly-shaped birthmark on Harriet's right hand.

"Because when I was out walking the other night, I saw her get into a car. After she was off work, you know." Clara took a bite of her prime rib, chewed, and swallowed. Several seconds elapsed while she methodically sliced another piece of meat.

Harriet leaned forward. "Come on, Clara, don't leave us hanging."

"She and the driver were arguing." Clara kept her gaze focused on her plate.

"How could you tell they were arguing if you just saw her get into the car?" Jessica asked.

"Because when they drove by, the window was open, and I heard them."

"Did you hear what they said?" Nina hoped to hurry along the narrative and perhaps learn something of importance.

Clara shook her head, setting her bobbed hair swinging. "Just angry voices."

"How do you know her boyfriend was in the car?" Harriet sat back and folded her arms.

"The voice I heard was male." Clara cast Harriet a frown. "Besides, I heard her talking once to one of the other teenage servers about her boyfriend. She didn't mention his name, though."

Sue heaved a sigh. "I remember those days. My beau used to pick me up after church—with my father's permission, of course. But we never argued. Oh my, no." She fluttered her fingertips against her lips.

"My father hated every one of my boyfriends." Lily pursed her lips. "He chased them all away. Except

George, and he lasted only because we ran off and got married."

"I never knew you had such a bad time growing up." Wally patted Lily's arm.

Lily's frown turned into a smile. "Oh, my father would've liked you, hon. He'd call you 'one of the good guys.'"

As the conversation wandered farther afield, Nina mentally filed away the information about Kimmie. The boyfriend issue definitely warranted looking into.

Kimmie returned with the drinks, which interrupted the discussion. Talk resumed, with Nina still thinking about Ellie. Then Harriet's deep voice broke into her thoughts.

"How do you like the beans?" Harriet pointed to her plate where a spoonful of string beans swam in a reddish sauce.

"I didn't eat any." Sue wrinkled her nose. "Beans aren't my favorite."

"I did." Clara speared a bean with her fork and popped it into her mouth. She chewed and swallowed.

"So?" Harriet gazed at Clara.

Clara sucked in her cheeks and shook her head. "Too sour."

"Too sour?" Harriet's mouth turned down. "The recipe is mine. I made the dish on my TV show. No one ever said the beans were too sour then."

"Oh, I beg your pardon." Clara widened her eyes. "I should know better than to comment when you ask how we like something on the menu. I forget you're asking because you had something to do with preparing the dish."

Nina followed the exchange with interest, noting

Harriet's need for praise. Why was she so insecure?

"Did you cook the beans, Harriet?" Stephen asked. "Which, by the way, I found very tasty."

Harriet's mouth turned up as quickly as it had turned down.

Nina hid a smile.

"I didn't cook them, but I supervised. I often do when the cook uses one of my recipes."

"I understand you're planning the menu for Ellie's memorial service." Nina scooped the last of her brown rice onto her fork.

Harriet straightened her shoulders. "Oh, yes. Would you like to hear what we're having? All Ellie's favorites."

"Lily and I will wait and be surprised." Wally pushed back his chair. "We need to be excused. We have a dog to walk."

"Wally's taking care of Nigel." Jessica looked around the group.

"I wondered what happened to him." Nina took another bite of her tossed salad.

Lily folded her napkin and placed it beside her empty plate. "He's such a cute little fella and well trained, too."

"Too bad he can't talk." Sue wrinkled her forehead. "Then he could tell us what happened to Ellie."

Wally stood and strode to the residents' walkers, lined up against the wall like a row of taxicabs waiting for their riders. He selected Lily's, with its bright pink basket, brought the walker to the table, and positioned it so that she could readily grasp the handles.

Everyone waved and exchanged "good-byes" and

"see you later."

When the couple was out of earshot, Sue smiled and sighed. "He is so good to her."

Clara sniffed. "Usually, the man is the one who has to be taken care of. My niece warned me when I moved here."

Several seconds elapsed with no more on the subject forthcoming from Clara.

Harriet folded her arms. "What exactly did your niece warn you of, Clara?"

Clara finished a bite of her cherry pie. "'Don't get involved with a man,' she said. 'Not at your age. If he's not already ailing, he soon will be, and he'll expect you to take care of him.'"

Sue nodded. "My friend Emella nursed four men. They kept dyin' on her."

"What does Wally want from Lily?" Clara snickered behind her hand. "Can't be what men usually want when they're younger."

"Some older ones are still kicking." Sue pressed her lips together.

Clara wrinkled her nose. "I wouldn't know about that subject."

Since a man still was present, Nina expected the women to be more circumspect in their conversation. She glanced at Stephen and saw he followed the talk with a smile rather than a frown.

Catching her gaze, he winked.

Nina gave a slight nod to indicate she appreciated his understanding and indulgence.

"I'm glad Lily has such a good friend in Wally."

Jessica's comment brought Nina's attention back to the discussion.

"I agree." Clara sipped her tea. "Especially since her only son is such a bum. He wants to be a rock star and comes around only when he wants money."

"He sounds like Ellie's nephew, Roger." Sue touched a napkin to her lips. "I have a couple kids who always need money, too." She turned to Harriet. "You're the smart one, Harriet. You chose a career over raising a family."

Harriet nodded. "My career was my whole life."

"Your career still is," Clara muttered.

"You're right about that, Clara." Harriet scooped up a forkful of her beans, chewed, and swallowed. "De-li-cious," she announced, and took another bite.

Nina found Harriet's preoccupation with her now-defunct career interesting. Why was living on her past glory so important? Did her friendship with Ellie enter in? If so, how?

****

After dinner, Nina, Stephen, and Jessica followed their established habit of playing pool in the downstairs recreation room. In addition to several pool tables, the facility offered space for card and board games, as well as jigsaw puzzles. In one corner, comfortable chairs and sofas stood grouped around a large-screen TV. In another, a mini kitchen allowed for food and drink preparation.

Games at two of the pool tables were already underway. The click of balls blended in with the cheers from a football game on the TV and the laughter from a group enjoying a board game. The aromas of coffee and popcorn floated along the airwaves.

Nina, Stephen, and Jessica claimed the third pool table. For the next hour, Nina concentrated on the game, always hoping to beat her grandmother, who was an expert. Stephen was a skilled player, too, and so the competition was tough. In the end, he won one game, while Jessica claimed two.

"Someday, maybe you'll teach us your strategy." Stephen teased Jessica as they left the recreation room and climbed the stairs to the first floor.

"Don't count on any help from her, Stephen." Nina shook her head and grasped the railing. "She won't even tell me how she learned to be such a good player in the first place."

"One of my deep, dark secrets." Jessica laughed.

They reached the first floor and stepped into the reception area. The air rang with good-byes, as residents accompanied their guests to the front door. At the desk, Hilda chatted with a couple visitors. The nearby snack bar was busy, too, with those who had chosen a lighter meal over the buffet or who wanted another cup of coffee before ending the evening.

Stephen turned to Jessica. "Can we see you to your apartment?"

Jessica smiled and patted his shoulder. "No, thank you. I'll be fine. You two run along."

Nina gave her grandmother a hug. "Are you sure? You're welcome to stay with me if you feel uncomfortable here."

Jessica returned Nina's hug then stepped back and raised both hands. "Oh, heavens no. I'm not that scared. But thanks for the offer. You two enjoy the rest of your evening. I'll talk to you later."

Soon, Nina was in Stephen's car and on the way to her condo. She settled back in her seat, clasping her hands in her lap. "I wish I could find out what the police have decided about Ellie."

"Maybe they'll announce the cause of death soon." Stephen braked for a traffic light.

"Even so, I'd like to know more.... Do you still have a special contact at the station?" She glanced at his profile clearly outlined in the streetlight beaming through the windshield.

"I do. But my inquiries might get back to Pete Russell."

She didn't want to deal with him again. "From your source? Why would he tell?"

"She."

Nina straightened. "Your source is a woman? Who?"

He gave her a solemn look. "You know I can't tell you, Nina." The light changed in their favor, and he pressed the accelerator, sending them through the intersection.

Nina turned to look out her window. The streetlights reflected in wavy lines on the wet pavement. A car full of teenagers passed them, the booming bass of their radio echoing into the night. Stephen's contact was a woman. Nina pressed a hand to her tensed stomach. What was their relationship? Was she old? Young? Pretty? Plain? Did they have coffee together? Lunch? What? "Will you, ah, be seeing her soon?" She hoped her voice sounded casual but, given her tight throat, couldn't be sure.

"Nina, stop fishing." He cast her a glance. "Oh, I get it. You're wondering if anything personal exists between her and me. Why would there be when I'm busy pursuing my relationship with you?"

"I don't know. Are you busy pursuing me?"

He slapped the steering wheel. "You see, Nina, our problem…part of it, anyway, is that you don't trust me. A solid relationship must be built on trust."

"You could reassure me." Lest she sound needy, Nina made her tone firm.

"I have tried in similar situations, but my reassurance hasn't done any good, which is why I want you to see Dr. Young."

Nina sighed. Well, she'd known the subject of Dr. Young would come up again, and tonight she provided the perfect opportunity. She folded her arms. "Never mind. I can investigate without information from your source."

Stephen slowed to turn a corner. "I haven't said I wouldn't ask. I only said my query *might* get back to Russell."

"How?" Was the person under Russell's supervision?

"Not because my source would tell. But if she has to dig, someone might get suspicious. Still, I'll see what I can do."

"I don't want to get anyone into trouble." Now she was sorry she'd asked for the favor.

"Don't worry. I'll handle the situation. But I sense you're withdrawing." He gripped the wheel.

"No, I'm not." *Liar.*

"Yes, you are. I feel your distress."

Her stomach churning, she again gazed out the window. "Please, let's not argue anymore."

"I don't want to argue, either."

His voice had softened. But no conversation, either hostile or friendly, was forthcoming, and they rode the rest of the way to Nina's condo in silence. She hated to end with dissention what had been a pleasant evening, but neither would she change her mind about not seeing Dr. Young. Would she and Stephen ever solve their dilemma?

****

Later, Nina lay in bed beside Stephen, unable to sleep. Last night she'd felt loved and protected. Tonight, a deep, dark chasm separated them. Did he feel their separation, too?

She finally fell asleep, but the image followed her into her dreams. She stood on the edge of an abyss, conscious of Stephen behind her. Then, without warning, another man appeared and ran toward her. She peered into the darkness to learn his identity, but he had no facial features. He came nearer and nearer. Her heart pounding, she turned and ran, forgetting that behind her was the cliff. She tumbled off the edge and spiraled down, down into the chasm. Her screams echoed off the surrounding walls.

Arms clutched her.

The faceless man? Her throat constricted. A light blinked on. She opened her eyes and squinted at the sudden brightness. No, the man who held her was Stephen.

"What's the matter, Nina?" His eyes were wide, his voice hoarse.

Gradually, Nina's senses returned her to reality. She leaned against him, grateful for his strength. "Sorry I woke you. I—I'm okay now."

"You were having one of those nightmares, weren't you?"

She pressed a hand to her forehead. "I don't know. I don't remember." She wouldn't admit he was right.

Her nightmares were one of the reasons he thought she should see Dr. Young "I'm all right."

"No, you're not." He frowned and gripped her shoulders. "You're shaking. Can I get you something?"

She shook her head. "Just hold me."

"Of course, honey." He drew her close, stroked her back, and nuzzled her hair with his sleep-warm lips.

You're okay. Stephen's here.

"Want to talk about it?" he asked after awhile.

"No, I want to go back to sleep."

They lay down again, and she curled up against his side. She was afraid to sleep, though, afraid her awakening was only a brief intermission in a macabre play whose end she didn't want to know.

The nightmare was not new. She'd dreamt it before, in different variations, many times. She called the sequence The Faceless Man Dream. A man without a face appeared and approached her. Although he was not particularly menacing, she was always afraid and ran away. Tonight was the first time his appearance sent her over a cliff.

Was the dream a symptom of deep psychological trouble, as Stephen thought? Trouble that needed the probing analysis of a professional? But everyone had nightmares occasionally, and recurring dreams were not uncommon. She was fine, Nina told herself, pressing a hand to her churning stomach. Just fine.

Chapter Seven

Monday morning, Nina returned to her job at the Seaview Library. After her upsetting weekend, she looked forward to answering questions at the information desk, to helping parents choose books to read to their children, and to working on a new book order. Nina's job brought her great satisfaction. For one reason, being in the library, where books stood in rows on shelves, fulfilled her need for orderliness. For another, because she loved to read, she enjoyed sharing books with others. Yes, Nina had found the perfect profession.

Still, Ellie's death preoccupied her, and she spent her lunch break sitting in her office creating a list of suspects. She divided a sheet of paper into three columns with the headings Name, Motive, Opportunity. Her entries were sketchy, but at least she'd made a start. First on the list, not necessarily because he was the most likely but simply because his name popped up first, was Ellie's nephew, Roger Blanton. He had the opportunity because he lived in the area, visited his aunt, and presumably knew her habit of walking around the lake. The motive stumped Nina, though. Gaining control of her money didn't fit, because he wasn't the principal heir. Still, maybe the sum of his inheritance was enough to kill for. She didn't know the amount and, other than asking him point blank, she had no idea how to find out.

After taking time to eat half of her tuna sandwich, Nina added Ellie's other heir, Dorleen Longman, to her list. Maybe she couldn't wait until Ellie passed away from natural causes to possess the money and had helped her along. Opportunity was a stumbling block, though, because Dorleen lived in Florida.

Dr. Ravensbarger was the next name she listed. She assumed he had opportunity, since he practiced in the area. Under Motive, she wrote, "Drugs," with a question mark.

Harriet Hambly, Lakeside's erstwhile home economist, came next. Opportunity, yes. Motive? She and Ellie had participated in a violent argument. Nina needed to find out more about that occasion.

Next was Person or Persons in the Boathouse. Perhaps Ellie discovered their hideaway.

She added Kimmie Hunter's name, not as a suspect, but as someone she wanted to know more about, since she had been a special friend of Ellie's.

Those names were all she could think of at the moment. She looked over her list. Not much to work with, she had to admit, and no one suspect stood out over another. Still, she felt better having made the list. All the roaming thoughts in her head were now organized.

Where to go from here? She would surely see Roger again. Dorleen she would meet at Ellie's memorial, to be held in a few days. Dr. Ravensbarger? Short of making an appointment at his clinic, she couldn't think how to discover more about him. Maybe a patient of his who lived here at Marley could help. She would need to be careful in her inquiries, though.

She wouldn't want word of her activities to reach Sergeant Russell.

****

"What do you want to do first?" Stephen asked. "The treadmill or the rowing machine?"

Gazing around the exercise room at the Evergreen Athletic Club, Nina pressed a finger to her cheek. Did she want to have sore legs or sore arms? "Treadmill," she finally said.

"I see two available, side by side, over there." He pointed across the room.

Eager to begin their exercise, Nina followed him to the machines. The club was a popular place, and today was no exception. Among the participants was a young woman wearing a white T-shirt and black tights using the stair-step. Her blonde ponytail bounced back and forth in time to her energetic steps. Farther on, an older, gray-haired man wearing headphones, his plump cheeks red with exertion, rode a bicycle, while a thirty-something guy with well-developed arm muscles lifted a barbell.

Nina and Stephen reached the vacant treadmills. Nina stepped onto what she called the conveyor belt, and punched buttons to select indicators such as "heart rate" and "calories burned." When she first joined the club, she regarded this room as a virtual torture chamber, full of mysterious machines that punished her body, all in the name of good health. Now, with Stephen's guidance, as well as help from Josie, her personal trainer, Nina had made friends with at least a few of the devices. She and Stephen visited the club an average of three times a week to work out and then soak in the hot tub. Being Tuesday, Nina's library shift was afternoon and evening, which conveniently left the morning for other activities.

Nina started the conveyer belt and walked with her back straight and her arms swinging loosely at her sides. In front of the machines, several television sets, each tuned to a different station, hung from the ceiling. A talk show, a soap opera, and a news report were in progress. In place of sound, closed captioned dialogue rolled across the bottom of the screens like ticker tape.

"I have information from the police," Stephen said, after they had both established their rhythm.

"You do? Fast work!" He'd seen his contact. Or not. Maybe they exchanged a phone call. But when? Yesterday? Last night? Nina pursed her lips. What was their relationship, anyway? Missing a beat, she grabbed the machine's frame to keep her balance.

Stephen shot her a glance. "Are you okay?"

"I just missed a step." Nina regained her footing and then her rhythm. "What did you find out?"

"The police are calling Ellie's death accidental."

Somehow, the decision didn't surprise her. "Did they find evidence of drugs in her body?"

"Yes, the ones Dr. Ravensbarger prescribed. She did overdose, probably by mistake."

"Do you"—Nina huffed a breath as she increased her speed—"know the names of the drugs?"

"I have them written down. I'll give you the list later."

"What was the actual cause of death?"

"Drowning. She had water in her lungs."

"She just waded into the water and"—she paused to whoosh another breath—"drowned? Seems unlikely, especially since she was in shallow water."

Stephen shook his head. "No, they figure she wandered onto the dock and fell off. Being doped up, she wasn't able to get up and out of the water. So, she drowned."

"Hmmm, I don't know if I agree...."

"Well, accidental drowning is the official cause. I'm shutting up now as I crank up the speed. We'll talk more later."

Later turned out to be after they finished the treadmill, spent time on the weightlifting machines, and at last relaxed in the hot tub. Nina leaned to let a jet massage her back. "Oh, this warm water feels good."

"Sure does." Stephen scooted closer. "Nice to have the place all to ourselves, too."

The hot tub room was an adjunct to the main building, with three walls of windows looking out onto the club grounds. Nina gazed at the pouring rain and the alder trees swaying in the wind, which made the warmth and coziness of the hot tub all the more pleasurable. She turned to Stephen. "Did your police source discover anything else?"

Stephen rested his outspread arms on the tub's wall. "That information is all for now. More may be forthcoming. In the meantime, something else has come up."

"Oh?" Nina rubbed her nose, tickling from the mist rising from the water.

"On Friday afternoon, I'm covering the opening of the Marsh Street Clinic."

"I see. Then you don't want to get together?" Her stomach knotted. Maybe he was using the occasion as an excuse to cut short their weekend. Maybe he wanted an out for the weekend altogether. They'd been getting along, but for her, anyway, the scars from their big argument last weekend still hurt.

Stephen frowned. "Nina, please stop jumping to conclusions."

The studied patience she heard in his voice calmed her.

"I'm not avoiding you." Stephen patted her shoulder. "On the contrary, I want you to go with me. Dr. Ravensbarger owns the clinic, and the opening would be a good chance for you to meet him." He raised an eyebrow. "That is, if you're continuing your investigation?"

His support both surprised and pleased her. "Oh, I am, until I'm satisfied one way or another. The clinic opening would be a good opportunity to meet the doctor. I've wondered how I might connect with him, short of pretending I need his services."

"Okay, then." He nodded. "We'll go to the opening and to dinner afterward."

"Sunday is Ellie's memorial...." She cast him a glance. Would he want to accompany her on that occasion?

"Looks as though we have our weekend planned." He moved closer and grasped her hand.

The knot in Nina's stomach eased. He wasn't leaving her. Not this weekend, anyway.

Chapter Eight

Nina sat in her living room that evening, a cup of tea at her elbow and her tablet computer on her lap. She researched the four drugs the police report said were found in Ellie's body.

The first drug was for relief of discomfort resulting from muscle spasm of the gastrointestinal tract. She read the article, focusing on the side effects, which included excitement, confusion, and disturbed behavior.

Those conditions described Ellie the night of her death. Granted, the side effects were labeled unusual, unexpected, and infrequent, but, still, the adverse reactions were possible.

Nina looked up the other three drugs on the list. The results were most enlightening, or perhaps horrifying would be a better word. One medicine, used to treat high blood pressure, also had possible side effects of confusion and disturbed behavior. So did the third, which treated depression, and the fourth, which corrected irregular heartbeat.

Did Ellie really need all the drugs? Nina wondered as she sipped her tea. She admitted she herself went to the opposite extreme, unwilling to take even an aspirin for a headache unless absolutely necessary. Still, Ellie's drug use seemed excessive. Also, the substances might react negatively with one another, creating even more undesirable and dangerous side effects.

Wouldn't a doctor consider the danger of drug interactions? Nina wondered about Dr. Ravensbarger. Did Ellie have legitimate illnesses, or did he prescribe the medications for some other reason?

The police were satisfied Ellie's death was accidental. She was just an addled old woman who didn't know what she was doing when she climbed onto the dock during the rainstorm.

Nina disagreed. Ellie's behavior and subsequent death were suspicious. She hoped attending the opening of Dr. Ravensbarger's new clinic with Stephen this Friday would provide new information. If not, she'd have to come up with something else to prove her theory.

****

"I've decided to begin our work sessions with a short meeting." Nina looked around the table at her Marley Manor library crew, which she had called together on Wednesday evening. Having another meeting to attend, Jessica was missing. But the others— Lily Ciliano, Mabel Whiteside, and Selma Bellari— faithfully arrived at the appointed time. While she enjoyed her project and was anxious to bring it to completion, Nina also hoped her presence at Marley would make her privy to information relevant to her investigation.

"Ah like meetings." Mabel smoothed her bell-shaped, maroon skirt and then fingered the artificial orchid tucked into her silver-blonde hair.

"Me, too!" Lily's magnified eyes sparkled.

Selma remained silent, her topknot tilting forward while she studied her fingernails.

"Selma?" Nina leaned toward the woman. "Is my

80

plan okay with you?"

"I suppose." Selma pursed her lips. "But when I worked as a teacher, we were meetinged to death. Faculty meetings, committee meetings, parent meetings, study group meetings, on and on."

"Ours will be short, I promise. Let's get started." Nina consulted the notes on her tablet. "We've sorted the books into two broad categories, fiction and nonfiction. Now, we'll put them into even smaller groups."

Mabel raised a hand.

"Yes, Mabel?"

"Are we puttin' numbers on the books? What do y'all call that? The Huey Decimal System?"

"The *Dewey* Decimal System." Nina smiled.

"You're thinking of Huey, Dewey, and Louie, Donald Duck's nephews." Selma giggled behind her hand.

"No, *you* are." Mabel glared.

Lily wrinkled her nose. "Maybe you were thinking of Huey Long, that awful southern governor."

"He wasn't so awful." Mabel lifted her chin. "He helped the poor."

"Well, somebody didn't like him, 'cause he was assassinated!" Lily made a fist and pounded the table.

"Ladies, please." Nina spread her hands in gentle protest. "Let's keep to the subject. We won't use the Dewey Decimal System—"

"I'm glad to hear that." Selma rolled her eyes. "Math was never my strong suit."

"We'll group the books into categories and put those names on the spines. Topics like Animals, Travel, History—you get the idea. I've made a list." Nina held up a sheet of paper. "Categories will make finding books easy for the users and for us to organize the books on the shelves."

"Won't we have a catalog?" Mabel's brow wrinkled.

"We will have a list on a computer, which I'll bring soon. Do most of you use a computer?" Nina looked around the group. After this initial period of instruction, she hoped to learn something useful to her investigation into Ellie's death.

Lily nodded. "My son set up mine and my email. He's the only one who ever emails me, though."

"Do you use your computer for anything else?" Nina asked.

Lily shook her head. "I could read news on it, my son says, but I'd rather read the newspaper or watch TV."

"How about you two?" Nina looked at Mabel and Selma.

Mabel frowned and folded her arms. "Why can't we have a card catalog like in the old days? Everyone who lives here will remember how to use the cards."

"A computer catalog is much more efficient." Nina kept a patient tone.

"Not if no one can use it." Mabel sniffed.

"I'm betting Marley has a lot of computer-savvy residents." Nina continued her attempt to bring the committee over to her side on the issue.

"My next door neighbor's a whiz on the computer." Lily looked around the table. "Maybe she could teach us."

"Great idea." Nina gave the woman an appreciative smile. "But, like I said, knowing how to use a computer will not be necessary in our library. We're sorting the books into categories and labeling them. People will find what they want by simply browsing. Then they will record what they borrow on this clipboard." She took a clipboard and held it up. "The computer will help us when we take inventory."

"Inventory." Selma frowned. "You mean counting the books?"

Nina put out a hand. "Yes, but don't worry about that task now. Inventory is far in the future."

"I had to take inventory when I worked at Maxwell's Mercantile." Lily pinched her nose with thumb and forefinger. "Bor-ing. I fell asleep."

Nina gave an inward sigh but kept the smile glued to her lips. "Like I said, don't worry about inventory now. Let's work on our book stacks. Here's the list of categories." She handed a sheet of paper to each woman. "An empty box on the table corresponds with each topic on the list." She pointed to the boxes. "Lily, while Mabel and Selma sort, you can put these labels on books I've already laid aside." She gave her several rolls of stick-on labels.

The women set to work.

Although she kept an eye on their progress, Nina also took the time to relax. Organizing the committee and keeping them on track took more effort than she had anticipated. Still, she enjoyed the women and knew their hearts were in the project.

A few minutes later, Harriet Hambly arrived. She wore her usual blue jeans and a sweatshirt with "Harriet Hambly Rules" written in big letters across the front.

"I just dropped in to see how you're doing." Harriet spread her feet, planted her hands on her hips, and gazed around.

Lily frowned. "If you're so interested, why don't you join our committee?"

"Oh, no, no, no." Harriet held up both hands, and the butterfly birthmark on her right hand spread its wings. "All I know about books is how to write them." She looked toward Nina. "By the way, have you decided where mine will be shelved?"

"I haven't, Harriet. We're still sorting and labeling." Nina pointed to the boxes and stacks of books on the table.

Harriet wandered around the room, stopping at a bookcase near the fireplace. She ran a hand over one of the shelves. "My books could go here, with a sign that says 'The Harriet Hambly Collection.' I'll have the sign printed." She smiled over her shoulder at Nina.

"I appreciate your wanting to help." Nina struggled to maintain her patience. "But let's wait until we see how many books we have in each category and how those groups fit on the shelves."

Harriet shrugged. "Okay." She reached into a box, pulled out a few books, and perused the titles.

"Are you looking for a particular book, Harriet?" Nina hoped to learn why Harriet showed such interest in the library project yet declined to participate.

Harriet frowned and dropped the books back into the box. "I'd really like to find the cookbook I loaned Ellie. Have you come across the books she donated?"

Ah, the cookbook Ellie borrowed. Could the book somehow be connected with her death? "No, we haven't. But I'll certainly let you know when I find her donation."

"Are you sure you don't have a box of her books?" Harriet folded her arms and planted her feet apart. "I could look through it myself."

"I'm sure, Harriet." The woman's persistence made Nina even more curious about the book's importance.

Harriet strode to the storage closet, opened the door, and peered inside. "What's in here?"

"Just supplies." Nina heaved a sigh. Didn't Harriet trust anything she was told?

Harriet shut the closet door. She wandered around the room for a few more minutes then finally left.

"Whew!" Lily swiped a hand across her brow. "I'm glad she's gone. She made me nervous."

"Why is she so fussed up about one cookbook when she gave the library a whole box of her books?" Selma propped her hands on her hips.

Mabel shook her head and narrowed her eyes. "There's somethin' strange about that woman."

"Strange?" Nina frowned. "What do you mean?" She, too, had always sensed something unusual about Harriet. Hopefully, Mabel had information she could add to her suspect list.

Mabel made a sweeping gesture to include the entire room. "She just doesn't fit in here at Marley."

"She's an outsider because she's so wrapped up in herself and her career," Selma said.

"She has accomplished a lot." Nina transferred a stack of books from her workplace to where Selma and Mabel sat.

"Maybe so, but does she have to keep reminding us? The rest of us weren't exactly dullards. I was once Teacher of the Year for my district." Selma straightened and lifted her chin.

Lily carefully removed a sticker from the roll and affixed it to the spine of a book. "My son's a dullard.

But, then, he takes after his father." She twisted her lips. "What I ever saw in that man I'll never know."

Lily's declaration led to a conversation about children and erstwhile husbands. Nina listened with amused interest.

Then Mabel waved her pendant watch. "Oh, my, I see it's time for mah date."

"Date!" Lily stared. "Who with? I thought I was the only one around here with a man."

Mabel giggled. "With Jeffrey Richards."

"Who's he?" Lily and Selma exchanged glances.

Mabel ducked her head and fluttered her eyelashes.

"Come on, Mabel," Selma begged. "Tell us."

"Oh, all right." Mabel waved a hand. "Jeffrey Richards is the doctor in that new show on channel seventeen. He is sooo handsome."

"Oh, you mean a TV date." Selma folded her arms. "Not a date with a real man."

"The best kind." Mabel patted her hair. "Ah don't have to cook for him or clean up after him. Ah can just sit there and admire him."

Nina joined in the ensuing laughter, glad her committee could enjoy themselves while contributing to the new library. At the same time, Harriet's appearance and her preoccupation with the book she loaned Ellie renewed Nina's determination to find out what that matter was all about. Did Harriet have something to do with Ellie's death, after all?

****

After the women left, Nina inspected their work and found they had sorted nearly a hundred books. Not bad, considering all the distractions. She stacked the boxes against one wall where they would be out of the way until the contents were shelved. As she worked, she thought again about Harriet Hambly. Her constant bragging was annoying, but Nina found something pathetic about her, too. She seemed such a loner. Ellie had been her friend, but now she was gone.

What about the book Harriet wanted to locate? Was the book really a cookbook? Nina had found no box of donations from Ellie. But perhaps she put her books singly in the donation barrel Nina placed in the lobby, where they became mixed with other people's books. Unless they were labeled with Ellie's name, identifying them would be difficult if not impossible.

Maybe she should check the storage closet. She'd told Harriet only supplies were inside, but she could be mistaken. Nina stepped into the closet and turned on the light. The shelves held boxes of bookends and office supplies, such as paperclips, pencils, and pens.

Underneath the bottom shelf sat several larger boxes. Nina pulled out the nearest container. An inspection of the contents revealed paper plates, cups, and napkins left over from when the room was used for meetings. Another box held old newspapers and a scrapbook someone had started about the home. She made a mental note to deliver the scrapbook to the office. Perhaps another resident would continue documenting Marley's history.

The last box was full of books, both paperback and hardback. Nina pulled out a paperback and opened the cover. "Ellie Larkin" was written on the flyleaf. Her heartbeat quickened. Had she located Ellie's donation at last? She examined a few more books and found all of them inscribed with Ellie's name. Who had put them in the closet, and why? Had they been separated from other donations by design or by mistake? Whatever the reason, she was relieved to have located Ellie's books. Now, to find the volume belonging to Harriet and, hopefully, to discover why Harriet was so obsessed over its return.

Nina tugged the box from the closet. Then the thought occurred that she might not want to be interrupted in her search. She went to the hallway door and looked out. No one to the left, but to the right, a shadowy figure stood in the recess housing the elevators. Harriet? Or someone else? She craned her neck for a better view but still couldn't identify the person. Presently, a ding sounded as an elevator door opened, and then a swishing noise as the door closed. Nina exhaled the breath she'd been holding.

Still, she waited. No one entered the hallway, and all was quiet. Empty hallways at Marley had never bothered her before. Now, all of a sudden, viewing the deserted, shadowy corridor sent a shiver down her spine.

Nina closed the door and twisted the lock, not only to shake the creepy feeling but also to prevent Harriet's interruption, should the insistent woman take a notion to return. Nina dragged the box of books to a table where she could sit and comfortably inspect them. The volumes numbered about three dozen and were an eclectic assortment, mostly old novels. A few travel guides were included, although too out of date to be useful, along with a book of world history that probably had monetary value in the book-collecting world. She grouped the categories together for future inspection and possible inclusion in the Marley library.

The next book she pulled out was titled *Cooking on*

a Budget. The cover showed a smiling, though younger, Harriet Hambly, wearing a chef's hat and chopping vegetables on a cutting board. Harriet had been right, Nina thought, experiencing a niggle of guilt as she paged through the attractive, lavishly illustrated book. Well, as soon as possible, she would personally deliver the book and set Harriet's mind at ease. Then the woman would have no more reason to disturb the committee's work.

Nina laid the cookbook aside and removed the last remaining book from the box. On the cover, in embossed lettering, was the word "Shasta" and under that, the date 1965. Ah, a high school annual. Shasta High was in Monroy, Iowa. Was this Ellie's high school annual? Nina searched the various class portraits and, sure enough, she found Ellie's picture in the seniors' section.

Attempting to reconcile the image with the confused and fearful woman she encountered at the lake, Nina studied the photo. Young Ellie, with a smile on her lips and her shoulder-length hair, appeared full of life and promise. What had happened to her in the intervening years? Had being abandoned by her fiancé soured Ellie on life and turned her into a bitter old woman?

My father abandoned me, and today I worry about Stephen leaving. We have something in common, Ellie and I. Even though Nina had been only five when her father left, she could, when reminded, still feel the emptiness and, yes, the fear, his absence created. Had Ellie experienced similar reactions?

Thinking about feelings froze her insides, and Nina shook her head to clear away the troublesome memories. She refocused on Ellie's annual. Maybe something in her past would cast light on what happened the night she died. What had Ellie accomplished in high school? What were her interests? Consulting the book's index, she located Ellie's name and several page references.

One page was for Math Club, which made sense, since Ellie had been an accountant later in life. Another reference led to a feature about the Science Club. A picture showed Ellie with several other students at work in the school laboratory. The last was for Home Economics Club. A picture of that group displayed several boys and girls in school's kitchen. Nina spotted Ellie, dressed in a white blouse, a pleated skirt, and saddle shoes, standing by the stove. At a nearby table, a student poured batter from a bowl into cake pans while several classmates looked on.

The student pouring the cake batter caught Nina's eye. Was that a butterfly birthmark on the person's right hand or a flaw in the photograph? A magnifying glass would help. She retrieved one from the cupboard and returned to the picture.

The magnifying glass examination confirmed her original supposition, and excitement rippled along her spine. The student had a birthmark in the shape of a butterfly on the right hand, just like Harriet Hambly. And yet, how could this person possibly be Harriet?

Tracing her finger along the caption under the picture, Nina gasped. The person pouring the cake batter was male, and his name was Harry Kirkwood.

Chapter Nine

As realization dawned, Nina continued to stare at the picture. The person who lived at Marley Manor as Harriet Hambly had been born Harry, or, more likely, Harold, Kirkwood. Flipping the pages, she looked up Harry's name in the annual's index. His portrait was in the senior class section, the same as Ellie's. The reddish hair, the snub nose, and the freckles showed an unmistakable resemblance between the young Harry and today's Harriet. While Harry's short haircut, suit jacket, and tie identified him as masculine, a softly rounded chin and full lips hinted at the latent feminine side.

When had Harry officially become Harriet? Nina did not think Harry was simply masquerading as a woman. No, the transformation appeared complete. He must have had a sex-change operation, after which, as Harriet, she carved out a successful career as the home economist icon. Years later, she and Ellie Larkin, perhaps by coincidence, came to live in the same retirement home. Ellie spotted the unique butterfly birthmark and recognized Harriet as her old school pal, Harry.

Gripping the book, Nina paced the room, putting together the scenario. Upon reconnecting, Ellie agreed to keep Harriet's secret. But then she had crazy spells where she talked about knowing people's secrets, and

Harriet feared Ellie would slip and reveal hers.

Even though Ellie might be dismissed as only confused, people would whisper and wonder. Worse yet, Ellie might show Harry's picture in the school annual to someone who would then know Ellie spoke the truth. Although many people who underwent sex-change operations were quite vocal and open about their experiences, Harriet might not be among that group. She could be particularly sensitive about her past life and not want anyone in her current life to know she had once been a man. Too, she had her reputation as Harriet Hambly, the renowned cook and TV icon, to protect.

Sinking back into her chair, Nina put in order the ensuing events. Harriet wanted Ellie to give her the annual, and she refused. As Ellie's confusion increased, her ramblings became more and more frequent. In desperation, Harriet followed Ellie to the lake on that dark, rainy night. Perhaps Ellie climbed onto the dock on her own, or perhaps Harriet, who was the bigger and stronger of the two, dragged her there. She pushed Ellie off the dock and into the cold water. Then, before Ellie could recover, Harriet ran to shore, waded into the water, and held down Ellie's head until she drowned.

The all-too-vivid scene sent a shiver down Nina's spine. Yet, the incident could have happened as she imagined. Harriet Hambly could very well be a murderer. The annual, not the cookbook, was the book Harriet was really looking for.

Nina ran her fingers over the annual's embossed letters. If the book was so important, why had Ellie donated it to the library? Perhaps in her confused state, she hadn't realized she'd included it in her donations.

Whatever, the annual might be an important piece of evidence. Still, with no actual proof of her supposition, she would keep the book at home while pursuing her investigation. Laying aside Harriet's cookbook to later give to the woman, Nina then put the annual into a manila envelope and tucked it into her tote. She straightened a few piles of haphazardly stacked books, gathered the category sheets strewn about the table, and dragged the now-empty box back to the closet.

She slipped into her parka and slung her tote over her shoulder, moving the bag around to the front so she could keep a grip on it, just in case. She thought about stopping by Jessica's apartment but decided the hour was too late. Besides, she wanted to be away from this place that had suddenly taken on an aura of danger.

Hurrying along the deserted hallway, she looked over her shoulder to make sure no one—namely, Harriet Hambly—was behind her. The elevator creaked and groaned in a way she had never noticed before and seemed inordinately slow lowering her to the first floor. The reception area, including Hilda's desk, was empty.

Before she reached the front door, someone jumped from a wing chair and stepped in front of her, blocking her way. Apprehension skittered down her spine and then changed to annoyance as she recognized Roger Blanton. "Roger! For heaven's sake, you startled me. What are you doing here so late?" Why was he here at all, now that Ellie was gone?

He stuck both hands on his hips. "Meeting with Director Marshall. Some last-minute details about Auntie's service on Sunday."

The use of the childish term "Auntie" by this fiftyish, barrel-chested man made Nina want to giggle.

But the fierce scowl on his face, obviously directed at her, quickly chased away the urge. A skitter of the fear she experienced a moment ago returned, and she tightened her grip on her tote. "Oh? Is the memorial all planned?" She stepped sideways to go around him.

He matched her steps, still blocking her way. "I guess so."

"Good. I'll be there. I'm on my way out now, though, so if you'll excuse me?" Nina glanced over her shoulder at the receptionist's desk. Still vacant. Where was Hilda? She needed a witness to this confrontation.

Roger finally moved aside.

Nina hurried to the sliding glass doors. They swished open, and she stepped outside. At the same time she realized he was still behind her, she heard the doors shut with a resounding click. At this time of night, the doors automatically locked, so returning to the building was not an option.

Turning, she faced him. "Did you have something else you wanted to say?"

"Yeah. I'll walk you to your car. Mine's in the same lot." He nodded to the parking lot.

Unease rippled through her, and she narrowed her eyes. "How do you know our cars are in the same lot?"

"I saw you when you arrived. C'mon." He took a step forward, stopped, and waited.

Nina had parked in the south lot, as she had the night Ellie died. Although the grounds were well lit, she didn't relish walking to her car with Roger. She neither liked nor trusted him. Reaching into her purse, she found her car keys, curling a forefinger around the vial of pepper spray attached to the ring.

Yet, did she really think he murdered Ellie? In light

of what she learned this evening, Harriet Hambly now seemed the more likely culprit. "What's on your mind, Roger?" she asked as they walked along. A cool breeze blew off the lake, and clouds hid the rising half moon.

"I want to know if you've discovered any of Auntie's secrets."

She'd never tell him what she just discovered in the library. "No, I haven't. Why?"

He stuck out his chin. "She was my aunt, and I should know if she had secrets. 'Specially now that she's dead."

Nina reached the end of the building and, eager to reach her car, stepped onto the path leading to the south parking lot. A thicket of evergreen trees lined the driveway on either side. To the left, tiny dots of light beamed from distant houses. To the right, spots of illumination came from the lamp posts in the parking lot. Although the rain had ceased, the roadway was slick. The wet surface would freeze overnight and in the morning be a silver sheet of ice. But tonight held a more immediate worry. Nina shivered and quickened her steps, anxious to be rid of the troublesome Roger Blanton.

"What do you know about Harriet Hambly?" Roger poked a finger at Nina.

Nina tensed but kept up her pace. What made him ask about Harriet? Had he spied on Nina in the library? No, impossible. She closed and locked the door before inspecting the album. "I barely know her. She was Ellie's friend, and she's built a reputation as a chef."

Roger waved a hand. "Yeah, but something's going on with her."

"What do you mean?" Nina hit gravel with the toe

of her boot, scattering the small stones into the nearby shrubbery.

"She wanted me to let her into Auntie's apartment tonight to look for a cookbook of hers she said Auntie had."

The cookbook? Or the school annual? "Did you let her in?"

"I don't have a key. Auntie changed the locks and forgot to give me one. I had a key before. I needed one, with her living alone and all."

"I see." Nina found Roger's information interesting. Most likely, Ellie changed the locks and forgot on purpose to give him a new key.

"Anyway, what about Harriet?" Roger frowned and leaned close. "Does she really want to look for her cookbook or for something else?"

Nina clutched her tote, feeling the outline of the school annual under her fingers. "Harriet also told me she is missing a cookbook. Just tonight, I found one of hers in a box of books Ellie donated to the library. I'll return it to her as soon as possible."

Roger's brow cleared as he stopped and planted his hands on his hips. "No kidding? She was tellin' the truth."

"Apparently so." Nina breathed a sigh of relief. Hopefully, he'd drop the matter and leave her alone. Still, he remained beside her as she continued walking. At the parking lot, she spotted her car. "I'll say goodnight to you here, Roger."

"Okay." He frowned again. "But, listen, you find out any of Auntie's secrets, you tell me."

As though a thought suddenly occurred, Nina stopped and faced him. Perhaps she could put an end to his badgering. "Maybe she had no secrets. Maybe your aunt was confused from all her medication."

He tilted his head and studied her. "Wait a minute. The other day at your grandma's, you asked me if I knew Ellie's secrets. Now, you've decided she didn't have any? What's going on?"

"I don't want to confuse you, Roger." Nina put out a hand. "I said, *maybe* she had no secrets."

He shook a forefinger. "No. She knew something bad about someone. I want to know what and who."

Nina gave an inward sigh. So much for diverting Roger's attention. "Goodnight, Roger." She put finality in her tone and turned toward her car.

"You tell me anything you find out, you hear?" he called after her.

Nina bit back a reply and kept walking. She half expected him to follow. Thankfully, he didn't. After she locked her car's doors and started the engine, she peered out the windshield into the darkness, hoping to see where Roger went.

Headlights blinked on a couple rows away. The vehicle backed out of the space and turned into the driving lane.

As Nina watched the dark-colored pickup truck drive by, she made out Roger's profile. She waited until the truck's motor faded away and then left the lot. The man was like a dog after a bone, she thought, as she headed home. None of her attempts to distract him from his mission worked. She only hoped his meddling didn't interfere with her meddling.

****

"Marsh Street Clinic looks like a fancy place." Nina surveyed the two-story office building she and

Stephen were about to enter. Tonight was the clinic's open house, an event Stephen was covering for his newspaper. Since the clinic's director, Edgar Ravensbarger, had also been Ellie Larkin's physician, Nina hoped to learn something to aid her investigation.

"The clinic is impressive." Stephen grasped her elbow and guided her onto the stone walkway.

Nina spotted a wooden sign listing the participating doctors, but before she could read them all, Stephen drew her toward the door.

Once they were inside, the décor captured Nina's attention. Chairs upholstered in turquoise fabric sat against walls painted a pastel peach. Coffee tables were a neutral cream color. The carpeting and even the pictures on the walls displayed only those pastel hues. Ordinarily, such a color scheme would have struck her as monotonous, but this design was oddly soothing.

At the far end of the room were a semi-circular reception desk and a hallway leading to offices. Both a wide, carpeted stairway and an elevator took patients to the second floor.

A group of thirty or so people were in attendance, chatting, drinking coffee and tea, and sampling hors d'oeuvres from a buffet table. Nina recognized several Marley residents, which was not surprising, since Dr. Ravensbarger specialized in geriatrics.

Stephen pointed to a young man with spiky blond hair and a camera bag slung over his shoulder. "There's Rob, my photographer. He and I need to work together for a while. Okay if I leave you on your own?"

Nina patted his arm. "I'll be fine. Do what you need to for the newspaper." When she was alone she went to the buffet table and filled a paper cup with coffee. Turning away, she spotted Sheryl Titus, Marley's nurse. Nina stepped to her side. "Hello, Sheryl."

Sheryl knit her brow. "Do I know you?"

Nina pointed to her chest. "I'm Nina Foster. My grandmother, Jessica Bingham, lives at Marley."

The woman's brown eyes lit. "Ah, so you're Nina."

Not sure how to take that remark, Nina chuckled. "Has my reputation spread?"

"Everyone at Marley knows you're investigating Ellie Larkin's death." She frowned. "But what's to investigate? Her drowning was accidental." Sheryl selected a chocolate chip cookie from a plate and took a bite.

Looking over the assortment of food, Nina chose a cracker topped with a slice of cheese. "Accidental is the official call, but some of us think differently."

Sheryl pursed her lips and shook her head, setting her silver hoop earrings swaying. She raised her cup to take a sip of coffee, revealing a matching silver bracelet.

Since she found the bee earring in the boathouse, Nina paid special attention to women's jewelry. She doubted the little bee belonged to Sheryl. The nurse's entire appearance, from her corkscrew, shoulder-length black curls, to her bright print tunic top worn over black stretch pants said Notice Me.

"What brings you here?" Sheryl waved at the crowd. "I don't see your grandmother anywhere. I don't see her often in our Marley office, either. She must be remarkably healthy."

"She is healthy, and for that we're both thankful. I came with Stephen Kraslow, from *The Richmond*

Review." She nodded to where Stephen, notebook and pen in hand, spoke with a gray-haired man dressed in a business suit. "How about you? Did you come with some of the residents? I see quite a few tonight."

"I'm attending because I also work for Dr. Ravensbarger here at the clinic."

Nina tucked away that interesting bit of news. "Were you on duty the night Ellie died?" She might as well take the opportunity to see if Sheryl had information helpful to her sleuthing.

Sheryl pressed a forefinger to her cheek. "Let me think. Her death was a week ago Friday, wasn't it? Hmmm, no. I was in my office during the day, but Janet Brunkel had night duty."

Nina wished she could question Sheryl about Ellie being Dr. Ravensbarger's patient and the medications he prescribed, but also knew the patients' privacy rules would prevent Sheryl from divulging any information. But perhaps the nurse could be helpful in another way. "I'd love to meet Dr. Ravensbarger."

"Of course." Sheryl smiled. "I'll be happy to introduce you."

Nina followed Sheryl through the crowd to where the doctor stood surrounded by a group of older women.

Favoring Sheryl with nods and smiles, they obligingly moved aside to admit her and Nina to the inner circle.

"Doctor, this is Nina Foster." Sheryl gestured toward Nina.

"Nice to meet you, Nina." Dr. Ravensbarger offered a hand.

"Pleased to meet you, too, Dr. Ravensbarger." His

handshake was firm and confident. He was a stout man, not much taller than Nina's five feet five, and in his late forties. He had bristly gray hair and black eyes under thick, expressive brows.

"Her grandmother lives at Marley." Sheryl sipped her coffee.

"Oh?" The doctor's thick eyebrows peaked. "Is she one of mine?"

Nina shook her head. "No, she isn't. She's in very good health and rarely needs a doctor."

"Indeed?" He folded his arms. "Can't be too careful, especially as one gets older. Am I not right, ladies?" He flashed his admirers a toothy smile.

The group nodded and chorused their agreement.

His smile still in place, he again faced Nina. "What brings you to our celebration?"

She was tempted to say, "I wanted to meet you," but instead said, "I came with Stephen Kraslow."

"Ah, the newspaperman. I spoke with him earlier this week. He promised to write a feature article about the clinic."

"Nina will find out who murdered Ellie Larkin," a voice piped up.

Gasping, Nina whirled. The speaker was Lettie, a Marley resident whom she knew only slightly

Lettie pushed her way forward until she stood next to Nina. "We residents asked you to investigate, and I know you won't let us down. Ellie was your patient, too, wasn't she, Doctor?"

"Indeed, she was under my care." Dr. Ravensbarger's smile faded. "I was most upset when I heard of her *accident* at the lake."

"No accident." Someone else spoke up. "She was

murdered."

More murmurs circulated the crowd.

"You're playing amateur sleuth, Nina? How brave of you."

Dr. Ravensbarger's black eyes glinted with malicious amusement, as though he and Nina shared a private joke. She lifted her chin. "If I am, you can be sure I won't be just playing."

The doctor turned to his fan club. "My, she sounds serious, doesn't she, ladies?"

Heat flamed her cheeks. The situation had rapidly progressed from bad to worse. She looked around for an escape, but the group had closed around her, Sheryl, and the doctor. She turned to him. "Your new facility looks like a wonderful clinic. Tell us how you came to build it."

Ravensbarger smirked. "Thank you. Having my own clinic, along with a group of congenial doctors, has long been my dream. I also wanted a lab for my research."

The doctor talked on, while his fans listened with rapt attention. He certainly had them under his spell. Was he really such a good doctor? Or just clever at making people think he was?

The doctor's monologue drifted back to his days in medical school.

Nina slipped farther into the crowd until she could leave. Sometime during the discourse, Sheryl, too, had disappeared. Stephen and Rob were near the entrance. Stephen interviewed a middle-aged woman, and Rob readied his camera for a picture.

Her encounter with Doctor Ravensbarger left Nina stinging with indignation and embarrassment. Thinking to separate herself from the crowd and calm her emotions, she drifted toward the hallway at the back of the room. A group of half a dozen people clustered around a young woman holding a clipboard. Her nametag said "Desi."

Desi met Nina's gaze. "We're touring the clinic. Would you like to join us?"

"I would." Nina stepped closer. Maybe seeing the rest of the facility would reveal useful information about the doctor and his practice.

Chapter Ten

Nina followed Desi and the rest of the group down the hall.

Desi stopped at the first open door and gestured to the room beyond. "Here's one of our offices. Since the space is unoccupied, we can take a closer look."

They entered a reception/waiting room. The yellow and green color scheme, while different from that of the main area, was similarly pale in tone.

Desi led them to windows overlooking a walled garden. "Since doctors' offices are frequently drab and confining, Dr. Ravensbarger wanted to make working here a pleasant experience." She nodded toward the window.

Chalk one up for the doctor, Nina thought, as she took in the wrought iron furniture, miniature trees, and flowering bushes.

They peeked into an exam room, a doctor's private office, and then continued down the hall. At the end were a spacious staff lounge, a door leading outside, and stairs to the second floor.

Desi pointed toward the stairs. "We'll go up to the lab, but first, let's take a look outside." She opened the door.

Nina followed the group into a courtyard decorated with stone walkways, statuettes of ancient Greek figures, and wrought iron furniture. In the center stood a fountain featuring a wood nymph pouring water from a jug into a circular trough. Quite a lavish addition to a medical facility, Nina thought.

"The courtyards Dr. R. saw on a trip to Greece so impressed him that he decided to have a similar courtyard here." Desi held her clipboard to her chest. "This one has a retractable roof, something very useful in the rainy Northwest." She pointed overhead to the building's second story.

"Is the yard for patients or staff?" a woman asked.

"For patients." Desi gestured down the hallway. "The other side of the building has a similar area for staff. Patients are welcome to wait here or to enjoy a cup of coffee after their appointment."

They trooped upstairs to the lab, a large room with high ceilings and skylights. Rows of testing equipment lined one wall, above which were cupboards, some with glass doors revealing bottles and stacked boxes. Desks with computer monitors filled another wall, and filing cabinets took up the remaining space.

Nina raised a hand. "What tests can the doctors perform in this lab?"

Desi gestured to the machines along the wall. "Routine blood work, urinalyses, X-rays—just about any test the doctors will need."

The tour ended, and they returned to the first floor. Looking around for Stephen, Nina spotted him at the buffet table. She was about to join him when she saw he conversed with an attractive, auburn-haired woman wearing a stylish, blue slacks suit set off by a white turtleneck sweater. They both held small plates filled with hors d'oeuvres. As they spoke, they leaned toward one another with an air of familiarity.

Nina's stomach twisted with an old, familiar pain. Who was the woman, and why were she and Stephen so friendly? Surely, she was not someone he had just met. He must have known her before today.

Nina hated the jealousy that flared up at the slightest provocation. Of course, as owner of *The Richmond Review*, Stephen knew many people, men as well as women. He was a friendly, outgoing person. He had been the one to initiate their relationship, persisting past the wall of shyness and separation she often put between herself and others.

Yet, right now, nothing dispelled the tight knot in her stomach or the choking feeling that invaded her throat. Should she join them? Or stay away?

Just then, Stephen looked around, and his gaze caught hers. His eyes lit, and his lips curved into a smile.

Surely, he wouldn't respond so pleasurably to the sight of her if he were interested in the other woman. Would he?

He beckoned to Nina.

Too late to escape. She swallowed and headed in his direction.

"Here's someone I want you to meet." He gestured to his companion. "This is Rebecca Young."

Dr. Rebecca Young? The woman's nametag confirmed Nina's fears. Yes, she was the psychiatrist Stephen wanted Nina to consult. Had he invited her to accompany him today, intending for her to meet the woman? Nina's stiff lips refused to smile, but she grasped Dr. Young's outstretched hand. "Hello, Dr. Young."

Rebecca Young smiled and nodded. "Pleased to

meet you, Nina. Stephen has told me about you."

I'll bet he has.

"Becky is one of the doctors here at the clinic." Stephen's gesture took in their surroundings.

Of course, she is. Nina avoided meeting Stephen's gaze. She wanted to turn and walk away, as she had that night at the restaurant. But on that occasion, only she and Stephen were involved. Now, Dr. Young was present. Nina must endure the meeting—as Stephen had known she would.

"Did you take the tour, Nina?" With thumb and forefinger, Dr. Young picked up a cracker from her plate and took a dainty bite.

"I did, just now." Still ignoring Stephen's gaze, Nina nodded toward the hallway.

"What do you think of our clinic?"

Although Dr. Young's tone was friendly, Nina's tension held. "Very nice. The lab upstairs looks especially well equipped."

Dr. Young smiled. "Dr. R. is always up on the latest technology."

"Have something to eat, Nina." Stephen handed her a plate from the stack on the table.

"Do help yourself." Dr. Young gestured to the array of food. "The caterers prepared a real feast."

Although she had little appetite, Nina obligingly took the plate and selected a square of bread topped with creamed crab. She took a bite, savoring the spicy taste. Then, wanting to at least attempt conversation, she turned to Dr. Young. "How did you come to share office space with Dr. Ravensbarger?"

Dr. Young sipped her punch. "A colleague introduced us. I was looking for new quarters, and he had built this clinic. Perfect timing for both of us."

Nina nodded to where the doctor still held court with a group of admirers. "He seems to be very popular, especially with older women."

"Geriatrics is his specialty. He's very knowledgeable and has the right temperament for dealing with the elderly."

"My grandmother's friend was the doctor's patient. She died last week under mysterious circumstances, although accidental drowning was the official verdict." Curious to know Dr. Young's response, she kept her gaze focused on the woman.

"Really?" Dr. Young's eyebrows peaked. "I've been out of town and haven't caught up on the local news. But I'm sure if Dr. R. knows anything helpful, he's been in touch with the authorities."

Was her response a polite way of saying Nina wasted her time with inquiries? Never mind, she was determined to press on. "Overdosing on several prescribed drugs was part of the autopsy findings."

Dr. Young sighed and shook her head. "Unfortunately, some patients deceive doctors. They go from one to the other, getting medication from each without the others' knowledge."

"Maybe some doctors scam their patients, too." Nina lifted her chin. "I wouldn't know about that crime, though, because I rarely have occasion to consult doctors."

Dr. Young raised her eyebrows. "You're fortunate to be so healthy."

"I think so. Although I'm sure not everyone would agree." She shot Stephen a glance, only to find he had turned away to sample the smoked salmon canapés.

Still, Nina felt sure he had heard her and that she had made her point—to him and to Dr. Young.

****

"I fell into your trap, didn't I?" Nina told Stephen later as they left the clinic. Dusk had fallen, and mushroom-shaped lights guided their way along the walk. Car doors opening and closing and the voices of the other guests saying their goodnights drifted along the air currents.

Stephen grasped her elbow. "I wouldn't call tonight a trap. You were interested in meeting Dr. Ravensbarger, and Becky is part of his clinic. I thought if you two met, you might change your mind about consulting her. Coming to the opening accomplished both objectives."

"You're *so* efficient." Still annoyed despite his explanation, Nina pointed to the sign listing the various doctors' names. *Dr. Rebecca Young, Psychiatry,* was included, as plain as could be. "Now I see why you hurried me past this sign. You were afraid that if I saw her name, I wouldn't go in."

"Okay, maybe I did." Stephen nodded at the sign and then turned to Nina. "But what do you think of her?"

Nina shrugged. "She seemed nice, but right now, I'm concentrating on learning about Dr. Ravensbarger."

"Uh huh." Stephen took her arm again and continued walking along the path. "Ravensbarger and his possible connection to Ellie's death. Focusing on him allows you to avoid dealing with your own issues."

"My, my, you're such a good analyst." Nina shook her head. "Why don't I just consult *you* about my so-called problems?"

They had reached Stephen's car, parked in the clinic lot. He unlocked the passenger door and helped her inside. "I'll ignore that remark and ask, where do you want to eat dinner?"

After some discussion, they chose a downtown café and during the meal avoided talking about either the clinic or Dr. Ravensbarger or Dr. Young. Afterward, they walked two blocks to Richmond's movie theater. Although the film was an amusing comedy, Nina had difficulty concentrating. She feared her stubborn attitude regarding her so-called problem would drive him away. At the thought of losing him, a sinking feeling akin to panic clutched her stomach, and the walls of the theater closed in.

Just when she thought she would have to bolt, offering the excuse for a drink of water or a trip to the ladies' room, Stephen closed his hand over hers. The gesture brought comfort, and she relaxed against his shoulder.

Still, in her dreams that night, confusion reigned again as disturbing images appeared—the faceless man, who became Stephen, then Dr. Ravensbarger, and then was faceless again.

Ellie, in her yellow slicker, drifted across the dream landscape. "Help me," she begged. "Help me!"

Nina awoke feeling as though she, not Ellie, had been the one crying for help.

****

Two days later, Ellie Larkin's memorial was held in Marley's chapel. The occasion could not be called a funeral, for Ellie's remains, once the police released them, were cremated and, presumably, claimed by her nephew, Roger Blanton. What he planned to do with the ashes wasn't made public knowledge. Nina hoped he would find them a respectful, secure resting place.

Bouquets of flowers lined the front of the chapel, their fragrances filling the air. On an easel stood a portrait of Ellie as a young woman, probably in her thirties, Nina guessed. The image was an older version of what she had seen in the school yearbook—an attractive woman with dark, curly hair and deep-set eyes. Certainly the image was far different from the anguished, haunted face which peered from the hood of a yellow slicker the night of her death.

However, the presence of her heir, the mysterious woman to whom she had left her fortune, upstaged Ellie. From the moment Dorleen Longman arrived, accompanied by Roger, a twittering swept over the other attendees.

The two arrived late, after everyone else was seated. Usher Wally escorted them to the reserved front row. Their walk down the aisle gave everyone, including Nina, who sat between Jessica and Stephen, a good look at the stranger.

Dorleen was in her late forties and overweight for her small stature. Her auburn hair looked dyed, but the soft color complemented her tanned complexion. She wore a brown skirt and a brown print blouse, clothing that appeared too lightweight for the Northwest's winter weather. But, Dorleen had come from Florida, the Sunshine State.

The two turned into the pew, and Nina glimpsed their faces. Although Dorleen's thin mouth was set in an appropriately solemn line, her chin was thrust forward, and when she glanced at the rows of people behind them, her eyes held a glint of defiance.

Nina expected Roger to wear his usual angry expression. Instead, he appeared calm and accepting, even offering Dorleen a smile as they turned toward each other before settling into their seats.

The organ music faded, and the minister approached the pulpit.

Nina focused on listening to the eulogy. Eloise Cecelia Larkin was seventy-five at the time of her death, the minister told them. She hailed from Dubuque, Iowa and had one older sister, Bernice. Bernice was Roger's mother and had passed away several years ago. Ellie attended Iowa State College, majoring in Math and History. After graduation, she taught high school for several years.

In the late 1970s, she moved to Seattle to be near her sister. Abandoning teaching, she used her mathematics expertise as an accountant for a large manufacturing firm. After her retirement, she moved to Marley. She liked to do needlepoint and read and play the violin. Until her health failed, she'd been an avid golfer.

"A dedicated volunteer, too," the minister added. "Ellie spent many hours at the Food Bank, the Fairhaven Shelter for the Homeless, and especially at Children's Hospital."

How simply one's life could be summed up, Nina thought. All the hours, the days, the joys and the sorrows, compressed into so few words.

After the minister finished, Roger stepped to the podium. "I never knew Auntie until she moved to Seattle. We played golf together. I was the one who taught her how. After she won the lottery, she took me on a cruise through the Panama Canal. She was"—his voice cracked—"a wonderful auntie." He bowed his head. When he straightened and again and looked at the other attendees, his eyes were misty.

"Crocodile tears," Jessica whispered to Nina.

"Cynic," she whispered back. Nina couldn't make up her mind about Roger. On this occasion, his demeanor seemed gentle and his emotion sincere. But, she also knew firsthand he could be rude and belligerent.

After the service concluded, everyone adjourned to a large conference room for the reception. The teenage servers in their green and black uniforms wheeled in carts loaded with sandwiches and cookies, plates and cups. Spotting Kimmie, Nina left Jessica and Stephen and approached the girl. "Did you attend the service, Kimmie?"

The teen placed a tray of egg salad sandwiches on the white cloth-covered table, and then looked at Nina. Her eyes were red-rimmed. "Uh huh. I sat in the back, so I could slip out to get started here." Her lower lip trembled. "I feel so sad."

Nina nodded. "I know. We all are sad." Still, Kimmie appeared to take Ellie's death exceptionally hard. But, from her work with teens at the library, she knew them to be, at times, overly emotional.

Kimmie set a dish of carrot sticks and cheese dip next to the sandwiches. "Are you still investigating her death?"

"I am." Nina waited, but Kimmie made no further comment. "Do you have something to tell me about her death?" She kept her tone gentle.

Kimmie shook her head. Her unevenly cut blonde hair flared, and then settled again into jagged layers. "I was just wondering."

"If you think of anything that might help me, you'll let me know, won't you?"

Kimmie lowered her gaze. "S-sure. But right now, I gotta do my job." Gripping the cart's handle, she headed toward the kitchen.

Nina stared after the teen. Was she exhibiting a normal reaction to the death of someone she cared about? Or did something else bother her? Maybe her distress was the boy trouble Clara mentioned at dinner last Sunday. Whatever, Nina planned to keep an eye on Kimmie.

She looked around for Jessica and Stephen. Jessica talked to Wally and Lily, while Stephen visited with the minister. Roger and Dorleen stood with two Marley residents. Nina waited until the residents drifted away and then approached the couple. Ellie's principal heir was someone she definitely wanted to meet.

Chapter Eleven

Roger introduced Dorleen to Nina, adding that she was "the daughter of one of Auntie's best friends."

"Pleased to meet you, Nina." Dorleen offered her hand.

Dorleen's lips smiled, but her gray eyes held a guarded look. Was she just uncomfortable in a room full of strangers, or was she hiding something? "I understand you're from Florida." Nina shook the woman's hand. "What part?"

Dorleen nodded. "South of Miami."

"Welcome to Washington. I'm sorry you had to come under such sad circumstances." Well, maybe not too sad, for Dorleen was now a very wealthy woman. "Is this visit your first to the Northwest?"

"It is." Dorleen shifted from one foot to the other and gazed toward the buffet table, where a line had formed at the coffee urn.

Her discomfort was to be expected, especially since she was a stranger among people who all knew one another. Still, Nina was determined to pry more conversation from the woman. "How do you like our part of the country so far?"

Dorleen grimaced. "I heard you have a lot of rain, but I didn't think the weather would be so cold." She shivered and hugged her arms.

"We prefer rain to snow in the winter. But,

hopefully, the weather will clear enough for you to see some of the sights."

"Oh, no." Dorleen frowned and shook her head. "I have to go home."

The finality of her tone put Nina on the alert. "Oh? Do you have family waiting for you?"

"No, but I have a business to run."

"Dorleen owns a resort." Roger smiled at his companion.

"Really?" Nina looked to Dorleen, hoping for more information.

"I do." A grin lighted her face. "Sun and Surf is south of Miami on the way to the Keys. We have snorkeling and scuba—and sunshine."

"We have scuba diving here in Richmond, near the ferry terminal." Nina hoped to convince Dorleen to stay. She needed to observe her and decide whether or not she was a suspect in Ellie's death. "I don't dive, but those who do say the underwater garden is spectacular."

"Too bad I won't have time to visit your site."

Roger frowned. "I thought you were staying a couple weeks? Didn't Loren Peabody talk to you about presenting checks to Ellie's charities?"

"Ellie's lawyer?" Dorleen's tan complexion paled. "He did contact me, but I can't possibly visit the charities. I need to get back to Sun and Surf. My manager quit, and I haven't yet hired a replacement."

"Come on, Dorleen." Roger stuck his hands on his hips. "Children's Hospital, for one, planned a tea in Auntie's honor. They want to meet you."

Dorleen shrugged. "Why can't you be the representative? I didn't even know Ellie."

"You're her principal heir. You should represent

her." Roger stuck out his chin.

"But I—"

"Director Marshall invited you to stay here at Marley in the visitors' apartment. Besides, I want to show ya around." Roger nudged her arm with an elbow. "We got lots of tourist attractions."

Showing Dorleen around would also give Roger a chance to talk her out of some of her inheritance for his downtown project. Nina saw the dollar signs dancing in Roger's eyes. She aimed a smile in his direction and then turned to Dorleen. "Extending your visit would give Ellie's friends time to know you better, too."

"Nina's right." Roger gave Nina a nod. "You can't run out on us so soon."

"I really need to go home." Dorleen's brow wrinkled.

Roger made a dismissive wave. "All settled. You can move into Marley tonight."

For once, Nina applauded Roger's aggressive behavior. Having Dorleen stay at Marley would give Nina a chance to know the woman. Did she really need to return so soon to her resort? Or was she eager to leave Richmond for some other reason?

****

"I saw you talking to the heiress," Stephen said when Nina joined him a few minutes later. He handed her a paper plate from the buffet table. "The crab salad sandwiches are good."

Nina selected one of the triangular sandwiches and inhaled the spicy aroma before taking a bite. "Mmm, delicious. Yes, I met Dorleen, and she'll be in town for a while." She related details from her conversation with Roger and Dorleen.

"She doesn't sound happy about staying." Stephen led Nina along the table.

Nina added a couple stuffed olives to her plate. "She's anxious to return to her resort in Florida."

"She just wants to take the money and run, huh?" Stephen grinned.

"Apparently. But Ellie's lawyer, Loren Peabody, and Roger have different ideas."

Stephen scooped a serving of potato salad. "Do you think they have ulterior motives?"

"I don't know Loren well enough to judge. Roger, maybe. He always goes where the money is, and now the money's with Dorleen."

"Is she married?"

"She said she doesn't have family. But even if she did, I doubt that situation would deter Roger…Oh, look, Gran's signaling us." She nodded to the chairs on the sidelines where Jessica sat with Wally, Lily, and an older man who was a stranger.

Nina and Stephen made their way across the room to join them.

"This is Joe McGarrity." Jessica introduced the man. "He knew Ellie and is a friend of Wally's, too."

Joe stood and extended a hand. "Pleased to meet you."

Tall and slender, he was neatly dressed in a gray suit, a white shirt, and a maroon tie. He had a pleasant smile and a firm handshake. Nina guessed his age as early seventies. "How did you know Ellie?" she asked, after they were all seated.

Joe sipped his coffee. "I was district manager for Harmon's department stores where she worked as an accountant. After a couple years, we went our separate ways. I haven't seen her since."

Nina sensed the relationship included more than Joe shared but decided to let the matter go. For now.

"Have you all met Dorleen?" Nina's gaze took in the entire group.

Everyone nodded.

"Not impressed." Lily wrinkled her nose.

"I thought Dorleen was nice." Wally brushed a cracker crumb from the sleeve of his pinstripe suit.

"Really?" Lily's eyebrows peaked.

He patted her hand. "Don't worry, honey. She doesn't have anything I want."

"Huh! She has millions!" Lily sniffed and turned away.

"Anyone after her money will need to get in line." Jessica nodded toward where Roger, smiling and leaning close, served Dorleen a cup of coffee.

Stephen winked at Nina. "Maybe Roger's just being a good host."

"Yeah, right." Lily rolled her eyes.

Wally finished a bite of sandwich. "I hope everything turns out as Ellie wanted. She carried a torch for Dorleen's father until the day she died." He turned to Joe McGarrity. "You know all about that situation, don't you, Joe?"

Joe frowned and looked down. "Oh, yeah. I know."

Catching the sadness in Joe's voice, Nina searched for a way to tactfully pursue the subject of Joe and Ellie's relationship.

"I have some news." Jessica waved a forefinger. "Ellie's lawyer, Loren Peabody, called yesterday. He told me Ellie designated me to take care of her personal belongings, including the contents of her apartment."

"Really?" Lily leaned forward to stare open-mouthed.

"She left small bequests to her friends—jewelry and such—that I am to distribute. I'm quite honored." Jessica pressed a hand to her chest.

"I hope I get a memento." Lily grinned. "Do ya think, Jessica?"

"I haven't seen the list, but I'm betting you will." Jessica turned to Nina. "I thought you'd like to help me. We might find some clues."

"Clues?" Joe's brow knitted. "Are you with the police, Nina? I thought Jessica said you were a librarian?"

"I am a librarian, but..." Nina searched for words to explain her amateur detecting to this newcomer.

"Nina's investigating to find out who murdered poor Ellie." Lily gave a vigorous nod. "She's very good at detecting. Only last year she helped to solve another crime, right here in Richmond."

Joe's gaze traveled around the group. "I thought Ellie's death was accidental."

"Accidental is the official word." Stephen nodded.

Lily stuck out her chin. "Maybe so, but we think she was murdered."

Joe raised his eyebrows and focused on Nina. "Playing detective is dangerous, don't you think?"

Nina shrugged. "Maybe. But if Ellie was murdered, I want to see the killer caught and brought to justice." She leaned closer. "By the way, do you live in the area?"

"I live in Lake City." Joe named a north Seattle suburb.

Wally sipped his coffee. "You oughta think about

moving to Marley, Joe, now that you're a widower."

"My wife passed away last year." Joe addressed Nina and Stephen.

"So sorry." Nina wrinkled her brow.

"My condolences," Stephen added.

Joe nodded and pressed his lips together. "Thank you."

"The food's good here," Wally continued, "and we have plenty of pretty gals." He winked at Lily. "Hey, you still play pool? You usta be quite a shark."

"I'm a bit rusty these days." Joe shrugged.

Wally smiled and gestured at Jessica. "Jessica here is our resident champ. We could use some new blood."

"No kidding? You play pool?" Joe smiled, and he leaned around Wally to address Jessica.

Jessica nodded. "I do, and Wally's right. We need new players. Beating the same people gets kinda boring."

"Come for dinner Sunday," Wally said. "We always play pool afterward."

"I'll give dinner a thought." Joe's gaze lingered on Jessica.

Nina hoped to ask more questions of the newcomer, but just then, Harriet Hambly joined them. She wore a long denim skirt and matching jacket over a white turtleneck sweater. Nina focused on Harriet's right hand and the butterfly birthmark, which, now that she knew Harriet's secret, took on new significance.

"Did you all try the mushroom puffs?" Harriet waved toward the buffet table.

Wally knitted his brow. "Hmmm. I think I might have."

"You'd know if you did. The puffs are

unforgettable. They're from my book, *Party Hearty With Harriet Hambly*. I supervised the kitchen helpers who made them today. We had such fun." Harriet's eyes sparkled as she surveyed the group.

"I'm sure Ellie thanks you." Lily sniffed. "From wherever she is right now."

Harriet turned to Nina. "Have you found any more clues?"

"I'm always looking." Nina purposely kept her reply vague. Her new knowledge of Harriet especially made her circumspect. Although she'd always sensed something unusual about the woman, she never would have guessed the matter had to do with Harriet's gender. The transformation from Harry to Harriet had been complete, as far as Nina could tell, anyway.

Lily frowned toward Harriet. "Even if Nina found any clues, she wouldn't say. Detectives don't tell what they discover."

Jessica finished a bite of her tuna sandwich. "We might find clues in Ellie's apartment." She explained to Harriet her assignment to sort Ellie's belongings and deliver her bequeathed mementoes.

"I'd be glad to help." Harriet beamed a wide smile from Jessica to Nina. "Maybe I'd find the cookbook of mine she borrowed."

"You don't have to worry anymore about the book." Nina raised a hand. "I found it."

Harriet's eyes widened. "You did? Where?"

"Mixed in with other donations. I'd be glad to bring the book by your apartment later today."

"I'm busy today." Harriet shrugged. "The next time you work in the library you can drop it off."

Harriet's casual attitude reaffirmed Nina's belief

that the cookbook wasn't the book she was anxious to possess. The volume she so desperately wanted was the high school annual.

Harriet leaned toward Jessica. "Are you sure you don't need my help sorting Ellie's belongings?"

"Thanks, but no." Jessica patted Harriet's arm. "Nina and I will manage just fine."

"Like Sherlock and Watson." Wally grinned.

Jessica laughed. "Yes, just like Sherlock and Watson."

Expecting Harriet to press the issue, Nina held her breath.

Instead, she waved to a woman passing by. "Oh, Midge, did you try my puffs?" Without a word to the others, she hurried to join Midge.

Still, Nina had the distinct feeling she hadn't heard the last of Harriet's covert search for Ellie's old high school annual. What if Ellie had refused to give Harriet the annual and had threatened to reveal her secret? If so, Harriet would have had a strong motive to do away with her old classmate.

****

Later, at Stephen's house, Nina stood looking out the picture window. When he moved to Richmond last summer, he purchased property and put down roots. The older home he chose needed repair, but the house sat on a prime piece of property overlooking Puget Sound. Tonight, a blanket of clouds reflecting lights from the city cast a faint illumination over the black water. Running lights from several boats, along with the faint hum of their motors, penetrated the darkness. Behind her, Stephen broke kindling and wadded up newspaper to start a fire in the fireplace. Nina left the window and placed a hand on his shoulder. "Need help?"

He looked up and flashed a grin. "No, thanks. But warming this room will be so much easier after I install the gas fireplace."

"The gas is next on your remodeling agenda?"

"That task and enlarging the deck." He crumpled another piece of paper and tossed it onto the grate. "I want to replace the stone, too. Something lighter. What do you think?"

Nina studied the slabs of charcoal-colored rock that framed the fireplace. "Hmmm, I guess."

"But you're not sure?" His brow wrinkled.

"You know interior decorating is not my strong suit."

"I know you had a professional do your place, but I want to see what I—we—can put together for mine."

Nina sighed. Remodeling his home was another touchy subject. He frequently asked for her input, and she never knew how to reply. She was only a weekend guest. She didn't know if she ever would be a full-time resident and therefore hesitated to influence his choices. Plus, if the home was hers, she would do exactly as she had done with her condo—hire a decorator. "Shall I make tea?" She hoped to end the discussion of the troublesome topic.

"Sure. You know where everything is."

Nina walked the short hallway to the kitchen. Stephen installed a hot water faucet for making instant drinks. Nina didn't particularly care for the device—she liked her tea water bubbling hot. But tonight, tired and preoccupied, she chose the faucet over waiting for water to heat on the stove or in the microwave.

A few minutes later, she carried the mugs of tea to the living room and set them on the coffee table, pushing aside a stack of Sunday newspapers. In typical Stephen-fashion, the table was littered with pencils and pens, notepaper, and two of the three ties he'd asked her opinion on wearing today. Nina picked up the pens and pencils and stuck them in the ceramic pencil holder, which, as usual, was empty.

She would never allow her own living room to become so messy. But, despite her and Stephen's housekeeping differences and their brief skirmish over remodeling, being here tonight felt comforting. In contrast to the thoughts of death and dying prompted by Ellie's memorial, the fire was a cheerful confirmation of life and warmth.

Finished with the fire, Stephen took off his tie and added it to the other two on the coffee table. He sat beside her on the sofa, stretching his arm along the back.

Nina kicked off her shoes, curled up her stockinged feet, and moved into the circle of his arm. They sipped their drinks in silence for a while, and then Nina put down her cup and posed a question that had been on her mind. "Do you have any contacts in Florida?"

He slanted her a glance. "Depends on what you want. Although I think I can guess."

"I want to check on Dorleen and her resort business. I can search for her online, of course, but important information may be available only to a professional investigator." She added, seeing his frown, "I'll pay for the person's time."

"Money's not the issue. What you learn about her might put you in danger."

Nina tensed and shook her head. "I can't be in this investigation halfway. I have to commit one hundred percent."

Stephen set his cup on the coffee table next to hers and shifted to face her. "Suppose we make a bargain. I'll get information on Dorleen if you promise not to do anything dangerous without checking first with me."

She stiffened. "Oh, like you're my protector?"

"Uh huh." He stuck out his chin. "I've had more experience than you."

"I know, which is why I'm asking your help. I thought you'd be willing because you like intrigue as much as I do. Your love of mystery led you to become an investigative reporter."

"True on all counts. But I also gave up investigating to fulfill my dream of owning a small town newspaper—and of finding you." He gripped her shoulder and pulled her close.

She sighed and relaxed against him. "You didn't know you would find me when you came here."

He chuckled. "Oh, but I did. I had the word of a very reliable Manhattan fortuneteller. 'You will find your dream in the West,' she said. 'I see a beautiful woman with brown hair and big blue eyes who is surrounded by books.'"

"I don't believe a word of your story." Nina struggled to keep her tone serious.

"Maybe this will convince you." Stephen grasped her chin and covered her mouth with a kiss. The kiss began softly and then grew more intense, with their tongues mingling, hands caressing, and bodies meshing together. "We could make love here by the fire," he murmured in her ear.

Sighing, she felt tingly inside. "We could."

"Would you like that?"

"I might."

He straightened and raised his eyebrows. "How about showing a little more enthusiasm?"

She smiled and gave his shoulder a playful slap. "Oh, hush, and get the blankets."

Later, as she lay beside him in front of the fire, her doubts about their relationship cooled the warm glow of lovemaking. Although she appreciated his concern for her safety, she wished he supported her investigation into Ellie's death. Plus, the issue of Dr. Young remained unresolved. Although he hadn't mentioned the woman tonight, Nina knew he hadn't given up.

Would they ever make their relationship work permanently? Did she want permanence? Nina worried that solving the mystery of Ellie's death would be easier than solving the troublesome issues between her and Stephen.

Chapter Twelve

On Monday, Nina worked the afternoon and evening shifts at Seaview. In the evening, the library was full of Westwood High students researching assignments for biology class. Nina and her staff assisted them at the computers and the reference shelves.

At eight o'clock, with an hour left before closing, Nina spotted Kimmie sitting at a corner table. She'd seen her earlier but hadn't had time to say a special hello. She approached her now. "Kimmie, how're you doing with your assignment?"

The girl looked up from her tablet. "Oh, hi, Miss Foster. Okay, I guess."

Kimmie's eyes wore gray circles, and her cheeks were pale. Nina glanced at her tablet. The word "Cloning" showed at the top of the screen, but the rest was blank. "Can I help you find information?"

Kimmie studied her fingernails. "No, thanks. I'm good."

A boy wearing a letterman's jacket approached. "Hey, Kimmie."

"Hi, Jason." Kimmie glanced at him and then looked away.

Keeping Kimmie and Jason in her line of vision, Nina moved to the adjacent table and scooped up some magazines.

"Want a ride home?" Jason adjusted the straps to his backpack. "I'm ready to split."

Kimmie waved a hand. "No, thanks. I already have a ride."

Jason curled his lip. "With that dork I see hanging around?"

"He's not a dork." Kimmie raised her head and narrowed her eyes.

"Who is he, anyway?" Jason spread his feet and propped a hand on his hip.

"He doesn't go to our school."

"I figured he was an outsider. Where's he from?"

Kimmie stuck out her jaw. "None of your business, Jason."

"Okay." Jason put up a hand. "Forget I asked." He turned and stomped off.

Well, that was an interesting exchange. Nina considered approaching Kimmie again but then decided to leave her alone. She didn't want the girl to think she wanted to meddle in her affairs. Which of course, she did, Nina thought with a covert grin.

By closing time, all the teens had left. The library looked like a cyclone hit. Nina dimmed the lights and, with the staff's help, loaded the scattered books and magazines onto book trucks to be shelved the following day. The sports magazines and graphic comic books mixed in with biology materials indicated not everyone had been diligent in their research. But, at least, the students were exposed to the library. As Nina pushed her book truck past the front door, she noticed Kimmie standing in the shadows. "Kimmie? You're still here?"

The teen stepped into the light. "Waiting for my ride. Can I stay inside until he comes? It's raining."

Nina gave a short laugh. "When is it not?"

Her remark drew a smile. "When it rains, my dad always says we're gonna move to Arizona. But when the sun finally comes out, he changes his mind and says we're staying here."

Nina nodded. "A day or two of sunshine and we're convinced the Northwest is the most beautiful place in the world. But, sure, stay inside until your ride comes." She steered the book truck into the workroom. The staff left, but Nina remained to clear her desktop and file stray papers. After completing those tasks, she checked the front door and was surprised to find Kimmie still waiting. "I need to lock up and leave now," she told the teen. "Since your ride hasn't come, I'll take you home."

Kimmie bit her lower lip. "Please, can I stay a little longer? I know he'll come, and he'll be mad if I'm not here."

"Well, okay, but only until I put on my coat and lock the office." Nina made her tone firm. She wanted to help Kimmie but needed to make clear she had a schedule to adhere to as well. A few minutes later, coat on and purse in hand, she emerged from her office to see Kimmie fly out the door and run to a car idling at the curb. She opened the car door, exposing an interior light. Nina strained to see, but before she glimpsed the driver, Kimmie jumped into the car and shut the door.

Nina ran to the library's front door and stepped outside. The car was an older model compact, dark in color. The darkness obscured the license plate, but the right front fender had a large dent that would aid in future identification. She waited until the vehicle disappeared into the darkness and then re-entered the library. Although thankful Kimmie found her ride, she had the feeling all was not well with the teen and the mysterious boyfriend.

****

The following evening, Nina walked along Marley Manor's first floor hallway. Turning a corner, she encountered Roger and the newly arrived heiress, Dorleen. "How are you two this evening?" Nina asked as they crossed paths.

"I've been showing Dorleen around town." Roger gestured to his companion. "We took a ferry ride to the peninsula. Probably not the best day to go, but who knows when the weather will clear? Sunshine could be weeks away."

Dorleen adjusted the strap of her shoulder purse. "Have you and your grandmother sorted Ellie's stuff?"

"Tonight's our first night. I'm on my way to Ellie's apartment now." She nodded toward the end of the hallway.

Dorleen raised her eyebrows. "I'd be glad to lend a hand."

"Me, too." Roger nodded.

They leaned toward Nina, anticipation lighting their eyes. She was tempted to say yes, just to see how they behaved once inside Ellie's apartment. She quickly squashed the impulse. She would need to check with Jessica first. "Thanks, but Gran and I can manage." She stepped around them and continued on. Reaching Ellie's apartment, she rang the doorbell.

Jessica opened the door, Nigel at her side. "Hi, honey." She stepped forward to give Nina a hug.

Nigel shot out the door and into the hallway. He ran to Dorleen and Roger, looked up at them, and barked.

Dorleen grimaced and jumped back. "Get away, dog!"

"Shoo!" Roger waved his hands at Nigel.

"Nina, get Nigel." Jessica pressed a hand to her chest. "He'll disturb the neighbors."

Nina ran to the dog and scooped him up in her arms. "Quiet, Nigel." She patted his head and carried him to Ellie's apartment.

Jessica quickly closed the door. "Thank you for rescuing him."

Nina set Nigel on the floor. "Judging from his bark, he doesn't like those two. Maybe he knows something. Aren't dogs supposed to be intuitive?"

Nigel scampered to the sofa and jumped onto a gold velveteen cushion. He circled several times and then lay with his head resting on his front paws. He shifted his brown-eyed gaze back and forth from Nina to Jessica.

"Nigel never did like Roger." Jessica straightened the cushions surrounding the dog's throne. "Now, Dorleen's on his blacklist, too."

"I'm not sure I trust those two, either." Nina laid her purse on an end table.

Jessica shot her a raised-eyebrow look. "You think they killed Ellie? They didn't know each other before now."

"That we know of." Nina raised a forefinger. "Maybe they did, and Roger told Dorleen he'd do the dirty deed for a percentage of the take."

Jessica's eyes widened. "Now, that theory's worth some thought."

"Stranger plots have been hatched, I'm sure. But, anyway, I thought Wally was taking care of Nigel?"

"He is, but he says whenever Nigel gets a chance, he heads here. He's homesick. I told Wally Nigel could keep us company while we sort tonight. And look at him, he's in his element." She nodded toward the dog.

Nigel raised his head, gave a big yawn, and snuggled into the folds of the cushion.

"Maybe he'd feel more at home at Wally's if he had his cushion." Nina patted the dog's head.

"Maybe. But nothing's to be removed from the apartment until everything is distributed according to Ellie's list." Jessica picked up a piece of paper, waved it at Nina, and then at the room. "Just look at this place. What a mess."

Nina gazed around. The small apartment was crammed with oversize furniture, including a sofa with a heavy mahogany frame and claw feet, and two fat, overstuffed chairs with huge cushions like the one Nigel claimed. The walls held impressionist oil paintings with wide gilt frames. Papers, books, coffee cups, and other miscellany were scattered across every available surface. She peeked into the kitchen and saw dishes, pots and pans, and silverware haphazardly piled on the counter. She guessed the bedroom and bath would be the same. Shaking her head in disgust, Nina returned to the living room. "How could anyone stand living in this mess?"

"Not everyone has your need for order, dear," Jessica said in a dry tone.

"I know, but—" Nina fought down the urge to escape. Environments such as this one made her claustrophobic.

"Ellie wasn't the neatest person in the world, but this clutter is a bit extreme." Jessica straightened a stack of magazines on an end table. "Perhaps the police visit contributed to the mess."

Nina made a mental note to ask Stephen about the police search. "Do you suppose Roger's been here taking stuff of value? He told me he has no key, but I bet he's not above lock picking."

Jessica nodded. "You might be right, but we can't make accusations without proof."

Nina ran a hand over the arm of an overstuffed chair. "Why would Ellie have such big furniture in such a small apartment?"

"The furniture came from her house—mansion, rather—on Queen Anne Hill."

"She lived in a mansion all alone?" Nina sank into the chair and wiggled. "Oh, this chair *is* comfy."

"She rented out rooms, like an old-fashioned boarding house. Anyway, she was quite attached to the furniture. Apparently, the pieces not fitting in here didn't bother her." She shrugged and pointed to her paper. "We'd better get busy. At least forty people are on this list."

Nina leaned forward and gave Jessica her attention. "What kinds of bequests did she make?"

Jessica consulted the list. "Star-shaped rhinestone pin and earring set to Clara. Cuckoo clock to Sue. Wedgewood tea set to me." She looked up. "So sweet of Ellie to leave me the tea set she always used when I came for tea."

"How organized of her to have a list. Maybe she knew she was going to die."

Jessica let out a peal of laughter. "Of course, she knew, my dear. Once you move into a place such as Marley you know you're near the end of the road.

Besides, having all your paperwork completed is an admission requirement. You know, your will and your wishes about resuscitation—"

Nina flinched and held up a hand. "Enough examples. I get the picture." She did not want to think about "the end of the road" with regard to her grandmother. "Put me to work."

"I assume you're looking for clues, so why don't you poke around while I locate items on the list? Then we'll tackle the rest of Ellie's belongings."

"What happens to the remainder?"

"All donated to charities. Some items, like personal papers, we'll dispose of."

Nina gripped the chair arms and pushed to her feet. "I'll start in the bathroom and see if I can find the pills she took."

"That way." Jessica pointed to an open door.

Ellie's pills were neither in the medicine cabinet nor among the counter clutter of hairbrushes, combs, and cosmetics but were tucked away in a drawer near the sink. Nina retrieved three plastic bottles and two paper envelopes. The bottles' labels had Dr. Ravensbarger's name, as well as that of a local pharmacy. Nina set aside the medication to take home and compare with the list Stephen gave her of the drugs found in Ellie's body.

Next, she returned to the living room to tackle the desk. The antique piece, made of oak, sat against the wall, bridging the space between the living and dining rooms. A keyhole gave Nina a moment's hesitation, but when she turned the handle, the drop front obligingly clicked open. She lowered the door, and papers spilled from the desk's crammed cubbyholes, some fluttering to the floor. Nina scooped them up and stacked them on the door panel, now the desk's writing surface. Then she pulled up a ladderback chair and sat.

Sorting through Ellie's papers brought a rush of guilt. She felt like a voyeur or a scavenger picking through the remains of someone's life. She imagined Ellie's spirit watching with patent disapproval.

Forgive me, Ellie. I want to find out what happened to you. Help me!

The papers yielded a mishmash of data—grocery lists, bill stubs from telephone and credit card payments, and miscellaneous sales slips. Purchased items included a nightgown, a down jacket, and a pair of slacks. Nothing unusual. Notes Ellie wrote to herself comprised another pile. "Call the vet about Nigel's booster shots." "Lunch with Clara and Sue." "Order new shoes from catalog." "Take blue dress to cleaners." Again, nothing of great interest. Searching a drawer, Nina found a rubber band and wound it around everything she had examined so far.

The cubbyholes held more paper detritus—recipes cut from magazines and coupons clipped from newspaper ads. Then she came across a small book that turned out to be Ellie's daily planner for the entire year. Her heartbeat quickening, she opened the book and perused the pages. Since the year began only a month ago, the entries were few. One notation read, "Shopping bus, 10:00 a.m.," which probably referred to the shuttle service provided by Marley. Another read, "Call Clara about bridge club," and another, "Pay bills." One entry in particular caught Nina's attention. For Tuesday, January 15, Ellie had written, "Benson Hotel, 1:00 p.m."

Located in downtown Seattle, The Benson Hotel was an elegant establishment offering amenities such as a five-star restaurant and sightseeing trips along Puget Sound. Why would Ellie go to the inn? Did she have a rendezvous with someone? A romantic tryst, perhaps. Nina giggled at the thought. No, probably not. What, then?

She paged through the remainder of the month, finding no other notations of interest until she came to the days prior to Ellie's death. Three days earlier, she had an appointment with Dr. Ravensbarger. "Bus at 10:00," she wrote.

The day before Ellie's death was blank, but the day of her death, she made the notation, "Sheryl, 3:00."

Sheryl? Oh, yes, the nurse who worked part-time here and also for Dr. Ravensbarger. Perhaps her visit to Sheryl was a follow-up to her appointment with the doctor. Nina made a mental note to have a talk with Sheryl and, despite patient privacy rules, see what information she could pry out of her.

The last item of interest was a manila envelope of medical papers. After studying the contents for several minutes, Nina decided she had never seen such a confusing mess. Included were photocopies of Medicare forms and bills from Dr. Ravensbarger. The papers were peppered with notes. "Talk to Dr. R. about this!" was penciled beside a notation for a spinal tap procedure. Spinal tap? Why would Ellie need a spinal tap? Another Medicare bill Ellie questioned was for X-rays. "I never had my feet X-rayed!" she wrote on that paper. Ellie questioned several other procedures for which Medicare had been billed.

Had she and the doctor discussed her questions

about these bills during her appointment three days prior to her death? If so, what was the doctor's response? Were the contradictions billing errors? Or was the doctor scamming Medicare? Or, had Ellie really undergone the procedures listed and, because of her periodic confusion, forgotten about them?

Maybe Jessica knew. Nina scooped up the papers and headed for the bedroom. Excitement surged through her veins. Had she just discovered the answer to Ellie's mysterious death?

Chapter Thirteen

Like the rest of the apartment, oversize furniture crowded Ellie's bedroom. A canopied bed filled most of one wall. Across from the bed, leaving a space only wide enough to walk along, sat a beautifully carved oak dresser and an armoire. Heavy draperies of green velveteen held back with gold cord adorned the single window. Jessica stood at the dresser, sorting through several boxes of jewelry.

Nina joined her and gazed at the glittering array. "Wow. You weren't kidding when you said Ellie liked jewelry." She picked up a ring with star-shaped stones. "Are these real diamonds and emeralds?"

Jessica shrugged. "I don't know. After I identify the bequeathed items, I'll have the remainder appraised."

Nina replaced the ring in its box. "Have you found many on your list?"

"A few." Jessica pointed to the bed where several pieces of jewelry rested on a piece of cardboard.

"I'll look at them in a minute. But first, I need to ask you a question." Nina showed Jessica the medical papers and pointed to the handwritten notes. "Do you know if Ellie actually had all these procedures? She questioned several."

Jessica studied the papers and Ellie's notations and then shook her head. "I'm afraid I can't help you. She doctored so much that after a while I gave up keeping track of her problems. She turned into a hypochondriac. Dr. Ravensbarger is the only one who'd know for sure what he did."

"Right, but he's not likely to reveal the real information—to me, anyway."

Jessica tilted her head. "Do you suspect Ravensbarger scams Medicare?"

"Uh huh, and that Ellie discovered the deception. As a former accountant, she was in the habit of checking figures. If she threatened to blow the whistle on him…"

"He'd have a motive to murder her." Jessica puffed her cheeks and blew out a breath. "Wouldn't exposing him as a murderer be a shock to everyone? But where's the proof?"

"Right now, I don't know, and please don't broadcast this theory to your friends."

Jessica frowned and put her hands on her hips. "I wasn't aware I ever *broadcast* anything to anyone."

"Sorry, poor choice of words. But this idea is best kept between us for now. What you can do, though, is listen for comments from the doctor's other patients. If he cheated with Ellie, he's probably using others, too."

Jessica returned to sorting the jewelry, leaving Nina to examine the pieces on the bed. Several rings, pin and earring sets, and bracelets were included, each with an accompanying note naming the bequeathed person.

One bracelet especially caught her eye. Closer examination revealed the bracelet was made of golden bees with diamond eyes. Nina's heart beat faster. The bees looked exactly like those on the earring she found in the boathouse. Although she didn't have the earring with her to compare, she was sure of the similarity. She consulted the attached paper to see who would receive the bracelet.

Kimmie Hunter.

Clutching the bracelet, Nina approached Jessica. "How do you plan to gift these mementos? At a ceremony, or a party?"

Jessica put down the rhinestone pin she examined under a magnifying glass. "Loren Peabody and I decided to give each bequest privately. Then recipients won't compare or feel conspicuously left out."

"Would you mind if I gave this bracelet to Kimmie Hunter?"

Jessica peered at the bracelet. "Oh, the little bee bracelet. Isn't it cute? Why, I suppose you can, but would you mind telling me your reason?"

Nina hadn't wanted to reveal finding the earring in the boathouse—not because she didn't trust Jessica—but because she might slip and tell someone else, and then the whole of Marley would know. She explained how she had discovered the bee earring.

"Attached to a sleeping bag?" Jessica frowned. "That place seems odd, although I suppose Ellie could have wandered into the boathouse in one of her dazes."

"I wasn't thinking Ellie lost the earring. What if she already gave the pair to Kimmie?" Nina studied Jessica for her reaction.

"Kimmie lost one in the boathouse?" Jessica rubbed her chin. "Hmmm, why would she be there?"

Nina thought she knew but chose not to share her suspicions. "Why she was there is what I want to talk to her about."

"I see. Well, you have my permission to give her the bracelet." Jessica consulted her wristwatch. "You might catch her yet tonight. She worked in the dining room at dinner, and I know the help stays to clean up."

Nina slipped the bracelet into her jacket pocket. "Great idea."

"Have you finished here?"

"No, but I'll be back." Nina picked up her purse and slung the strap over her shoulder. "Next time, I'll help you rather than poke around on my own."

Jessica walked with Nina to the front door. "All right, dear. But I hope Kimmie's not in any trouble. She's such a *nice* girl."

Nina agreed, but right now, the clues led to exactly the opposite conclusion.

****

A few minutes later, Nina pushed through the swinging doors leading to Marley's kitchen. No one was in sight, and although the aromas of corned beef and cabbage lingered in the air, the cleanup had been accomplished. The stainless steel counters and sink gleamed from recent scrubbing. Pots and pans hung from a rack near the industrial-size stove, and white porcelain dishes were stacked on open shelves above the work area.

However, the murmur of voices indicated someone was still present. Advancing farther into the room, she spied two people. A man wearing a white jacket and a chef's hat stood at a butcher's block in the center of the room. The cook. He would know about Kimmie.

Dismay dampened her eagerness when she recognized the second person as Harriet Hambly. She was dressed in her usual jeans and sweatshirt and held an open book. One of her cookbooks, no doubt.

"I know everyone would love my pot roast," she told the cook. "This recipe is very easy to follow." She pointed to a page in the book.

Nina struggled to recall the cook's name. Dino? Darby? No, Darren, that was it. She stepped forward. "Ah, Darren, excuse me."

The two looked up.

The cook's lips curved into a smile.

In contrast, Harriet's brows folded into a frown.

"I'm looking for Kimmie Hunter." Nina gazed from one to the other. "Is she still around?"

"She just left." Darren waved toward the back door.

"Why do you want Kimmie?" Harriet propped a hand on her hip.

Noting suspicion in Harriet's tone, Nina thought fast. "I'm helping her with a school assignment."

"A school assignment?" Harriet's eyes narrowed.

Recalling Kimmie's class's visit to the library, Nina nodded. "She's writing a report on cloning." Before Harriet could say more, Nina turned and headed toward the back door. Outside, she stood on the stoop peering into the darkness. No rain fell, but the air was cold and heavy with moisture. She zipped up her jacket and hugged her arms. Where was Kimmie? Was Nina too late to catch up?

Then she spied a person about the teen's size walking along the path toward the parking lot. Nina stepped onto the path. She considered calling out to see if the person was indeed the girl, but a new thought held her back. If Kimmie was meeting her boyfriend, perhaps Nina could catch a good glimpse of him and even learn his car's license number.

The figure passed under one of the tall lamps lighting the path. The light caught the jagged haircut and the faux fur trim on the same blue parka she wore at the library. Yes, the person was Kimmie.

The path came to a Y. One way led to the parking lot and the other to the lake. Nina expected Kimmie to head toward the parking lot, where the boyfriend must be waiting. But no, she turned toward the lake. Nina continued following at a discreet distance. Once she heard a rustling behind her. She jerked to a halt and turned but saw no one. The noise was probably a stray cat out for an evening's prowl.

The lake came into view, a dark, flat pancake of cold, silent water. Nina shivered. Since Ellie's death, she no longer regarded the lake as a pleasant, enjoyable place. Especially at night the expanse of water took on dangerous and deadly aspects.

Instead of catching the path bordering the lake, Kimmie stayed on the grass, weaving in and out of the trees and bushes.

Nina hung back but kept the girl in sight. What was she up to? When Nina glimpsed the boathouse in the mist, she guessed Kimmie's purpose. She stepped behind a tree and waited to see if her hunch was correct.

Kimmie approached the ramp leading to the boathouse's double doors. Another figure appeared from the shadows of the doorway. The two merged as one for a moment and then together climbed the ramp. The door opened, and they disappeared inside.

Nina waited a few minutes, to see if they would emerge again, but all remained silent. Her mind whirling with her newfound information, she headed back to the parking lot. Kimmie and her boyfriend used the boathouse as a rendezvous. Their presence didn't prove the girl lost the earring there, but Nina would bet she had, especially since the trinket was found in the sleeping bag.

What Kimmie did was none of Nina's business. Still, she was underage, and surely her behavior would receive parental disapproval. Plus, she doubted the Marley management would appreciate their boathouse used as a hideout for teenaged lovers.

Nina still mulled over the situation when she reached the parking lot and spotted her car. In the next row, a shadow moved. The quick, furtive shift indicated the person did not want to be seen. Was someone now following her the way she had followed Kimmie?

She froze, her heart thudding against her ribcage. Then, pulling her key ring from her purse, she aimed the car's remote control toward the door. Before she could press the button to unlock the car, the ring slipped from her hand and fell to the asphalt with a loud clatter. A glance at the neighboring row of cars showed the shadow still lurked, telegraphing danger.

Swallowing against the fear threatening to choke her, she scooped up her keys. She pressed the button on the remote, knowing the resounding "beep" might further alert the person but having no other choice. Once inside, she secured the locks and started the engine. Peering through the windshield, she glimpsed the shadow darting between the cars. Not enough details were visible to discern either features or gender.

Nina left the parking lot, mulling over what had just happened. Who was the mysterious person? Had Kimmie known she was being followed and sent the boyfriend to stalk Nina? Was Roger surveilling her, hoping she'd lead him to Ellie's secrets? Or was the stalker Harriet Hambly? She displayed a keen interest in Nina's need to locate Kimmie. Although Nina was curious to know, putting distance between herself and the mysterious person took precedence.

Even in the safety of her condo, the unsettling experience kept Nina's nerves on edge. She stood at the window watching the street below to make sure no one followed her. When half an hour passed and the street remained empty, she went to the kitchen and brewed a cup of tea. Then she sat on the living room sofa with the tea and her list of suspects. Everything she learned tonight reeled in her mind. Recording the details would help put her new knowledge into perspective.

She studied the list. Roger Blanton, Dorleen Longman, Dr. Ravensbarger, Harriet Hambly, Person or Persons in the Boathouse, and Kimmie Hunter. One obvious change needed to be made. She now knew Kimmie and her boyfriend were the boathouse intruders. Of course, what she saw tonight didn't *prove* they used the sleeping bag or that Kimmie lost the earring there, but chances were, that scenario was the case.

Roger and Dorleen appeared too friendly with one another for having recently met. Had they been previously acquainted? Or was Roger making up to Dorleen hoping to benefit from her newly acquired millions? Did he want her to invest in the downtown mall, just as he tried to involve Jessica?

Or, as Nina had mentioned to her grandmother earlier that evening, suppose Roger and Dorleen conspired to murder Ellie? Maybe Dorleen promised

Roger part of her inheritance if he would drown his aunt. Nina wouldn't put such an evil deed past the slimy nephew. She didn't know Dorleen well enough to judge her character. Stephen promised to find someone to investigate the woman, but so far, he hadn't reported anything.

Nina sipped her tea and considered the next person on her list, Dr. Ravensbarger. The papers she found this evening in Ellie's apartment hinted at Medicare fraud. If Ellie discovered his cheating and confronted him, he would have good motivation to silence her. Had he committed murder? If so, how brazen—not to say risky—to sneak onto the Marley Manor grounds and lie in wait for his victim.

If the doctor wanted Ellie dead, would he act alone, or enlist help? Sheryl Titus, perhaps? Nina added the nurse's name to the list.

Was anyone else to be considered? Nina recalled Ellie's memorial and the newcomer, Joe McGarrity. He'd known Ellie in the past, and Nina had the feeling their association was more than casual. He seemed such a nice man, though. She certainly didn't need another suspect. She had more than enough to keep her busy. Nevertheless, she added Joe's name to the list. Then she made a few more notes:

Find out more about Dorleen.

Talk to Kimmie.

Talk to Sheryl.

Learn more about Dr. Ravensbarger's practice.

She debated which task to tackle first when the phone chimed. Caller ID showed Stephen's smiling face. "Did you go to Marley this evening?" he asked after they exchanged greetings.

"I did, and I might have discovered something important. I'll tell you the details when I see you. How are you doing?"

"Missing you."

His plaintive tone struck a chord, and she smiled. "We've been apart only two days."

"Seems longer."

"Well, I miss you, too." She pictured him sitting in front of his fireplace, sleeves rolled up, mug of steaming coffee at his elbow, working on an article for the newspaper. A wave of emotion rolled over her. Her apartment, which she always loved and found comfortable, suddenly became cold and lonely. Maybe they *should* be together all the time. But, was a permanent relationship what she *really* wanted?

"Are we still on for our workout at the club tomorrow?"

Stephen's question brought her back to the present. "Yes, I'm looking forward to our racquetball game."

"I am, too. Oh, I'd better not forget the other reason I called. I found someone who will check on Dorleen."

Nina straightened her shoulders. "Really? Who?"

"A former journalist buddy. Like me, he opted out of the New York rat race. But instead of coming to the Northwest, he headed south. He's been lazing around the Florida Keys for the past couple months, on an extended vacation until he decides what to do with his life. Anyway, he said he'd be glad to do some digging."

"I'll certainly pay him for his trouble." Nina added the information to her notes.

"No payment necessary. He owes me a couple favors."

"You are wonderful, Stephen. I really appreciate your help."

"Thanks. But wait until he turns up something before you get too excited."

Nevertheless, after they ended the call, excitement surged through her veins. She could hardly wait to learn what Stephen's contact would discover.

****

The following day, while Nina performed her duties at the Seaview Library, she considered the next step in her investigation into Ellie's death. She had thought of a way to find out more about Dr. Ravensbarger's practice. But, since the idea was dangerous enough to be absolutely insane, she considered dismissing the plan. She was still debating when she saw Kimmie enter the library.

The teen stopped to push back the silver, faux-fur-trimmed hood of her blue parka and smooth her blonde hair, which fell into its jagged layers.

Catching Kimmie's sweeping gaze, Nina smiled and waved. Kimmie's returning smile appeared lukewarm and wary. Nina would have to tread carefully. She recalled how the girl bristled when Jason questioned her about her mysterious boyfriend.

Nina covertly watched Kimmie weave her way through the library.

She passed a table of youths her age and stopped to exchange a few words. Then she sat alone at a corner table. She took her tablet, a notebook, and a pen from her backpack. Setting up the tablet, she stared at the screen, twirling the pen between her fingers.

Nina allowed several minutes to pass and then approached. "I bet you're here to work on your cloning report. Right, Kimmie?"

The girl looked up. "Uh huh. I haven't even started."

The sight of Kimmie's tired eyes jolted Nina, and sympathy filled her. Obviously, the teen was under great stress. She tore away her gaze to focus on Kimmie's tablet. As before, except for "Cloning" written at the top, the rest of the screen was blank. "I'd be glad to help you find information."

"Maybe later." Kimmie tapped her pen on the table.

Nina slipped into a chair. "I need to talk to you. Let's go into my office where we won't disturb anyone."

Kimmie's back stiffened. "I don't want to answer any more questions about Ellie."

Gaining Kimmie's cooperation was more difficult than she'd anticipated, but the girl's defiance made her all the more determined. Nina took a deep breath. "Yes, I want to talk about Ellie. I have something of hers to give you."

Kimmie frowned. "You do? What?"

"Ellie made several bequests in her will to special friends, like you. My grandmother is in charge of distributing the gifts. I told her I'd be seeing you, so I have yours."

"Really?" Her eyes widened. "Cool. What did Ellie leave me?"

"Your bequest is in my office." Pushing away a niggle of guilt at having to bribe Kimmie, Nina gestured to the area behind the checkout desk. "Bring your tablet and books. We'll discuss your report, too."

Kimmie gathered her belongings and followed

Nina to her office.

Okay, so she used a bit of trickery. She was justified. She did have a gift for Kimmie, but, as the teen would soon find out, the gift came with strings attached. Would she cooperate? Or would Nina's plan to discover more about her only strengthen Kimmie's defenses?

Chapter Fourteen

"Please have a seat, Kimmie." Nina shut her office door and pointed to several straight-backed chairs reserved for visitors.

Kimmie sat, positioning her backpack on the floor beside her chair.

Nina unlocked her bottom desk drawer and dug inside her purse for the fabric pouch containing the bee bracelet and also the matching earring from the boathouse. Instead of sitting at the desk, she pulled up a chair beside Kimmie. Opening the pouch, she pulled out the bracelet.

"Wow!" Kimmie stared. "The bee bracelet."

"You're familiar with the bracelet, then?" The girl's reaction didn't surprise Nina.

"I, uh, Ellie told me about it. Actually, she showed me the bracelet. Oh, this is so cool. I love it." She clapped her hands. "Ellie told me the stones are real diamonds."

"Then the bracelet is quite valuable. Here, put it on." Nina held out the jewelry, hoping Kimmie appreciated Ellie's generous gesture. Under the office's fluorescent lights, the bees' diamond eyes winked and sparkled.

Kimmie took the bracelet, wound it around her wrist, and snapped the clasp.

Nina helped her attach the safety chain.

The girl fingered the jewelry. "I've never had anything like this before."

"What about the matching earrings?" Nina kept her tone casual.

Kimmie jerked up her head, her eyes narrowed. "What earrings?"

"I know Ellie already gave you the bracelet's matching earrings."

She stuck out her chin. "How do you know?"

"Because I found one of the pair."

"You did?" Her voice rose a notch.

"Caught in a sleeping bag." Nina drew the earring from the pouch and placed it in her palm.

Kimmie stared, but then she drew back and folded her arms.

Nina kept her gaze on Kimmie. "The sleeping bag was stuffed into a rowboat in the boathouse at Lake Mead."

Her mouth set in a stubborn line, Kimmie remained silent.

Nina leaned forward. "I know you and your, ah, *friend* use the boathouse. I saw you enter there last night."

Kimmie gasped. "You spied on us." She clapped a hand over her mouth. "I didn't mean to say that," she mumbled through her fingers.

"You might call my observation spying, but invading your privacy wasn't what I intended." Nina explained her trip to the kitchen to give her the bracelet and then following her to the boathouse. "As you know, I want to find out what happened to Ellie. But I'm concerned about you, too."

Kimmie shifted in her chair. "You don't think we

killed her, do you?" She shook her head. "We had nothing to do with her death."

"No, I don't think you would harm Ellie. But who is your friend?"

"I can't tell you." Kimmie looked away.

Nina leaned closer. "Are you in some kind of trouble? Is your friend in trouble?"

The girl hugged her arms and turned sideways. "Quit bugging me. My life's none of your business."

Surely, a person needed the patience of Job when dealing with teens. Nina searched for a diplomatic way to handle the situation. "Maybe your being in the boathouse is not my business, as you say, but I do care, and I'm worried you might be in trouble. Were you at the lake the night of Ellie's death?"

"We didn't see anything."

Nina's breath quickened. Perhaps she'd learn some useful information yet. "Then you *were* there that night."

"Will you tell on us?" Kimmie's eyes narrowed.

Nina debated. What exactly was her responsibility? She finally formed a reply. "I won't mention your trespassing to anyone if you will talk to someone about your relationship with your friend. How about a counselor at school or another adult you feel comfortable with? I'm guessing your parents wouldn't be your first choice."

Kimmie ducked her head. "They'd kill me if they knew."

"Do you know someone else you can trust?"

"I'll think about it." She folded her arms.

"All right, I'll trust you will. Here's something else I want you to think about." Nina toughened her tone. "If you do know something about Ellie's death and you don't tell the authorities, you'll be withholding evidence. When you're discovered, you—and your friend—can be prosecuted. You will be found out, too, because I'm not giving up my search for the truth about Ellie." As a thought occurred, Nina tilted her head. "By the way, did she know about you and your friend and the boathouse?"

Kimmie bit her lip and looked away.

"She did. Oh, boy." Nina rolled her eyes.

"But we didn't kill her."

Kimmie's decisive tone convinced Nina, and she raised both hands. "I believe you. But remember what I said about withholding evidence."

A couple seconds of silence rolled by, and then Kimmie cast Nina a sideways look. "Are you taking back the bracelet?"

"Of course not." Nina waved a hand." According to Ellie's will, the bracelet is yours with no strings attached. But I will keep the earring while you and your friend decide what to do." Expecting Kimmie to protest, Nina tensed.

Instead, the girl clamped shut her jaw and stared at the floor. Tears rolled down her cheeks.

Nina's heart went out to her. How could she help the troubled teen? She pulled a tissue from the box on her desk and held it out. "I'm sorry our talk upset you, Kimmie. I'd hoped to help you with your report, too—"

Kimmie took the tissue and dabbed at her wet cheeks. "I don't want your help. Can I go now?"

"Of course." Kimmie's reluctance to accept help disappointed Nina, yet she knew better than to push the troubled teen, especially at this time.

"Will you keep my secret?"

Nina held up a hand. "You have my word—for now. But if I need to go to the police with the information, I will."

Kimmie glowered. Then she jumped up, grabbed her backpack, and marched from the office.

Nina leaned back in her chair and let out a breath. Had confronting Kimmie been a mistake? But, when she thought about abandoning her purpose, Ellie's image popped into her mind. She saw again the woman's woeful, distressed face peering at her through the rain and heard her plea. "Help me! Help me!"

No, Nina would not give up, no matter how many roadblocks people such as Kimmie put in her way.

****

On her break a few days later, Nina took her coffee into her office and closed the door. She sat at her desk and stared at her cell phone lying on the desktop. Next to the phone was a business card. She put down her cup and reached for the phone. Then she shook her head and drew back her hand. All day, she'd been undecided about making the call. Yes, she should. No, she shouldn't. Yes, the idea was brilliant. No, the idea was insane.

Regarding her investigation, the last few days were a stalemate. She returned twice to Ellie's apartment but found nothing more of interest. On both occasions, she peeked in Marley's kitchen to say hello to Kimmie and ask how she was faring. Each time, chef Darren told her Kimmie had called in sick. Nina worried the pressure she put on the girl contributed to her absence.

Dorleen and Roger kept to themselves, according to Jessica. Ellie's friends hoped to get to know Dorleen, but, apparently, the woman didn't share their feelings. Bringing her thoughts back to her dilemma, Nina stared again at the phone. *Just do it.* She picked up the phone and entered the number written on the business card.

A receptionist answered the call. "Dr. Young's office. How may I help you?"

Nina swallowed. "I, ah, I'd like to make an appointment."

"Certainly. Do you have a particular date in mind?"

"As soon as possible." She gripped the phone. "Does the doctor work evenings? I work during the day."

"The doctor is in on Tuesday and Thursday evenings."

Today was Wednesday. She could wait until next Tuesday... No, she might lose her courage by then. "Do you have any openings tomorrow?"

"Just a minute. Let me check."

Nina's heart thudded. *I'll take whatever happens as a sign. No Thursday openings will mean I shouldn't pursue this scheme. If openings are available, then I should.*

The receptionist returned to the line. "You're in luck. We've had a cancellation tomorrow night for eight o'clock. Would that suit you?"

"Ah, all right... I'll be there at eight." Nina gave the receptionist the rest of the needed information and then hung up, biting her lip. Had she just taken the first step in what was a brilliant plan, or was she headed for a disaster?

****

The following evening, as the appointed hour neared, Nina considered calling Dr. Young's office and cancelling. She paced her living room, thinking she couldn't go through with this crazy idea. Not only crazy but also downright dangerous. Nevertheless, while deciding whether or not to keep the appointment, she put on her coat, gathered up her purse, climbed into her car, and drove along the streets of Richmond until she reached the two-story office building.

She marched up the stone walk, past the mushroom-shaped lamps, and past the sign listing the doctors' names. At the glass doors, she came to an abrupt stop. Here was a significant threshold to cross. She could return to the car and cancel the appointment using her cell phone.

You've come this far, don't back out now. You can do this. Nina gulped a breath and opened the door.

Inside, the clinic was eerily dim, with only perimeter ceiling lights to illuminate the pastel peach and turquoise decor. The atmosphere was silent, too, without the usual daytime noises of telephones ringing and people talking. No one sat behind the reception desk. The door leading to the hallway was closed. Nina stood at the desk waiting for the door to open and an employee to appear. She was expected. Someone would come to greet her and check her in. She glanced at her wristwatch. Two minutes to eight. Okay, she was a little early. Still, the longer she must wait, the more tempted she was to bolt.

The door to the hallway finally opened, and Dr. Young appeared. Her thick, auburn hair swept away from her face like wings, accenting her deep-set eyes and high cheekbones. She was dressed not in a suit, as she had been at the clinic's opening, but more casually in rust-colored slacks and a beige turtleneck sweater. A vest decorated with colorful sequins added a stunning decorative touch.

"Hello, Nina." Dr. Young smiled. "I've been waiting for you. Come to my office." She gestured toward the hallway.

"Good evening." Nina took a deep breath and followed Dr. Young.

Once in her office, Dr. Young closed the door and waved to an overstuffed chair. "Please sit, Nina, and make yourself comfortable."

Comfortable? Not likely. But Nina mustered a smile and sat. She kept her back rigid and both feet planted firmly on the floor.

Picking up a clipboard and pen from her desk, Dr. Young sat in a high-backed, brown leather chair facing Nina. "We have some business to take care of first." She pointed toward the clipboard. "Usually, my receptionist has new patients fill out forms, but she's not here tonight. Rather than complete them now, you can take the forms home and bring them with you next time." Removing several stapled sheets of paper from the clipboard, she handed them to Nina.

Nina barely glanced at the papers before tucking them into her purse. She wouldn't tell the doctor a next time would not happen and that this was a one-time visit because she came tonight under false pretenses.

Dr. Young sat back in her chair, resting her elbows on the wide leather arms. Her nails were painted with clear polish, and a gold-banded watch peeked from under the cuff of her sweater.

"I really appreciate your seeing me tonight." Nina forced a smile. "Coming here after hours seems strange. I mean, the office is so…deserted. Are we the only ones around?" She hoped her question sounded innocent. She must be careful not to arouse the woman's suspicions, but knowing if others were in the building was vital to her purpose.

Dr. Young waved a hand. "Dr. Ravensbarger usually works late in his laboratory…"

"Oh." Nina's heart sank. His presence would ruin her plans.

"…But tonight he's not here, so we are alone." The doctor tilted her head. "Does the absence of others make you uncomfortable?"

"Oh, no. I was just…making conversation." Inwardly, she gave a relieved sigh.

Dr. Young held her pen poised over the clipboard. "What brought you here, Nina?"

"Stephen Kraslow recommended I see you."

Dr. Young nodded, made a note, and then looked up again.

"I have nightmares." Nina felt her stomach tighten. Admitting her problem was always difficult. "My bad dreams upset him."

The therapist's eyebrows peaked. "Do the nightmares upset you?"

"No. Yes. I don't know." Nina shifted in her seat. "I've had so many I should be used to them."

"Tell me more about your disturbing dreams."

Nina licked her dry lips and glanced at her wristwatch. Only ten minutes after eight. How would she ever get through the interview and on to her real purpose for being in the clinic tonight?

She didn't want to talk about her nightmares. Yet, she mentioned them, so she must give Dr. Young at least some information, or she might suspect her sincerity. Too late she realized she could have made up a fictitious problem for the occasion. Then she wouldn't be quite so distressed. Nina took a deep breath and clasped her hands in her lap. "The dreams always start with a man who has no face."

Dr. Young took more notes, but most of the time, her dark eyes stayed riveted on Nina.

Ten minutes later, Nina finished describing the nightmares. "I have never known the man's identity."

"Do the dreams always awaken you?"

"Not always. Whether or not I wake up depends on how frightened I become...I guess...I don't know." She shrugged. "What do the dreams mean?" Anticipating the doctor's response kept her nerves on edge.

Dr. Young smiled. "I'll need to work with you awhile longer before coming up with any theories."

"How *do* you work?" Nina was suddenly interested in the doctor's methods.

"Basically, I'm a Jungian." She tilted her head. "Carl Jung?"

Nina nodded. "I'm familiar with his work from a college Psychology course."

"I'll recommend books that discuss his theories. But his aren't the only techniques I use. I'm more eclectic, and I'm a licensed hypnotherapist."

"I see." Although Nina knew little about hypnosis, she found Dr. Young's training impressive.

The doctor turned to a fresh sheet of paper on her clipboard. "Tell me more about yourself and your family."

Nina tensed again but reminded herself she must respond enough to keep the doctor from becoming suspicious. "My mother worked in real estate. She died shortly after I graduated college. My grandmother lives at Marley Manor. Her husband died, oh, about twenty years ago."

Dr. Young nodded. "How about your father?"

Nina swallowed over sudden dryness in her throat and lowered her voice. "He left my mother and me when I was five."

"Do you have siblings?"

"None." Nina shook her head. "My mother never married again. She was an only child, too. My grandmother's relatives live in the Midwest, but I've never met any of them."

"What word or words would you use to describe your mother?"

The answer to that question brought a rush of sadness. "Busy with her career. Selling real estate was more important than anything else."

"Hmmm." As she recorded a note, Dr. Young's brow wrinkled. "And your grandmother?"

"She keeps busy, too. But she has more time for, for—" What was she saying? "For me," she finished.

"You mentioned you're a librarian."

As Nina told Dr. Young about her job, she felt her tension ebb. Talking about her profession was easier than discussing her family.

At last, the doctor put down her pen and leaned forward. "I'm afraid our time is up, Nina. Let me get my book, and we'll set up another appointment."

The reminder she was expected to return jolted Nina. "No! I mean, I, uh, I'll need to check my schedule at the library. I work different hours each week." As branch manager, she determined those hours, but the doctor didn't need to know that fact.

"All right. I'll wait to hear from you. Just give my office a call, and Jenny, my receptionist, will set up an appointment."

Despite Nina's sudden outburst, Dr. Young's tone remained calm. After learning the fee for the session, Nina took out her checkbook and wrote a check. She handed the slip to the doctor, added a verbal "thank you," and was surprised to find she meant the words.

Dr. Young led Nina to the office door.

Nina stopped, exaggerating having a sudden thought. "Do you have a restroom I could use before I leave?"

"Yes, the restrooms are at the end of the hall toward the back of the building." Dr. Young pointed down the hallway.

"From there, could I leave by the back door? That exit is close to where I parked my car."

"Of course."

After again thanking the doctor for the session, Nina went down the hall to the restroom. She hadn't faked her request, either, because nervousness prompted her kidneys to work overtime. After visiting the restroom, she continued on to the back door. She pushed the bar to open the door but did not step out. Then, with a resounding bang, she slammed shut the door. She hoped Dr. Young heard the noise and would think she left the building.

Remaining in the building after her appointment was the point of tonight's visit. She hoped what she discovered would be worth the risk.

Chapter Fifteen

Nina gazed around the hallway. She needed a place to hide until Dr. Young left. The restroom was a bad choice because the doctor might visit the facility before leaving. Spotting a door marked "Storage," she grabbed the handle and opened the door. Smells of soap and ammonia drifted out. Several large trash barrels, buckets, mops, and brooms filled the space. *Perfect.* Nina stepped inside the room and closed the door. Soft light from a small window near the ceiling allowed her enough light to make out objects.

In case Dr. Young or someone else might have a reason to come inside, Nina ducked behind a trash barrel. She made herself as comfortable as possible and settled to wait. She hoped she wouldn't have to stay long in the storeroom. The strong odors made her want to sneeze.

The waiting gave her time to reconsider. Did she really want to go through with this crazy plan? If she were caught, she'd be in big trouble.

A door closed, and footsteps approached. Dr. Young was leaving. As she heard the steps come nearer, Nina held her breath and then exhaled when the person passed by. The back door opened with a creak and closed with a bang.

At last, Nina was alone. She waited a minute or two more before abandoning the protection of the trash barrel. Then, leaving the room, she approached the stairs leading to the second floor. Upstairs was Dr. Ravensbarger's office and tonight's true target. Her heart thudding, she hurried up the stairs. Even though she was alone now, she didn't want to linger longer than necessary.

At the top of the stairs was a hallway lined with doors, similar to the downstairs floor plan. Thankfully, a few lights had been left on, allowing her to locate the doctor's office. As she expected, a lock—a deadbolt— secured the door. However, she came prepared. Digging in her purse, she pulled out a small leather case. Opening the zipper, she surveyed the exposed tools, selecting the tension wrench and the pick.

A couple years ago, just for fun, she took a course for mystery writers taught by a private detective. As a mystery reader, she enjoyed learning tricks of the detective trade.

One of the topics the instructor covered was lock picking. He pointed out that possessing lock-picking tools was not only for criminals but also for someone locked out of a house or car.

After the class, Nina purchased a set of tools online. She practiced with them on her front door, on her jewelry box, and on her basement storage unit. Tonight would be the first attempt picking someone else's lock. Her heartbeat quickened.

Manipulating the two tools took precious moments, but at last the lock snapped open and Nina slipped inside. The interior was dark, but, again, she came prepared. She pulled a flashlight from her purse, switched it on, and played the light over a waiting room with a reception desk and chairs. The doctor chose pale blues for his color scheme. But never mind such details—she must locate his patient files. The records were on his computer, of course, but she counted on finding paper copies, too. Her doctor kept hard copy files, and so did Jessica's. She hoped Dr. Ravensbarger did as well. The files wouldn't be here in the reception room, though.

She opened another door. Her flashlight revealed an examine room, with a paper-covered examination table waiting for the doctor's next patient. Nina shuddered and closed the door.

Next, she found a room with a computer, a printer, a copy machine, and a metal file cabinet. Giving an inward cheer, she hurried to the cabinet and tugged the handle of the top drawer. Locked. No problem—hopefully. Opening her tool case, she selected a pick she thought would work. She stuck the tool in the file lock, but it didn't fit. Neither did the next one she tried. Or the next. Beads of sweat broke out on her forehead. A paperclip was supposed to work, too, but she didn't want to take time to search for one and, besides, she hadn't practiced with a paperclip. Holding her breath, she tried yet another pick, and the lock finally popped.

Stuffing away the tools, she yanked open the drawer. Files crammed the inside, so close together she could barely push her hand between them. The doctor certainly had a lot of patients. Nina shone her light on the folder tabs. Thankfully, they were in alphabetical order. She located the L's and then narrowed down the names to Lark, Millicent, Larkes, Adele, and, finally, Larkin, Eloise. She pulled out the folder, marking the correct place with another one turned sideways.

Ellie's file was jam-packed. Fortunately, all the

papers were secured at the top of the folder, or they would have fallen out when Nina opened it. She put the open file on a counter and, holding her light, scanned the pages. She quickly realized the hopelessness of her task. She couldn't possibly sort through all the records to find the information she sought. Stealing the entire file was out of the question. Yet, she was determined not to leave empty-handed.

Her gaze fell on the copy machine. *Yes!* She scurried to the copier and flipped the On switch. The machine's hum sounded inordinately loud in the otherwise-silent building. She tapped her foot while the copier warmed up. When the machine finally was ready, she duplicated the more recent records in Ellie's folder, including those dealing with Medicare.

She made as many copies as she dared and then turned off the machine. She returned the folder to the file cabinet and shut the drawer. The drawer wouldn't be locked, but she couldn't worry about that now.

Now, she had to get out of there. Her purse bulging with the papers, she left the office. Thinking the door's deadbolt was more important to secure than the file cabinet's lock, she took the time for that task. Then she hurried down the stairs and headed for the back door. From there she would make her way through the courtyard, the alley, and around the block to her car.

She was about to push open the heavy steel door when a sign caught her eye. CAUTION—AFTER HOURS ALARM. Next to the door was a keypad where one could punch in the code. Nina froze. Of course, the clinic would have a burglar alarm. Why hadn't she noticed the warning and the keypad earlier when she opened the door? The sign was large enough.

But, then, she was preoccupied finding a place to hide until the doctor left.

The alarm was turned off while Dr. Young was in the building and expecting Nina to arrive. Now, however, the doctor had gone home. Surely, she activated the alarm system before leaving. If Nina opened the door, everyone within hearing distance would be alerted. Her car was parked a block away. Could she reach the car without someone seeing her, or being caught by security cameras?

What now? Was she stuck here until morning? Even then, how would she escape undetected? The realization of how stupid she was hit Nina like a lead weight, and she sagged against the wall. She'd be discovered, arrested, and hauled off to jail. Her career as a librarian was over.

What was she thinking? How could she put her life on the line to play detective?

All the self-recriminations and chastising didn't help her now. She must find a way out of this dilemma. She had her cell phone, but she didn't dare call Stephen. He'd worry about her or bawl her out. Probably both.

She finally decided to hunker down for the night and hope that when the building was unlocked in the morning, she'd sneak out without being observed. While looking for a place to hide, she heard a car approach. No, the sound was deeper, more like the engine of a truck or a van. Sucking in a breath, she waited. The sound ceased. Then voices and footsteps sounded. People were coming. Nina's heart raced.

She'd better hide and quickly. Nina scurried down the hallway to the storeroom where she hid earlier. She ran inside and ducked behind the same large trash barrel. As before, the smells of soap and ammonia tickled her nose. She was barely situated when she heard the outside door open. The steps and voices drew near. Nina held her breath.

The door to the storeroom opened and light streamed in.

Nina pressed together her lips and squeezed into a tighter ball.

"You turn off the alarm while I get the bucket," a man said. "We can use the bucket to prop open the door."

"Okay," a woman replied.

The man approached the trash barrel where Nina hid. He reached for a bucket on rollers sitting beside the barrel.

Nina stifled a gasp. In the next moment, he would discover her.

Instead, the man grabbed the bucket and retreated. "Hurry up!" he called to the woman. "We got five more jobs after this."

Nina risked a peek from behind her barrel. Both workers wore gray coveralls with Acme Commercial Cleaners printed on the back.

The sound of their footsteps, along with the squeak of the bucket's rollers, faded. The door to the outside opened. She waited but did not hear the door close. The man said something about propping open the door. Dare she hope the unalarmed exit would offer her an escape?

Nina crept to the door of the storeroom and peered out. Yes, the outer door stood propped open with the bucket. The couple was nowhere in sight. They'd probably gone to their truck for cleaning supplies.

Did she have time to escape before they returned? This opportunity might be her only chance before morning. Hugging the wall, Nina scurried along the hallway toward the door. Breathing fast, she stopped and peered through the opening. A large van was parked in the alley beyond the courtyard. The cleaners were probably unloading their supplies from the back end of the van, which was hidden behind the courtyard wall.

Nina leaped over the bucket and out the door. Free at last.

Just then, a flashbulb popped squarely in her face.

"I wondered if you'd ever come out," said a deep, familiar voice.

Gasping, she skidded to a stop. She peered at the person, but spots of light from the camera's flash danced before her eyes, obscuring her vision. Still, she recognized the voice and the outline of the burly-chested figure. "Roger. What are you doing here?"

"Huh! Why are *you* here?"

The slamming of the van's doors resounded from the alley.

"They're coming." Nina glanced around the immediate area. If she ran from the courtyard, she'd meet the cleaning crew. She turned in the opposite direction and dashed around the corner of the building.

Roger stayed close on her heels. "I saw you…go in the clinic tonight."

His alcohol-tainted breath turned her stomach. She wanted to stuff a rag in his mouth and probably would have, had one been handy. "Shut up, or they'll hear us."

Finally, the cleaners finished transporting their equipment into the building. The man picked up the bucket holding the door. He disappeared inside, and the door closed.

Nina stepped from behind the building and hurried across the courtyard to the alley. Aware Roger was still behind her, she reached the alley and squeezed past the cleaners' van.

Roger huffed a breath. "Whadja find in there?"

"What makes you think I was looking for something?" Had her flashlight been visible through the window?

"Aw, come on, I wasn't born yesterday. You were in ol' Doc Ravensburger's office."

"Ravens*barger*," Nina automatically corrected and then, realizing she'd given away her location, winced.

Roger waved a hand. "Whatever. Anyway, he was Auntie's doctor. You're lookin' for something has to do with her. Whadja find?"

Walking at a brisk pace, she rounded the corner leading to her car. The farther away she was from the clinic, the better. If only she could escape Roger before he figured out any more about her mission.

He leaned toward her.

She caught another whiff of alcohol. "Roger, you're stalking me. Stalking is against the law."

"Stalking? Is that what you call wanting to know what you find out about my auntie? I don't think so. But go ahead and complain. I have this nice picture of you comin' out of the clinic late at night. The picture tells the date and the time." He patted his parka pocket where the camera made a bulge. "Wonder what the police will make of that."

"Blackmail is against the law, too."

He snorted. "Wanna put the law to the test?"

What an insufferable jerk. She rounded another corner.

On the other side of the street, a man walked his dog. His gaze on them lingered.

"Wait until we get to my car, Roger." She nodded toward the man with the dog.

Roger took the hint and kept quiet.

Finally, they reached her car. Nina could hardly wait to drive away from the obnoxious man. She unlocked the door and yanked it open.

"Hey, wait a minute." Roger loomed over her. "What about what you found in the clinic?"

She turned and glared. "You're only assuming I found something."

"Look, I'm warning you, Nina Foster." He shook a finger. "Don't play games with me. You better come clean, or I'll find a good use for the picture I took tonight."

Nina slid onto the car seat and then shut and locked the door.

Roger beat his fists on the window.

Starting the engine, she put the car in gear and stepped on the gas. In her rearview mirror, she saw him standing in the middle of the street, hands on his hips, jaw agape.

Hoping to stop her hands from shaking, Nina gripped the steering wheel. Tears crowded her eyes, blurring her vision. Yet, somehow, she made the trip to her condo. She expected Roger to follow her, but he didn't. Hers was the only car on the street, and no others came into sight as she punched in the code to open the gates to the condo grounds.

In her apartment, Nina tossed her purse on a table

and sank onto the sofa. Hugging her arms, she leaned back against the cushions. Carrying out her plan was daring enough without being trapped in the locked building. Then, to find a way out, only to face Roger and learn he caught her escape on film. He was clever. But, oh, what a mess.

Pressing a hand to her stomach, Nina took deep breaths, and, gradually, she relaxed. At last, she felt steady enough to make a cup of tea. As she returned to the sofa with her steaming brew, she noticed her purse bulging with the purloined records. No, she did not want to look at them tonight. She sat and sipped her tea. Maybe she should get rid of the papers, in case Roger made good his threat, and the police arrived with a search warrant.

Quit jumping to conclusions. Roger was a big blowhard full of threats, nothing more. Yet, he was a loose cannon, too, and therefore potentially dangerous. She had no idea what he might do. Tonight, she might have pushed him too far.

Oh, Ellie! I want to find out the truth about what happened to you. Instead, I've created a mess.

Nina waited for Ellie's pleading, distraught image to fill her mind, which always reassured her about her involvement. Tonight, however, the only image she saw was Roger's menacing face.

Chapter Sixteen

The following evening after dinner, Nina examined Ellie's medical records. Sitting on the living room sofa, she read through most of the stack without finding anything of interest. Then she came upon the record of a visit that coincided with the Medicare billing found in Ellie's apartment. A paper titled Attending Physician's Statement had several columns listing various procedures and diagnoses. Studying the record, Nina saw Dyspepsia was checked, as was High Blood Pressure. Both confirmed what she knew of Ellie's illnesses and her medications.

However, further reading revealed another Attending Physician's Statement for the same date. In addition to the identical items marked on the first record, under Laboratory Profiles, Thyroid and Liver were indicated, along with corresponding fees. A handwritten note on the second statement said "Medicare."

Nina placed the two papers side by side on the coffee table and studied them. The one with the Medicare notation had four more items checked to be charged than the first statement. She located Ellie's copy of the billing statement and compared it with the other two. Ellie's matched the Medicare bill. The added items were those she'd marked to question the doctor.

Taking a deep breath, Nina sat back. Dr.

Ravensbarger was committing Medicare fraud. But why had he sent Ellie a copy of the bill with the bogus charges? Did he think she wouldn't notice the discrepancy?

The amended bill must have been sent by mistake. Maybe he discovered the error and prescribed more medication to keep Ellie in a confused state, so she would not report him. Or, if she did, she would be written off as crazy.

Had she discovered a motive for Ellie's murder? Nina set aside the papers and went to the kitchen to make a cup of tea. While the water heated, she paced, preoccupied with her newfound knowledge. If the doctor cheated Medicare, who else in his office knew? Confiding in the entire staff would be risky. Perhaps only one or two participated in the fraudulent practice. The person who did the actual billing might be an accomplice, and perhaps nurse Sheryl.

Nina poured the boiling water over the teabag in her cup, wondering what to do about her discovery. She couldn't take her evidence to the police without exposing her own illegal activities. Even if the doctor was a crook, that fact didn't prove he murdered Ellie.

****

On Sunday, Nina and Stephen joined Jessica for the midday meal at Marley Manor. Upon entering the building, she found Jessica waiting in the reception area. Other residents also greeted their guests, and the room buzzed with activity. The aroma of freshly brewed coffee and pastry wafted from the nearby cafe.

Nina hugged her grandmother and then stepped back and regarded her outfit. "My, don't you look dressed up today. Is that blouse new?" The garment was a colorful blue-and-green print with a cinched-in waist that flattered Jessica's slight figure.

"Brand new." Jessica stood on her toes and twirled. "Took the shopping bus to the mall yesterday. Also had my hair done." She patted her curls.

Nina noted Jessica's glowing expression. "A new shade?"

"A bit more blonde." She turned to Stephen. "You like?"

"Very becoming." Stephen put an arm around Jessica's shoulders and drew her into a hug.

In the dining room, Nina filled her plate with baked chicken, mashed potatoes, and coleslaw at the buffet table and then, by prearrangement, the three joined Wally and Lily. Seeing Joe McGarrity sitting with the couple surprised Nina, but then she remembered that at Ellie's memorial, Wally invited him to a Sunday dinner.

Jessica sat next to Joe, leaving Nina to sit at one end of the table and Stephen at the other.

Nina's seat faced the window. Outside in the courtyard, white, yellow, and purple crocuses waved in the breeze, forecasting the coming spring. On the lake, a small flock of ducks trailed across the pewter-colored water, leaving a wide V wake behind them. Today's peaceful scene was a sharp contrast to the stormy night Ellie died.

Joe leaned in Nina's direction. "How's the investigation?"

Although accustomed to queries, Nina never divulged anything important. "Oh, I'm still gathering information." She kept her tone casual.

"Here comes a couple that would top my suspect list." Lily nodded toward the door.

Nina turned to see Roger and Dorleen join the buffet line. Roger looked more dressed up than usual in black slacks and a plaid, Western-style shirt. His shoes, however, were the same scuffed work boots he always wore. Dorleen had on pale green slacks and a blouse decorated with palm trees. Her blonde hair was tied haphazardly in an off-center ponytail.

"I'm surprised they condescended to join us." Lily sniffed. "I thought she stayed here so we could get to know her, but we haven't had a chance."

"Whenever we do see her, she's with Roger." Wally spread butter on a roll.

"I thought she'd see through him by now, but I guess not." Jessica shook her head.

"Shhh!" Lily put a finger to her lips. "Here they come.... Oh, hello, you two."

"Hello." Dorleen's gaze roved the table and then focused on Nina.

Nina flinched inwardly. Had Roger told her about the episode at the clinic? She certainly hoped not. She pasted on a smile. "Nice to see you, Dorleen."

Roger shot her a grin. "Hey, Nina, how's your investigation these days?"

She lifted her chin and kept her tone firm. "Just fine, thank you."

"Is Roger showing you around town?" Stephen's question to Dorleen drew everyone's attention.

"Oh, yes." Dorleen rolled her eyes. "We took a ferry boat ride—in the rain. We shopped the stores—in the rain. We went to a waterfront restaurant, but all we could see of the view was—"

"The rain." Nodding, Stephen chuckled. "If you stick around long enough, the sun will shine."

"We're having a bus trip to Skookioomie Falls next week." Jessica waved a hand. "You should join us, Dorleen. You, too, Roger. We have great fun on our bus trips. The TV weatherman promised sunshine."

"Yes, come along. Give us a chance to know you better." Lily looked at Dorleen. "Wasn't becoming acquainted the purpose of your stay here at Marley?"

"I'm remaining until I fulfill Ellie's charity obligations." Dorleen pursed her lips.

Joe sipped his coffee. "You probably don't remember, Dorleen, but we met when you were a kid of about, oh, four or five."

Dorleen stepped back and narrowed her eyes. "We did?"

"Yep." Joe put down his cup. "I visited your parents in Florida. Your hair was curly then."

"I don't remember that occasion." Dorleen frowned and shook her head.

Roger looked at his plate. "We'd better find a table before our food gets cold."

"Sorry we don't have room here."

Lily's cheerful tone, which obviously didn't match the sentiment, brought a smile to Nina's lips.

"No problem." Roger shrugged. "I see an empty table by the window. C'mon, Dorleen."

"Nice to see you all again." Dorleen turned to follow Roger.

"Think about joining our trip to the falls," Jessica called after them.

The two made their way across the room. Others nodded and waved, but Roger and Dorleen kept on track to their intended table.

Nina let a few minutes elapse while everyone

resumed eating then turned to Joe. "I'm interested in your visit to Dorleen's parents. Would you mind telling us more?"

He nodded and put down his fork. "Ellie and I knew each other when we were in our thirties. I liked her, and I thought she liked me, but she always kept her distance. Finally, she told me that her fiancé, Wyatt, and her best friend, Anna, ran off together."

"Wyatt didn't break his engagement to Ellie first?" Stephen frowned.

"Apparently not. She showed me her ring. Such a shock, she said. She'd never trust any man again. I tried to convince her she should move on and give another guy—namely, me—a chance, but she wouldn't listen." Joe picked up his fork and took a bite of chicken.

Nina let him chew awhile. "How did you meet Wyatt and Anna and their daughter, Dorleen?"

"Oh, yeah." Joe nodded. "Well, when my job took me to Florida, I decided to look up Wyatt and Anna. I wanted to see what the guy she couldn't forget was like. Ellie knew exactly where they were. I found them and told them I was a friend of Ellie's."

Jessica touched her napkin to her lips. "How did they react?"

"They were standoffish at first, but then they relaxed, and we had a nice visit."

"And Dorleen?" Wally leaned forward.

Joe waved a hand. "Cute kid. I remember she had a doll she wouldn't let go of. Carried it with her everywhere."

"I remember my favorite toy." Lily smiled. "A mechanical dog my uncle gave me for Christmas. I named him Henry and walked him on a leash, just like a real dog."

"Mine was a fire truck with a ladder that went up and down." Wally gestured with his forefinger. "And a siren, too…."

Nina sighed. So much for Joe's experience with Dorleen. Actually, though, she learned quite a bit. As she concentrated on eating, she gazed around. Had Kimmie recovered from her illness and returned to work?

Just then, the teen came through the kitchen's swinging door pushing a cart filled with teapots. She headed in their direction, but when she met Nina's gaze, she veered away.

Okay, Kimmie avoided her. At least, she was back on the job. Looking around the room, Nina spotted Harriet Hambly. Accompanied by her usual hand gestures, Harriet entertained her tablemates, no doubt with a story related to her cookbooks or her TV show.

Harriet tossed back her head in a laugh and caught Nina's gaze. She clamped shut her mouth and gave Nina a glare before turning back to her companions.

What was Harriet's anger all about? She couldn't possibly know Nina discovered her secret. Could she? Nina sighed. Kimmie, Harriet, Roger—so many enemies she'd made, and all because she wanted to learn the truth about Ellie's death.

"Nina?"

The sound of Jessica's voice jolted Nina to attention. She turned and met her grandmother's inquisitive gaze. "Yes?"

"I asked if you and Stephen are joining us downstairs for pool."

Nina nodded. "We always do. Right, Stephen?"

She looked to him for confirmation.

Stephen put down his coffee cup. "Absolutely. Today might be our lucky day, and we'll win for a change."

"We'll all have a new challenge today." Jessica gestured toward Joe. "Joe will join our game, too."

"Since Wally told me about Jessica's skill at playing pool, I decided to see her in action." Joe smiled and nodded in her direction.

Jessica shrugged. "I've been known to win a tournament or two."

"You should see the trophies in her apartment." Wally spread his arms.

"Really? Maybe I'll be invited sometime." Joe's eyebrows peaked.

"Maybe you will." Jessica met his gaze and then lowered her eyelids.

Were they flirting? Nina stared at Jessica and then at Joe. *No, never.* Jessica wasn't interested in men. Not in that way. Not at her age. She was too set in her ways. She had male friends, of course, but no...*romantic* interests. Yet, downstairs in the poolroom, during Jessica and Joe's game, Nina watched in astonishment as Jessica missed several easy shots.

Joe won the game. Not by much but enough to emerge the victor. Jessica won the following game, but the third went again to Joe.

Nina had never seen her grandmother play so poorly. Oh, she still did well by the average player's standards, but she was definitely not up to her usual performance.

While Stephen showed Joe the rest of the basement facilities, Jessica and Nina put away the pool equipment.

Nina placed the balls in the triangular pool rack. "You let him win those games, didn't you?"

Jessica hung a cue stick on the rack. "Let's just say I had an off day. Joe is a very good player, though, and I might have met my match."

"Yeah, right." Nina's flat tone expressed her disbelief. "And at dinner, you two flirted."

A smile hovered over Jessica's lips. "You might call our exchange flirting."

"You knew Joe was coming today, too. Was that why you bought a new blouse and got a new hairdo?" Nina straightened and faced Jessica. "What's going on?"

Jessica met Nina's gaze. "What I'm doing ought to be obvious. I find Joe attractive."

"But—but—"

"You think I'm too old for romance?" Jessica stuck her hands on her hips. "Too old to date Joe?"

"D-date him?" Nina sputtered.

"Yes, dear. In my day, we called going out together "dating." And no, he hasn't asked me yet. But he will." Jessica's lips curved into a smile. "And when he does, I plan to say yes."

What would happen then? Nina wondered. Joe was on her lists of suspects. Was he really the nice guy he appeared to be? Or was he hiding something?

****

"You're quiet tonight," Stephen said when he and Nina were on their way home from Marley. "Are you worried about what Dorleen and Roger might be up to?"

Nina turned from gazing out the window at the

rain-slick streets. "They do seem awfully thick for two people who've just met."

"My guess is, he's pressuring her to invest in the downtown mall project." Stephen braked to turn a corner.

"Very likely. Have you looked into that situation, by the way?"

"I have, and if they don't get big money in a hurry, the complex won't be built. Dumping that idea would please me and a lot of others in this town." He stopped for a traffic light and studied her. "Has Roger bugged you for money, like he did Jessica that day at her apartment?"

Feeling guilty, Nina looked away. She hadn't told Stephen about her adventure at the clinic. "No, but he still wants to know if I've found out anything about Ellie."

Stephen slapped a palm on the steering wheel. "Don't let him badger you. If he does, let me know. I'll set him straight."

"Okay." *Maybe.*

"Joe seems like a nice guy." The light changed, and Stephen stepped on the gas.

"Yes, but I hope Gran will be careful."

Stephen's forehead wrinkled. "You don't want her to go out with him?"

"She told me he hasn't asked for a date."

"He plans to. While I showed him around the basement, he asked me for restaurant suggestions."

Nina tensed. "I'm surprised she's interested…"

"In men? In romance? Come on, Nina, give her a break. Getting together would be good for them both."

"I hope he's not just after her money." Nina folded

her arms.

Stephen grinned. "You'll approve if he's just after her body, then?"

Nina shifted in her seat. "They're kind of old for that, aren't they?"

"No, they're not. I hope I'm never too old for...that." He laughed, and then sobered. "Seriously, you know what I think? You're a little bit threatened."

Nina stiffened. "What do you mean?"

"If your grandmother develops a relationship with Joe, then she won't have so much time for you. You'll be abandoned, like you were when your father left."

A sharp pain arrowed through her chest. "I wish you'd stop analyzing me."

"Honey, please don't be angry. I care about you. If you'd just go see Becky..."

Steeling herself against his plaintive tone, she hugged her side of the car. "We're back to that argument, are we?"

He shot her a glance. "Have you thought any more about consulting her?"

"I don't need to think about it." *If he only knew.*

"You know I just want you to be happy."

"I am happy!" Nina turned away and looked out the window. They were almost to her condo. Good. She suddenly felt like a prisoner who couldn't wait to escape.

They rode the rest of the way in silence.

At the condo grounds, Stephen punched in the code to open the gate then continued on to her unit.

Nina debated whether or not to invite him in. Not wanting the day to end with both of them upset, she finally decided she would.

But when they stood on her doorstep, he grasped her hands and looked at her with solemn eyes. "We both need space, and I'll say goodnight now."

"We do. But, Stephen, I'm sorry, I—"

"Shhh." He placed a finger over her lips. "No need to apologize. We'll work out our problems. Have faith. I do."

"Faith." Nina mustered a faint smile. "All right, I'll try."

"I'll call you tomorrow." He gave her a soft kiss on her cheek, and then he was gone.

Later, as Nina made ready for bed, guilt at her deception nagged. What would Stephen say if he knew she had in fact visited Dr. Young, and that the visit was a sham, that she used Dr. Young only to gain access to Dr. Ravensbarger's records. He'd really be angry then.

Yet, she had to admit talking to Dr. Young wasn't as threatening as she'd feared. The therapist skillfully put Nina at ease. Discussing her feelings with a professional was different than with someone she knew, like Stephen, or Gran. Still, she didn't plan to return because she did not need a doctor.

Then what did she need? Despite her protests to the contrary, something dark and dangerous festered inside her. Occasionally, the menace, whatever it was, erupted as nightmares and sudden rushes of panic. Would she ever find the answer to her dilemma?

Chapter Seventeen

On Monday evening after work, Nina went to the new library at Marley Manor and set up the computer the home's director authorized her to purchase. Then she went to Nurse Sheryl Titus's office, hoping to learn about Dr. Ravensbarger's treatment of Ellie. The nurse's schedule, posted with Marley's receptionist, Hilda, indicated Sheryl was on duty tonight.

Nina stepped into the nurse's waiting room where a row of vinyl-covered chairs faced a desk and a door leading, presumably, to an examination room. No one was in sight, but muffled voices sounded behind the door. Concluding the nurse was with a patient, Nina sat, picked up a *Senior Living* magazine from a nearby table, and idly perused the pages.

At last, the door opened, and a woman hobbled out on a cane.

Nina recognized her as Lorna, one of Jessica's friends. In her nineties, she had stiff, white hair and wrinkled, brown skin. Bone disease curved her spine, and arthritis turned her hands into claws. Sadness at the ravages of old age filled Nina.

Sheryl, dressed in black slacks and an emerald green smock, followed Lorna. "Don't worry, dear." She patted the older woman's shoulder. "Dr. Ravensbarger will get your blood pressure lowered."

Lorna frowned. "I don't know if I want to see him

anymore."

"Why not?" Sheryl's eyebrows peaked.

Lorna tilted her head to look up at the nurse. "Some of us wonder about Dr. Ravensbarger—after Ellie's death, you know. Maybe I should see Dr. Janssen instead."

Sheryl placed an arm around Lorna's shoulder and gave her a hug. "Dr. Ravensbarger had nothing to do with Ellie's death."

"Some people think the pills he prescribed made her goofy."

"Rest assured, the doctor prescribes only what is necessary. If the medications affected her thinking or reasoning ability, she wasn't following his directions for taking them."

Lorna looked around and saw Nina. A smile deepened her wrinkles. "Oh, here's Nina. She'll find out what happened to Ellie."

Sheryl frowned at Nina. "Is that so?"

Lorna nodded. "What have you discovered, Nina?"

"Nothing significant yet." Nina noted Lorna's uncertainty about continuing to consult Dr. Ravensbarger.

Leaning on her cane, Lorna took a step. "Well, I hope you do soon. We're all counting on you."

Sheryl led Lorna to the outer door. "You take care now, and I'll set up your appointment with the doctor." After the woman left, she turned to Nina. "Is something wrong with Jessica?"

"No, she's fine. I'm here on my own." Nina laid aside the magazine and stood.

Sheryl's bright red mouth tightened. "If you're here to talk about Ellie, you surely know that due to doctor-patient confidentiality, I can't tell you anything about her treatment."

Nina nodded. "I know, but I saw on her daily planner that she had an appointment with you on the day of her death."

"Just how did you have access to her calendar?" Sheryl stuck her hands on her hips.

Nina took note of Sheryl's defensive posture. "I'm helping Jessica sort her belongings."

"I see."

The nurse's cold gaze told Nina that although she might understand, she clearly didn't approve. "Then you did see her that day?" Nina pressed on.

"All right, yes, I treated her. She came periodically to have her blood pressure checked. A lot of the residents do. Like Lorna." She nodded toward the door.

"I thought you might have noticed something different or strange about Ellie's behavior."

Sheryl shrugged. "She was her usual self. She talked about Nigel, the rain, and seeing a play at the senior center."

Surprise rippled through Nina. "Then she was lucid."

"Of course. I never saw her confused or acting crazy, like people have said."

Nina shifted her feet and folded her arms, intent on pursuing her questioning despite Sheryl's obvious reluctance. "But she was seeing Dr. Ravensbarger."

"Yes, she was under his care. But, like I said, I can't go into details." Sheryl turned away to straighten the magazines on the end table.

Nina took a deep breath. "I know why she saw him."

Sheryl dropped the magazines and turned. "Oh, really? How do you know?"

"I found copies of paperwork Ellie received from Medicare and her supplemental insurance carrier."

"My, you have been busy snooping haven't you?"

Sheryl's mouth turned down and her voice dripped with sarcasm. Did she wonder if Nina had seen the duplicate papers? Did she even know about them? "How long have you worked for the doctor?"

"What does my employment record have to do with Ellie or any other patient?" Sheryl folded her arms and planted her feet apart.

Nina spread her hands and softened her tone. "I'm just curious. You don't have to tell me if you don't want to."

"I have nothing to hide." Sheryl stuck out her chin. "I've been with him for about seven years."

Sheryl's answer, however curt, encouraged Nina. After seven years of employment, surely she knew about the fraud. "Where were you before that?"

"I worked at a hospital in Boston—where I got my training."

"What brought you to the Northwest?" Had job opportunity prompted her relocation? Or something else?

"A couple of my colleagues moved here and suggested I join them." Sheryl consulted her wristwatch. "I have another resident coming soon. We'll have to cut short your interrogation."

"I'm sorry if my questions upset you." Nina secured the shoulder strap to her purse and turned toward the door. While she had no way of knowing the truth of Sheryl's statements, she would add the information gleaned from this meeting to her investigation data.

"I'm not upset, but some of your questions are inappropriate." Stepping ahead of Nina, Sheryl opened the door. "Ellie's death affected us all, including Dr. Ravensbarger. She was our patient. We cared about her. But the police ruled her death an accident. Why don't you stop wasting your time attempting to prove otherwise?"

Aware of Sheryl's defensive tone, Nina moved into the open doorway. "I appreciate your concern, but I don't feel my inquiries are a waste of time. We all have our jobs to do, and right now, finding out more about Ellie's death is mine."

Sheryl pursed her lips and shook her head. "You're asking for trouble, Nina."

As Nina walked away, she felt a chill ripple down her spine. Did the nurse have Nina's best interests at heart? Or had she just been issued a warning?

****

The following evening, Nina phoned Jessica. "I've been thinking about your trip to Skookioomie Falls. Do you know if Dorleen is going?"

"I believe I saw her name on the list. Roger's, too. Why?"

Nina shifted in her seat on the sofa. "I'd like to be included, if there's room on the bus. I'd like the opportunity to get to know Dorleen better before she returns to Florida."

Jessica laughed. "If you can get past Roger. I swear, you'd think he was guarding the crown jewels."

Gazing idly out the window, Nina spotted several of her condo village neighbors on an evening walk. "In a way, he is. Dorleen's a very wealthy woman now."

"True. But, yes, we have extra seats. The weather's supposed to be mild, with even a little sun."

"Sounds like fun," she said to Jessica. "I'll come."

"Great. We're leaving at nine a.m., having lunch at the falls' lodge, and will return around four. Stephen could join us, too."

"I'll ask him." Having his company would make the occasion even more enjoyable.

Stephen declined, though, saying he had to meet several deadlines for the newspaper's next issue. "I'll be waiting when you return," he told Nina. "Give me a call at the office, and we'll go out for dinner."

The trip was all set. Nina looked forward to the outing and hoped the day would yield something fruitful to her investigation.

****

On Saturday morning at eight forty-five, Nina joined Jessica and a couple dozen other Marley residents waiting in front of the home for the bus to arrive.

Lily and Wally stood at the front of the line.

"Today will be fun!" Lily announced to the group in general. "I love bus trips."

Behind the couple stood Nina's library helpers, Mabel and Selma.

Mabel, wearing a faux fur-trimmed maroon parka, caught Nina's eye and waved.

Selma, too, spotted Nina. "When will we have another meeting?"

"Soon." Nina smiled, glad to hear Selma's enthusiasm about the library project.

Nina glanced over her shoulder to see Harriet

Hambly step into the line. She wore black slacks and a red plaid wool jacket with a matching hat. A large thermal pack hung from her shoulder. Nina surmised the pack contained a food treat Harriet made for the occasion. "I still have your cookbook," she reminded the woman.

Harriet nodded and folded her arms. "Of course, I want the book, but have you and Jessica finished sorting Ellie's belongings? Did she leave anything to me?"

"No, we're not finished, and I'm sure she didn't forget you. She was a very *loyal* friend."

Harriet's mouth turned down. "She was until she let Dr. Ravensbarger dope her up with all those pills."

Nina heard the bitterness in Harriet's voice. "You sound really down on doctors."

"Wouldn't go near one." She made a dismissive wave.

Nina was tempted to say that if it weren't for the skills of certain doctors, Harriet would still be Harry. "How did Ellie's pill-taking change her loyalty?"

Harriet peered through narrowed eyes. "You were the one who mentioned loyalty."

"Yes, but—"

"Oh, look, there's Jessica's new friend. I told the girls he would come."

Hearing the sound of a car's engine, Nina turned to see a white compact car pull into a visitor's parking space. Jessica's "new friend" must be Joe. Sure enough, the driver's door opened and Joe McGarrity stepped out. Nina had to admit he was attractive. Tall and trim, he lacked the bowling ball-shaped stomach many older men carried. Nor had he been afflicted by aging baldness. His thick hair was a shiny silver still harboring flecks of its original black.

Joe locked his car then hurried to join them, stepping up to Jessica.

"You made it." Jessica beamed.

"Was there ever a doubt in your mind? I wouldn't miss this trip." He aimed a smile at Nina. "Hello, Nina."

"Good morning, Joe." Nina shivered against the sudden chill that accompanied his arrival. Now that Joe was in their lives, would Jessica still have time for her? Then she chided herself for her selfish worry and vowed instead to be happy for her grandmother's newfound companionship. She wished Stephen had come, though. Then she, too, would have a special friend.

A bus with Marley Manor written on the side in gold letters wheeled around the corner of the building and pulled to a stop at the curb. The doors folded open, and a tall, heavy-set man stepped out. Booted feet spread, hands on his hips, he surveyed the crowd from under a Seattle Mariners baseball cap. "Good morning, everyone! How's everyone this fine morning? For those who don't know me, I'm Bill Blazer, your driver and tour guide."

"Good morning, Bill!" chorused the crowd.

Smiling, he opened his arms. "Are we ready to have some fun?"

"We're ready!" Nina joined in the group's hearty response.

"Okay, hop aboard." He made a sweeping gesture toward the vehicle's open door. "Everyone with walkers and canes come first, as usual. You know the drill."

Nina had been on bus trips with Jessica where Bill was the driver. Middle-aged but still young enough to be like a son to many of the residents, he knew how to relate to the older generation and make sure they enjoyed their outings.

The crowd shifted as those with walking aids made their way to the front of the line. Leading them was Nurse Sheryl, who often came along on trips to assist the less able and to deal with any health emergency that might arise.

As Jessica, Joe, and Nina neared the door, Jessica turned to Nina. "You don't mind if Joe and I sit together, do you, dear?"

"Of course not." Nina stuffed down her disappointment and mustered a smile.

On board the bus, Nina took a seat behind Joe and Jessica. No one joined her, and she resigned herself to sitting alone.

Leaning on her cane, Lorna hobbled down the aisle. "Is this seat taken?" She pointed a crooked forefinger toward the empty place beside Nina.

"No, please join me." Glad to have the woman's company, Nina patted the seat.

Lorna settled herself, propping her cane at her side.

Nina turned her attention to the people still boarding the bus. She hadn't seen Dorleen and Roger. She would be greatly disappointed if the two didn't join the excursion. She counted on this opportunity to observe their behavior and, hopefully, to speak to Dorleen as well.

The two finally appeared.

"Just in time, folks." Bill's voice resonated

throughout the bus. "You almost missed the party."

"Hi, everybody." Roger waved to the seated assemblage and then pointed toward his companion. "In case you haven't met her already, this here's Dorleen Longman. She's Ellie's, ah, what you call, heir."

Nina watched Dorleen's gaze dart around like a trapped rabbit's. Her lips turned up for a second or two then drooped into a sulky pout. At least she was dressed for the occasion, in a parka the same olive green color as Roger's. He'd probably taken her shopping at his favorite army surplus store. Although seats were available farther back in the bus, Roger and Dorleen chose the first seat, which left their backs to everyone. A good way to avoid interacting with the others, Nina thought.

Bill brought the folded walkers on board, stacked them in an enclosure behind his seat, and at last, the bus was underway. He provided a running commentary of trivia and jokes while they made their way through stop-and-go freeway traffic. Once they left the city behind, traffic thinned, and the bus steadily rolled along. During a lull in Bill's monologue, Nina turned to Lorna. "How're you doing?"

"Pretty good." Lorna patted her stiff, white hair. "'Cept my stomach bothers me again. Didn't know if I should come on this trip or not."

"Did Nurse Sheryl set you up with Dr. Ravensbarger?"

Lorna nodded. "I see him next week."

Recalling the snippet of conversation she heard between Lorna and Nurse Sheryl, Nina slanted her a glance. "Do you like him?"

"He's awfully nice and really thorough.

Sometimes, too thorough, I think."

"Oh? In what way?" Most people Nina knew felt doctors didn't take enough time with them.

"He's always running tests. X-rays, blood tests, motor skill tests—he has one for everything. Not just one. When I went to him for a stomachache, I had my feet X-rayed." Lorna frowned. "What do my feet have to do with my stomachache?"

"Did you ask him?" Lorna's concern sounded reasonable to Nina and reminded her of Ellie's excessive tests.

"Yes, but he just laughed, patted me on the shoulder, and said, 'Doctor knows best, Lorna.'"

Ellie questioned her foot X-rays, too. Thinking she might have discovered another clue, Nina tucked away the information.

Lorna opened her tapestry purse, removed a cloth hankie, and dabbed the end of her nose. "Same thing happened to my friend, Arlene, who lives next door. She went to Dr. R about her hearing loss."

"And also had her feet X-rayed?"

Lorna nodded. "Her arms, too. But you need to trust the doctors. What choice do you have when something ails you? Everybody at Marley goes to Dr. R. He and Nurse Sheryl make such a good team." She leaned close to Nina. "I heard that she and the doctor, well, you know. But he's married, with five kids. They're all college age, too. Bet he has a lot of expenses educating them. Don't know why people have so many kids. I had two, that was enough."

Nina felt her pulse quicken. "About the doctor and Sheryl. Were they, ah, seen together? Out somewhere? Like on a date?"

Lorna drew back and clasped her crooked fingers on her lap. "I really shouldn't gossip."

"I won't say a word to anyone." Nina raised her eyebrows and put a forefinger to her lips.

Lorna sniffed into her hankie, looked around, and then leaned close again. "One of our residents, I won't say who, left her scarf in his office after a visit. When she went back to get it, no one was in the outer office. So she walked into the exam room, and, well, there they were."

"Doing what?" Not that Nina wanted to hear salacious details, but she did want to confirm the two were having an affair. If Sheryl were personally involved with the doctor, she might also be privy to his scamming patients.

Lorna's eyes widened. "Why, my dear, I didn't ask for the details. My ears were already burning."

The bus slowed, catching Nina's attention. She looked out the window in time to see a "Rest Stop Ahead" sign flash by.

"Time to take a break, folks." Bill slowed for the turnoff. "We have a real fine treat coming up."

Harriet's treat, no doubt. Nina looked forward to sampling the former cook's creation. At the same time, she also hoped to exchange a few words with Dorleen.

Chapter Eighteen

The treat turned out to be mini Danishes, which, as Nina had surmised, Harriet Hambly brought in her thermal pack. After everyone left the bus and assembled at several picnic tables, Harriet stacked the pastry on paper plates and passed them around. "The rolls are from my recipe, of course." She held up one of the plates. "Our cook made them especially for this occasion."

Bill produced thermoses and cups and poured coffee for everyone.

Nina selected a Danish with an orange marmalade center. The tangy orange tasted delicious. Whatever had happened in Harriet's life, one thing was certain—she turned out to be a good cook. Watching Harriet beam with pride as she passed around her goodies, Nina had trouble believing the woman could be a murderer. But, then, people often weren't what they seemed.

While enjoying her roll and coffee, Nina gazed around. The rest stop was a pleasant place. A warm winter sun peeked through the maple and pine trees, beaming on paths where travelers could stretch their legs. In addition to the restrooms, another building offered coffee and light snacks. A separate area provided a retreat for people with pets.

Bringing her attention back to their group, Nina saw that Dorleen and Roger sat apart from the others.

She wanted to talk to Dorleen while at the same time avoid Roger. As Jessica had said, though, he guarded the woman as though she were the crown jewels. Others who approached and spoke to them soon moved away.

Nina saw her chance when Dorleen left Roger's side and headed toward the restroom, the one place where he couldn't accompany her. Nina quickly caught up with the woman. "Enjoying the trip?"

Dorleen wrinkled her nose. "Um, I guess. Seeing the falls might be interesting."

Nine kept up with the woman's pace. "I've never been to Florida. Do you like living there?"

"I do. Today, the temperature is in the 70s, and the sun is shining. I really miss the sun."

Sighing, Dorleen gazed at the overcast sky.

Inside the ladies room, conversation lapsed while they each disappeared into a stall but resumed a few minutes later when they stood at the sinks.

"Have any of the charity events been scheduled?" Nina turned on the sink's hot water.

Dorleen squirted a glob of liquid soap into her palm. "The first one is next week. Thank goodness. I really am anxious to go home."

She cast Nina a forlorn look that begged understanding. "I'm sure Ellie's many friends enjoy having you here—what little they've seen of you." Nina soaped her hands and held them under the water.

Dorleen frowned.

"Well, Roger has been monopolizing your time."

Doreen rinsed her soapy hands. "I can't ignore him. He was Ellie's nephew."

A sudden inspiration seized Nina. "I have an idea. Why don't you and I have lunch one day? An outing would give you a break and us a chance to visit."

"Why, uh, I don't know if I'll have the time…" Dorleen lowered her gaze.

Why was she so reluctant to accept her invitation? "What day is your charity event?"

"Thursday."

"Okay, we'll do lunch on Friday."

Dorleen waved her hands under the automatic drying machine. The air whooshed on, spreading heat to the surrounding area.

Nina stepped to the adjacent machine, allowing two other women to take their places at the sinks. The dryers' noise prevented further conversation.

When they were outside, Nina cast Dorleen a sideways glance. "Too bad you never knew Ellie. You didn't, did you?"

Dorleen frowned and pushed out her lower lip. "No, of course not."

Dorleen's firm denial put Nina on alert. "Did you ever hear anything about her?"

"Not that I can remember." She picked up her pace.

Nina lengthened her stride to keep up. "You had no idea she was leaving you an inheritance?"

"No." Dorleen pointed ahead. "Oh, look, the group is packing up and boarding the bus. We'd better hurry. I'd hate to be stuck here."

"Don't worry. Bill will make sure everyone's on board before taking off."

Still, Dorleen ran ahead, creating a bigger gap between them.

She certainly acted guilty. Why? Nina took the hint and dropped back. Then she helped clean up, which made her one of the last to board. As she squeezed past

Lorna and took her seat, she glanced out the window at a car parked nearby. A black sedan, like dozens one saw on Seattle's streets, yet something struck her as familiar. She leaned closer to the window, and as the bus passed the car, she saw the crumpled right front fender. *Just like the fender on the car Kimmie's elusive friend drives.* Nina felt her pulse quicken. She twisted her head to glimpse the license plate, but another vehicle appeared and obscured her view.

"What's the matter, dear?" Lorna leaned around Nina to gaze out the window.

"Oh, nothing. I just thought I saw a familiar car."

"The one with the bashed-in fender?"

Nina widened her eyes and turned to the woman. "Why, yes."

"I've seen one like it, too, at Marley. I think the car belongs to one of the help. But the one we just saw is probably not the same."

Nina sank back into her seat. "Probably not." They'd been traveling for an hour, so a coincidence was unlikely. And yet, the image of the black car lingered in her mind. She'd keep an eye out for the vehicle, just in case. If the car was the same one she'd seen at Marley, was it here by chance? Or was the occupant of the car following them?

****

The bus traveled the freeway for another hour and then along a winding road leading into the hills. The trees thickened, in places blocking the sunlight. The lack of traffic and slower travel speed allowed a more peaceful ride, and Nina sat back and enjoyed the view from her window.

At last, Bill pulled into the parking lot at

Skookioomie Falls.

As Nina stepped from the bus, she thought of the black car and looked around to see if it followed. Although she saw no sign of the car, she vowed to keep an eye out.

Then, along with the others, she turned her attention to the spectacular waterfall cascading down the mountainside. Pristine water made a sharp contrast to the surrounding dark-colored rocks and moss-covered trees. The roar of the rushing water filled the cool, pine-scented air, and as she lifted her face, a soft mist settled on her cheeks.

Nearby stood a lodge made of traditional cedar planks decorated with Indian motifs. A cement patio with a cluster of chairs offered a place to rest and view the falls.

"The falls are six hundred feet high." Bill stood in front of the assembled group. "A legend has to do with the daughter of an Indian chief who fell in love with a young man her father didn't like."

Mabel stepped forward. "Tell us."

Grinning, Bill folded his arms and spread his feet. "Okay, the story goes like this. The old man wanted his daughter to marry a guy from a neighboring clan he needed to get in good with. But a' course she loves this other guy, one he don't approve of."

Bill settled his cap more firmly on his head. "So, one day she and the boy she loved came to the falls. They climbed way, way up to almost where it starts." He pointed to the top of the falls. "The other boy followed them. The two guys fought, and one fell over the cliff into the falls. Anybody want to guess which one?" He quirked an eyebrow.

Lily raised a hand. "I know—the one the Indian girl loved."

"Right." Bill grinned at Lily. "Anyways, when the girl saw what happened, she jumped off the cliff after her lover."

"Sort of like Romeo and Juliet," someone said.

"Wait a minute." Jessica looked around the group and put out a hand. "The guy who was left was the only witness, wasn't he? What if he wasn't telling the truth?"

Wally chuckled. "Jessica, Nina has you turning everything into a mystery." He winked at Nina.

Bill shrugged. "The story's all written up in pretty language, better'n I can tell it, in a book for sale at the lodge gift shop."

"Can we hike up to the falls?" Selma pointed toward the cascading water.

"Yep. There's a path with lookouts along the way. One is the Lovers' Leap, and you can see for yourself where the guy fell. The path's kinda steep, though, so you have to be real careful. Those who don't want to hike can stay here." He indicated the chairs on the cement patio.

"I'm ready for a hike." Roger pulled a camera from his inside jacket pocket. "I want to get me some pictures. I'm a pretty good photographer, aren't I, Nina?"

He cast Nina a sly look. Nina recognized the camera as the same one he used to photograph her at the clinic, and her stomach clenched. "I wouldn't know." She straightened and narrowed her eyes, hoping to call his bluff. She had no idea what she'd do if he did blab. Worry kept her nerves on edge.

"How 'bout you, Dorleen?" Roger turned to his

companion. "You want to see the falls up close, don'tcha?"

Seeing Roger's attention diverted, Nina relaxed a bit and focused on Dorleen.

The woman gazed at the waterfall and knitted her brow. "I don't know…I'm not real crazy about heights."

"Aw, c'mon." Roger grasped her elbow.

Dorleen grimaced and pulled away. "I can look at the falls from here."

However, when Bill assembled the hikers at the bottom of the path, Dorleen was among them. The others included Roger, Nina, Jessica and Joe, Harriet Hambly, Sheryl, Mabel and Selma, and about half a dozen others. After settling Lily with the group to stay behind on the patio, Wally joined them, too.

Nina followed the others up the path, with Bill leading the way. On one side rose a cliff, thick with moss-covered trees and leafy ferns. On the other, a wooden rail protected them from another cliff that dropped vertically to the ground level. The mist-laden air cooled Nina's cheeks, and the scenery was spectacular, with each turn offering a different view of the roaring falls.

Roger and several others who brought cameras stopped here and there to take pictures.

Halfway up, Nina and the group came to a cement bridge that spanned the middle of the falls. They lingered, oohing and ahhing over "nature's grandeur," as Wally described the setting.

"Lovers' Leap is up there." Bill huffed a breath and pointed toward the opposite side of the bridge. "The climb is steeper than the path we're on now, but I'll lead whoever wants to tackle it."

While several members returned to the lodge, others—including Nina—accepted Bill's offer. The climb was steep, as he had warned, but they managed to reach Lovers' Leap, a small ledge set in the rocky side of the cliff, almost at the top of the falls. A low stone wall protected the drop off. Peering over the wall, Nina glimpsed the group waiting at the bottom. She shivered and stepped back. Although the view was spectacular, Lovers' Leap needed to be approached with caution.

Roger scurried around, taking pictures.

"Hey!" Bill waved at Roger. "Don't go out of bounds. Could be dangerous. Only this here section is protected."

"I see a shot I wanna take." Roger plunged into the bushes.

Nina shook her head as she watched Roger disappear. Did he really have a photo in mind? Or was he just showing he was above following orders?

Bill pursed his lips and mumbled under his breath.

When the group had rested a few minutes, Bill led them down the path. After collecting the others, he took them to the lodge for lunch.

A totem pole topped with an eagle marked the entrance. Inside, a hostess escorted the group through a spacious and attractively furnished lobby then into the restaurant. Nina gazed around, noting the ceiling and three walls of glass, which enabled diners to view the falls.

After being seated with the others, she looked up to see Roger and Harriet outside on the deck.

A flush reddened Roger's face, and he poked a finger at Harriet.

Harriet propped her hands on her hips and jutted

out her chin.

Wishing she could read lips, Nina covertly watched. When Harriet and Roger finally entered the restaurant and joined the others, they sat at opposite ends of the table. They exchanged one last glare then ignored each other.

The cocktail server arrived. Most of the group, including Nina, ordered a glass of wine.

Roger requested whiskey and soda. When the drinks arrived, he raised his glass. "Here's to success."

Lorna leaned toward him. "Whose success are you referring to?"

"Mine." Roger looked around the table. "We're finally gonna get our downtown mall."

"No kidding." Wally's eyebrows peaked. "I thought the opposition killed the project."

"Money talks." Roger nodded. "Money talks."

Nina glanced at Dorleen. Had Roger convinced her to invest in his venture? If so, she gave no sign she was even remotely interested in the subject and instead gazed at the falls while sipping her wine.

"One day you'll all thank me for my fine leadership." Roger drank his whiskey and then hiccupped.

"I doubt that'll happen," Lily muttered into her napkin.

"The mall's gonna be real nice, with trendy shops and covered parking." Roger regaled them with details of his pet project.

Finally, the server appeared again to give highlights of the buffet menu.

Several of the group excused themselves and went to select their food.

Thinking she'd heard enough of Roger's monologue, Nina trailed them. At the buffet, a dazzling array of choices awaited, including poached salmon, barbecued ribs, potato salad, and several kinds of pies, for which the lodge was famous. Tantalizing aromas filled the air, making Nina's mouth water.

She finally made her choices and returned to the table. For the next few minutes, she enjoyed her food, especially the poached salmon's tangy sauce and the nutty flavor of the green beans almondine.

The server brought Roger another drink. Having finished his talk, either by choice or because he lost his audience, he sat back and gazed out the window.

When lunch was over, Bill pushed back his chair and stood. "Okay, folks, we leave in half an hour. I'll bring the bus to the patio, and we'll board there."

Most of the women visited the restroom and then the gift shop.

The men gathered outside to examine the totem pole and other carvings that decorated the lodge environs.

Roger and Dorleen left the table together. Roger tripped over his chair, and Dorleen grabbed his arm to steady him.

After perusing the gift shop and purchasing two copies of a children's book on Indian legends—one for the library and one for her own collection—Nina joined the others on the patio.

Sheryl ministered to a woman who picked up a splinter on the hike.

Harriet Hambly fussed with her thermal bag.

Joe and Jessica stood to one side, talking.

Dorleen sat by herself on a bench.

Where was Roger? He'd stayed close by her side the entire trip. Why had he suddenly abandoned her? Nina was about to ask Dorleen when the bus rumbled down the driveway.

Bill parked the vehicle, alighted, and approached. "Okay, folks, time to go. Is everyone here? Let me count noses." As he counted, he pointed a finger toward each person. "One missing. Who?" He looked around.

"Roger," chorused several of the group.

"Ah, fer Pete's sake." Bill folded his arms and tapped his foot. "Where'd he go? Anybody know? Dorleen?"

Dorleen turned up her hands. "He lost his camera and went to look for it."

"I knew that guy was trouble." Bill pursed his lips. "He better hurry up. If we don't leave soon, traffic is gonna be impossible."

Nina and the others waited for several minutes, but Roger failed to appear.

"Did you see which way he went?" Bill asked Dorleen.

"He headed back up the path to the falls." She pointed toward the walkway.

Bill rolled his eyes. "Oh, great."

Along with the others, Nina scrutinized those who emerged from the path, but Roger was not among them. She looked toward the parking lot. Maybe he wandered there, although for what reason, she couldn't imagine. But then, when the subject was Roger, who knew?

Scanning the vehicles, she spotted the car with the dented right front fender and started. The car certainly looked like the one Kimmie's mysterious friend drove. A shiver slithered down her spine. Had the car followed them? If so, why? She kept a steady eye on the car, hoping to catch sight of the driver.

"Look!" someone shouted. "Up there!"

Nina lifted her gaze just in time to see a figure tumble into the falls. Head first, arms flailing, the hapless person plummeted all the way to the bottom and disappeared into the backsplash of water rushing over the boulders. A glimpse of a green parka, black pants, and brown boots told Nina the victim's identity. She gasped and pressed a hand to her mouth.

Chapter Nineteen

"I still can't believe Roger's gone." Nina shook her head and leaned against Stephen's shoulder. They sat on the sofa at his house, relaxing after a meal of his homemade clam chowder and freshly baked sourdough bread. The nourishing food and the warmth of the fire blazing in the hearth helped to ease Nina's tension and distress since witnessing Roger's horrific death.

"If talking about the incident makes you feel better, I'm listening." Stephen took her hand and massaged her fingers.

"Thank you, Stephen. Yes, reviewing the incident might help." Nina took a deep breath. "Okay, after he fell, employees from the lodge attempted to rescue him, but they couldn't reach him. Finally, firemen arrived and crawled across the rocks to where he lay. They pulled him out and pronounced him dead." Nina shivered at the awful memory of seeing Roger's battered body. "Then police arrived. They took those who witnessed his fall into a lodge conference room for questioning."

"I imagine you all were in shock." Stephen leaned forward to pick up his cup from the coffee table.

"I think I still am. I doubt anyone liked Roger, but even Lily allowed he didn't deserve such a fate."

Stephen sipped his coffee. "Was anyone from your group missing at the time he fell?"

Nina shook her head. "No. We were all within sight of each other."

Everyone except the occupant of the mysterious car with the dented fender, she amended to herself. She couldn't mention the car to Stephen, though, without revealing her knowledge of Kimmie's friend.

"Then his fall—and death—was an accident." Stephen shifted to study her.

"Apparently. Several hikers who saw Roger on the path said he stumbled and staggered. One person reported he climbed out of bounds at a lookout. He asked Roger what he was doing, and Roger said he was searching for his camera."

"Was the camera ever found?"

"Not that I know of. The police told us only that he fell from Lover's Leap." She turned to face him. "Maybe you could find out their conclusions."

He brushed a lock of hair from her forehead. "I don't know. The falls are in a different jurisdiction than ours. But I'll see."

Relieved to have his help, she grasped his hand. "I'd appreciate your help. I didn't like Roger, but I didn't wish him dead, either."

Stephen drew her back into the shelter of his arm. "How did Dorleen react to his death?"

Nina frowned. "Hard to say. She shows little emotion about anything. She sat by herself on the return trip, in the same seat they shared earlier."

"Do you think he could have jumped on purpose?"

"Committed suicide?" Nina shook her head. "At lunch, he bragged about the acceptance of the proposed mini-mall. He was so pleased with himself. What do you know about the project, by the way?"

Stephen rubbed his chin. "I heard someone found a wealthy investor from out of state."

"Dorleen, maybe?"

"Could be. Maybe Roger convinced Dorleen to invest her inheritance in his pet project. Speaking of Dorleen, I have some information."

Nina straightened. "You do? Great."

"I'll be right back." Stephen stood and left the room. He returned a few moments later with a manila envelope. "Here's the info my friend Don collected."

Her pulse quickening, Nina took the envelope and pulled out a sheaf of papers. The report began with Dorleen's background, including her parents and place of birth, which agreed with facts Nina learned from Ellie's friends. She shuffled through the papers looking for information on Dorleen's adult life.

"Ah, here's something of interest." She pointed to one of the documents. "Dorleen bought a resort near the Keys, just like she said."

Stephen leaned to look over her shoulder. "Yes, but she originally had a partner. Read on."

Nina spent the next several minutes studying the report then looked up. "Dorleen and someone named Cora Wilson planned to buy the resort."

"But the partnership never happened. Take a look at this." Stephen pulled a newspaper article from the envelope.

Nina accepted the article and read aloud the headline. "*'Woman Dies in Freak Accident.'*" She cleared her throat.

"*'Floby, Tennessee. A woman drowned last Thursday when her car left the road and plunged 500 feet into Lake Floby. Due to recurring ice storms, several days elapsed before divers recovered her body. The victim, Cora Wilson, 53, of Brasham, Maryland, was on her way to Florida when the accident occurred.*

A passenger in Wilson's car, Dorleen Longman, 51, escaped and swam to shore. "I tried to rescue Cora," Longman told investigators, "but she was unconscious and a dead weight. I just couldn't save her."

The stretch of highway where the accident occurred is known for danger, especially during bad weather conditions. "Maybe now they'll put up a cement wall instead of just that flimsy guard rail," commented Floby resident Jacob Stillings."'

"When did this accident happen?" Nina searched for the date at the top of the page. "Ah, just about a year ago."

"According to Don's report, Dorleen and Cora lived together in Brasham." Stephen pulled another sheet of paper from the stack. "They both had ex-husbands but no kids. They decided to go to Florida—Dorleen's original home, you remember—and buy a resort."

"Which Dorleen went ahead and did, after Cora drowned."

"Right. Here's something interesting. Dorleen was Cora's beneficiary. They both had life insurance policies on each other."

"Lots of business partners insure the other person." Nina figured she knew where Stephen was headed, but how did that situation relate to the current situation?

"True. Just thought I'd mention that fact." He gave her a sideways glance.

"Okay, you've caught my attention. How much

money did Dorleen collect?"

"Not nearly as much as she inherited from Ellie, only a few hundred thousand, but enough to make a down payment on the resort."

Nina frowned. "Are you thinking Dorleen could've saved Cora if she really wanted to?"

"The thought occurred to me, yes."

Nina sat back and tapped the papers with a forefinger. "Or, maybe she made sure Cora didn't survive and then murdered Ellie, too." She glanced at Stephen and saw his solemn nod.

"Having both inheritances would secure her resort."

"Okay, but what about Roger?" Nina straightened. "She couldn't have murdered him. She was with our group when he fell from the cliff."

Stephen shrugged. "Roger's death might have been an accident. She didn't have any reason to kill him, did she?"

"Not that I know of." Still, she'd exchanged only a few minutes of conversation with Dorleen.

Stephen snapped his fingers. "Unless he found out she murdered Ellie. Maybe Roger was blackmailing Dorleen."

"I wouldn't put blackmail past him." Since Roger had threatened to blackmail Nina with the photo he took of her at the clinic, she spoke from experience, but of course she could not share that information with Stephen. "But I know she didn't push him off the cliff, nor did anyone in our group." Nina recalled the mysterious black car in the parking lot, which might belong to Kimmie's friend. Could two murderers be on the loose?

Later that night as she lay in bed beside Stephen, another worry plagued her. Now that Roger was dead, what would happen to the photo he took at the clinic? She had no idea who would inherit his belongings. She'd never heard of any relatives except Ellie and several ex-wives. If only she could think of some way to gain possession of the incriminating picture.

****

The following Monday evening, Nina met with Mabel, Selma, and Lily to work in the Marley library. After the unsettling events of last week, turning her attention to her project provided a welcome diversion. Nina gathered the group around the new computer then held up a book from a nearby stack. "Our next task is to enter data on all the books in our collection."

"Like title and author, I bet." Behind her thick glasses, Lily's eyes sparkled.

Nina nodded. "Right, plus publisher, date of publication, and the book's category, so the user can find it on the shelf." She raised her free hand, fingers spread. "Each entry includes five items. Who wants to be the first to do them?"

Mabel waved a hand. "Ah will."

"Great." Seeing Selma's and Lily's disappointed expressions, Nina made a decision. "We'll trade off every half hour. That way, everyone will have a turn. I have plenty of other tasks. Lily can stamp the books with the Marley Manor Library stamp, and Selma, you may sort the magazines. Arrange them according to title and then by date. We'll decide later which ones to keep. I'll look at the new books donated since we last met."

Everyone settled down to work. Nina allowed time to elapse and then broached the subject she was sure was on everyone's mind. "Have you all recovered from our bus trip?"

Mabel stopped typing and hugged her arms. "Wasn't that accident awful? Mah heart stopped when Ah saw that man fallin'."

"I couldn't sleep that night." Selma clutched a magazine. "I still have nightmares."

"He was a bad man, but he didn't deserve such an awful death." Lily stamped a book's flyleaf.

"Now, wait a minute, Lily." Mabel frowned. "Sometimes, he was nice to Ellie. Remember the beautiful poinsettia he gave her at Christmas, which she brought to the dinin' room?"

"Anything nice he did was to get her money." Lily stuck out her chin. "Same reason he played up to Dorleen."

Nina pulled a handful of books from a box of donations. "Does anyone know who will settle his affairs?" She hoped more conversation would add to her knowledge of Roger.

"One of his ex-wives." Selma wrinkled her nose.

Without knowing the ex-wife, should she make contact and tell her Roger had a photo he promised her? Did she want the woman to see the picture and perhaps question its purpose? Maybe the photo hadn't turned out. The night sky had a thick cloud cover and no stars or moonlight. Of course, he'd had his flash, but still…

"Nina, can you help, please?" Mabel waved. "Ah can't find the publisher's name for this book."

"Of course." Nina joined Mabel at the computer and pointed to a spot on the book's title page.

"Roger was good at making enemies." Lily reached for another book. "Did you see him and Harriet arguing at the falls?"

Selma straightened a stack of magazines. "I saw them. She sure was mad." Her topknot wobbled and then settled into place.

"I noticed, too." Nina returned to her sorting. "Do any of you know what they argued about?"

Lily waved her rubber stamp. "She accused Roger of having one of her books that Ellie borrowed."

"Do you know the title?" Nina visualized the high school annual. What would Harriet do if Roger discovered her secret?

"I didn't pay attention." Lily shrugged. "One of the cookbooks Harriet wrote, I suppose. The way she brags, you'd think she was the only one ever wrote a cookbook."

"I always liked Fannie Farmer's cookbooks the best." Selma picked up another magazine.

"Betty Crocker was mah favorite." Mabel bent over the computer keyboard and punched a key. "She guided me through the early years of mah marriage to Sydney. I remember believing she was a real person."

"She was." Lily nodded. "I saw her on TV."

Selma pursed her lips. "No, Lily, Betty Crocker was just a made-up name."

The debate continued, allowing Nina to put together a scenario involving Harriet and Roger. Harriet thought Roger had the high school annual. Even though he didn't possess the book, Roger made Harriet believe he did. He told Harriet he knew why she wanted the book, even though he didn't know. He might have been blackmailing her. If so, then Harriet would have good reason to want Roger dead.

But Harriet was present with the group when Roger

fell. Nina remembered seeing her standing next to Jessica and Joe. So much for that theory.

Maybe Roger's death was an accident, after all. All the alcohol he drank made him dizzy and disoriented on the return climb to Lover's Leap to look for his camera. He strayed from the path, as he had earlier, and fell to his death. Yes, that sequence of events was logical.

One loose end needed to be tied up before Nina could accept that scenario—the black car she saw at the rest stop and again at the falls. She must make sure that even if the driver was Kimmie's mysterious friend, he wasn't involved.

After the committee left and Nina closed the library, she stopped in the dining room, hoping to find Kimmie. Given the teen's hostility on previous occasions, she dreaded questioning her again, but gathering as much information as she could was important. When Nina reached the kitchen, she found Kimmie putting on her blue parka. Nearby, Chef Darren chopped celery at the stainless steel counter.

When the girl's gaze landed on Nina, Kimmie whirled and headed for the back door.

"Kimmie, wait!" Nina hurried after her.

"I can't talk to you now, Miss Foster," she called over her shoulder.

"I only need a minute."

Kimmie stopped and turned. "I can't talk to you. Davey's waiting. Oh!" She clapped a hand over her mouth.

"Davey? Your friend who drives the black car with a dented right front fender?" The teen's eyes flashed defiance.

"Okay, so now you know his name. So what?"

"I also know he was at Skookioomie Falls last Friday, at the same time as the group from Marley. The same day Roger Blanton was killed when he fell from Lover's Leap. You heard about Roger's death, didn't you?" She studied Kimmie's face to see her reaction.

"Yes. Everyone's talking about his accident."

"Maybe Roger didn't fall by accident."

Kimmie's eyes widened. "Are you accusing Davey of murdering Roger?"

Nina gritted her teeth. "I'm not accusing Davey of anything. I thought he might have seen something that would help the police's investigation."

"Well, he didn't." Kimmie propped a hand on her hip.

"The car *was* his." She was right about the black car's ownership. Nina gave herself a mental thumbs-up. "Was he following our bus?"

"I can't talk here." Kimmie rolled her eyes toward Chef Darren.

Looking around, Nina spied the chef's office. "May we use your office for a few minutes?" she called to Darren.

He looked up. "Sure, go ahead."

Before Kimmie could refuse, Nina grasped the girl's arm and guided her into the room. She closed the door and pointed to a straight chair. "Okay, sit and tell me about Davey."

Kimmie sank into the chair and heaved a sigh. "All right. He wasn't following the Marley bus. Not at first, anyway. He was driving along the highway when he saw the bus at the rest stop."

Nina nodded and sat in an adjacent chair. "I first saw him there."

"You saw him? You actually saw him?" Kimmie's voice rose.

"No, I saw the car. We left before I spotted the driver. But why did he stop at the falls?"

Kimmie looked away. "I talk a lot about the people I wait on. He was curious about them, and when the bus pulled off at the falls, he turned off, too."

Nina frowned. Why would a teenage boy care about a bunch of senior citizens? "Did he climb to the falls?"

"He said he didn't." Kimmie brushed a strand of hair from her forehead. "He bought a hot dog at the outdoor stand and then left."

Nina stiffened. "His car was still there when Roger had his accident. Did he witness Roger's death?"

Kimmie dipped her head. "Okay, he saw Roger fall, but when the police came, he took off."

Nina leaned forward. "Why? Is he in some kind of trouble?"

Kimmie bit her lip and looked away.

"You might as well tell me." Nina folded her arms.

"If I tell you, will you promise not to turn him in?" Kimmie twisted her fingers together in her lap.

Nina slumped her shoulders with the weight of another secret. Should she agree? Or not?

Kimmie heaved a sigh. "Okay, a woman identified Davey as the guy who threatened her with a knife and stole her purse. He was judged guilty and sent to Glenhaven. You know, the juvie detention center north of town?"

"I know about Glenhaven. But did he threaten the woman?" Nina hoped not. What she'd already heard was serious enough.

"Davey wouldn't hurt or steal from anyone." Kimmie shook her head.

"Did he serve his time?" If wrongfully sentenced, would he still pay for the crime?

"No, he ran away. He wants to find the guy who really robbed the woman and clear himself."

Maybe Davey followed the tour group looking for that person. "I know Davey hides in the boathouse." Nina held her breath. Would Kimmie protect her boyfriend? Or had Nina gained her trust?

Kimmie lowered her gaze. "He stays there at night, sometimes."

Relieved she made progress with her questioning, Nina blew out a breath. "Where does he stay other times?"

"Oh, around...I don't know, exactly." She waved a hand.

"What will he do if he doesn't find the guy? Will he just keep hiding and running for the rest of his life?"

Kimmie shrugged. "I don't know."

"Haven't the police been tracking his car?"

"He's not driving his car. He borrowed a friend's."

Unfortunately, that behavior made him look guilty. Nina stood and walked around the desk, glancing at the cookbooks piled in one corner, wondering idly if Harriet Hambly's books were among them. Probably. She turned back to Kimmie. "How did you get mixed up with Davey in the first place?"

"I met him at the skating rink. He goes to a different school, but my dad let me go out with him. But when Davey got in trouble, my dad said he'd better not catch me associating with him ever again." She looked at her wristwatch. "I gotta go. Davey doesn't like to wait."

Concerned about Kimmie's relationship with a young man who evaded the police, Nina put out a hand. "Someone else might discover you use the boathouse."

Kimmie stood and zipped her parka. "We're not staying there tonight. Davey's gonna take me home."

"But I thought your father said—"

"I tell Dad Jason gives me a ride." Kimmie shrugged. "Dad doesn't know the difference. He's always watching TV, and Mom will be in bed with one of her headaches."

"Well, be careful, and let me know if you need help, okay? You can always reach me at the library. Here, I'll give you my work and my home numbers." Nina pulled a business card from her purse. Picking up a pen from the desktop, she wrote her home number on the card and passed it to Kimmie.

"Thanks, Miss Foster." Kimmie smiled but then sobered again. "I have to go."

Nina followed her through the kitchen, reaching the outer door in time to see her jump into a black car idling at the curb. Light from a nearby streetlamp shone on a dented front fender.

The driver gunned the motor, and the car roared down the driveway.

Nina watched the vehicle disappear into the darkness, pleased she'd finally learned about Kimmie's mysterious friend. Still, a shiver snaked down her spine. What, if anything, did Davey have to do with Ellie's death?

Chapter Twenty

Nina drove along the quiet streets of Richmond to her condo, still thinking about Kimmie and Davey. With both the authorities and her parents to fear, no wonder Kimmie always appeared upset and stressed. In another scenario, her loyalty to Davey might be admirable. But what if he *had* assaulted the woman? Maybe Ellie found out and threatened to turn him in. Would he go so far as to murder her?

If Davey were prone to violence, Kimmie might be in danger, too. If something happened that Nina could have prevented, she would never forgive herself. Nina hugged her arms. Already, she carried guilt for abandoning Ellie the night of her death. She didn't need another, similar situation to add distress. But what if Davey were innocent of the alleged assault, as he and Kimmie maintained?

As she drove through the condo's security gate, Nina mulled over the problem. Once inside the building, she stopped at the wall of mailboxes, opened hers, and removed a handful of envelopes.

Kimmie and Davey occupied her thoughts through drinking a cup of tea and preparing for bed. While turning out the living room lights, she spotted the unopened mail on the coffee table. A small manila envelope especially caught her eye. Her name and address were printed in block letters, and no return address showed on either the front or the back. A shiver coursed down her spine.

Calm down and open the envelope.

She picked up her silver letter opener and, taking a deep breath to steady her hand, slit the envelope. Inside, she found only two items—a photograph and a folded piece of paper. The photo was the one Roger took the night he discovered her at Dr. Ravensbarger's clinic. Roger's aim had even captured the sign on the door that said "Marsh Street Clinic." Also, as he had told her, the date and time were printed in the picture's lower right-hand corner.

Nina's pulse raced. Her hope the photo had not turned out was now squelched. The accompanying paper was probably a blackmail note. A mixture of disgust and anger tempted her to rip the paper into shreds.

But Roger was dead, and, unless he told someone else about the photo, his blackmail threat was no longer a concern. Still, steeling herself against discovering the worst scenario, she unfolded the paper and read:

Nina,

Here's that naughty picture I took. You were a bad girl, but I don't need it now. I am better at finding out secrets than you are. Ha ha. This print is the only one, and I have deleted it from my camera. Trust me.

Roger

Blowing out a breath, Nina sank onto the sofa. Roger was not blackmailing her. The clandestine search of the clinic would remain undiscovered. Another thought surfaced. Roger hadn't needed to blackmail her because he found out something on his own. Had he discovered the secret Ellie insisted she knew, the secret that ultimately led to her death?

The photo and the note created another dilemma. If Roger's death was connected to the secret he discovered, then his fall wasn't an accident, and his death was murder. Nina should report her knowledge to Detective Russell. But if she did, he would learn about her after-hours stay at the clinic. She'd end up telling him everything. She wasn't ready for such a confession.

Nina put her head in her hands. Her so-called investigation was an impossible mess. She sat a moment and then straightened and looked again at the items Roger sent. What should she do? Toss them into the fireplace and reduce them to ashes? Maybe. But, if she ever discovered the truth about Ellie's death, she might need to confess her illegal entry into the clinic, despite the consequences. With a deep sigh, she returned the photo and note to the envelope and tucked it away in a desk drawer. Another clue had better turn up soon. Time was running out.

****

Two days later, Nina joined Jessica in Ellie's apartment, ready to help sort Ellie's belongings.

"I found something that might interest you." Jessica pointed to a rectangular metal box amid the clutter on Ellie's dining room table. "The box was locked, but I found the key in a kitchen drawer."

Nina sat and opened the container. Inside were letters addressed to Ellie. She pulled out half a dozen and held them up. "Did you read any of these letters?"

Jessica nodded. "I did, and guess what? They're from Wyatt. You know, the fiancé who ran off with her best friend. The guy who became Dorleen's father."

Surprise rippled through Nina. She took one of the

letters and laid the rest aside. "No kidding? You mean he wrote to her through the years, even though he married someone else?"

"Evidently." Jessica added a silver-plated spoon to a box of silverware.

Nina scanned the letter and then, her eyes wide, looked up at Jessica. "He says he's still in love with her and wishes he'd married her instead."

Jessica huffed. "Pretty gutsy admission, I'd say."

The next letter in the stack included a snapshot of a baby. On the back was written, "Dorleen Rose, six mos." Nina waved the photo. "He sent her a picture of Dorleen."

"Uh huh. The letters are full of pictures." Jessica scooped up several knives and forks and put them in the silverware box.

Jessica was right. Most of the photos showed Dorleen in various stages of growth and participating in different activities, from tricycle and horseback riding to sitting behind the wheel of a new car. Nina examined several more letters and then sat back. "Now I understand why Ellie left Dorleen the bulk of her fortune. She witnessed her growing up through Wyatt's letters and pictures and thought of her as the daughter they should have had."

"That guess was mine, too." Jessica nodded.

Nina picked up another envelope and pointed to the postmark. "This letter was sent twenty years ago."

"Just about the time Wyatt and his wife died."

"How did they die?" Her interest piqued, Nina gave Jessica her full attention.

Jessica sank into a chair and rested her arms on the table. "In a freak boating accident while on vacation.

I'm not sure how Ellie found out, though."

Nina pointed toward the box. "Do you think we should give these letters to Dorleen?"

Jessica shook her head. "Reading them might raise doubts about her father's loyalty to her mother."

"But doesn't Dorleen wonder why Ellie chose her as heir?"

"Good question. Since no one's become acquainted with her, due to Roger's hovering, we don't know what she thinks about Ellie's bequest."

"Maybe Roger learned about the letters. On the trip to Skookioomie Falls, I asked Dorleen to go to lunch."

Jessica's eyebrows peaked. "Did she agree?"

"Reluctantly, but I'll insist. I want to talk longer than just in passing." Nina returned all the letters to the box. "Since we're not giving these letters to Dorleen, would you mind if I take them home? I have several yet to read, and I'd like to study them all more thoroughly."

"You go right ahead, dear." Jessica waved a hand.

A knock sounded on the door.

"Who could that be?" Nina frowned. "Probably Harriet, nosing around, as usual."

"I don't think our caller is Harriet." Jumping up, Jessica patted her hair and straightened her skirt. "Do I look okay, or am I a mess?"

"You look fine, but why—" Before she could finish with "do you care?" Jessica opened the door and Nina saw the answer to her question.

Joe McGarrity, dressed in black slacks, white shirt, and a gray topcoat, stepped across the threshold. "Not too early, am I?"

Jessica gave him a wide smile. "Not at all. Nina and I are finished here, aren't we, dear?"

Nina shrugged. "I can be through any time. Are you two going somewhere?"

"Out to dinner. Didn't I tell you?" Jessica's eyes sparkled.

"No, you didn't mention you and Joe had plans." Fearing she had intruded, Nina stiffened. "I could've come some other day to help."

"Today was fine. I knew we'd have some time before Joe arrived."

But not time enough to chat about Nina's day at work and Jessica's life at Marley, like they always did. A familiar knot twisted her stomach.

Joe approached the table where Nina sat amid the silverware and other items Jessica sorted. "Have you found anything of special interest?"

"Today I came across letters Wyatt wrote to Ellie over the years, including pictures of Dorleen." Jessica pointed toward the metal box.

Joe's eyebrows drew together. "No kidding. His hold on Ellie might explain why I was unable to get close. Was he promising to divorce his wife?"

"Not in any of the letters I read." Nina tapped the box with a forefinger.

"Ellie was a sad case." Joe slowly shook his head. "She never got over Wyatt and moved on. When something bad happens, we need to grieve, get mad, be sad, whatever it takes to work through the pain, and then get on with our life." He shrugged. "That's my opinion, anyway."

Joe's observation hit a nerve. "But suppose Ellie didn't know exactly how to grieve, or get mad, or be sad? Then what?"

"She could've sought help." Joe folded his arms

and planted his feet apart. "I told her to talk to a counselor or a minister, but she refused. 'I don't have a problem,' she insisted. 'I'm happy.'" He shook his head. "Yeah, right."

I don't have a problem. I'm happy. Nina cringed inside. How many times had she said those same words to Stephen—and to Jessica—while at the same time knowing she lied and was miserable?

Would she end up like Ellie, stuck for a lifetime in an emotional rut unable to move forward to a more fulfilling life? No, of course not. Her experience was vastly different from Ellie's, yet she couldn't shake the feeling Joe's assessment applied to her, as well. Joe's voice broke into Nina's thoughts.

"How much more do you need to do tonight, Jessica? I made reservations for seven." He turned to Nina. "I'm taking your grandmother to dinner at my golf club's five star restaurant. I hope to get her on the links soon."

"I told Joe I don't know how to play golf, but he said he'll teach me." Jessica gave him a smile.

"How nice." Nina secured the lid on the metal box.

Jessica clapped her hands. "Anyway, Joe, I'm ready to go except for a big box in the bedroom I'd like you to move out here."

"Show me the way." Joe made a sweeping gesture toward the bedroom.

As she watched them leave the room, Nina pursed her lips. She would have moved the box if Jessica asked her. Obviously, she saved the task for Joe. Was her request supposed to make him feel important?

Nina waited, listening to the sounds of Jessica's giggle and Joe's deeper, masculine laugh coming from the bedroom. Finally, she shrugged into her coat and picked up her purse and the metal box of letters. On the way to the door, she called "Good-bye" over her shoulder. They evidently didn't hear her, though, for she heard no reply. Never mind. She had a box of letters to examine. Would they yield more clues?

Chapter Twenty-One

"Wyatt wrote to Ellie over the years about Dorleen," Nina told Stephen the following evening during a phone call. She sat on her sofa, the letters spread around her. Outside the nearby window, the condo grounds' floodlights illuminated the falling rain and the swaying branches on the maple and pine trees.

"You must have found out a lot about Dorleen's growing-up years."

Stephen's deep voice came over the line. "I did, but the box also contained several notes Dorleen wrote to Ellie. In one, she thanked Ellie for—get this—a plane ticket." Nina picked up the letter in question, laid it in her lap, and idly ran a finger over the Key West, Florida, postmark.

"No kidding? A ticket to where?"

"To SeaTac. From there she was to hire a car to downtown Seattle where Ellie would meet her at the Benson Hotel. Her arrival was the Wednesday that just happened to be a week before Ellie died."

"Whoa, that information is news. Why would Ellie want to meet Dorleen?"

Stephen's voice raised a notch. "I don't have a copy of the letter Ellie sent, but I'm guessing she wanted to meet because she'd decided Dorleen would be her heir. She'd heard about her over the years from Wyatt and felt a close kinship."

"Would she have told Dorleen the purpose of her visit?"

"I don't know. Maybe she said only that she was an old friend of both her parents and therefore wanted to meet her." Nina shook her head. The puzzle of Ellie's and Dorleen's relationship contained many missing pieces.

"Do you have any proof Dorleen actually came?"

Nina shifted in her seat. "No, but I saw on Ellie's daily planner a notation for the Benson Hotel on the Wednesday in question. Getting Dorleen to admit she was here will be proof enough, won't it?"

"Huh! Good luck with that plan. Dorleen hasn't been forthcoming about anything, so far. But if anyone can get her to talk, I'm betting you can."

His compliment warmed her. "Thanks, Stephen. I appreciate your support."

Their talk turned to other matters, such as their upcoming visit to the Evergreen Athletic Club, topics for her book review column for the newspaper, and where to have dinner Friday night. Nina heard soft music playing in the background. She pictured him sitting in front of a cozy fire, sipping his coffee while they talked.

A longing suddenly filled her, and she wished she were with him, instead of alone in her condo. She could be; he'd indicated often enough he wanted a permanent relationship. But, she just couldn't commit—for so many reasons. Would she ever take the next step?

She gave her shoulders a shake. Never mind that dilemma. Now, she must solve the mystery of Ellie's death. After that, she'd make a decision about her future with Stephen.

Maybe.

****

On Friday, Nina drove to Marley Manor to pick up Dorleen for their lunch date.

The woman waited under the yellow-canopied entry, protected from the chill breeze.

Nina pulled up to the curb and reached across the seat to open the passenger door.

Dorleen hurried to the car, climbed in, and shut the door.

"You look like a real Northwesterner." Nina nodded toward Dorleen's black slacks and olive green parka, the same outfit she wore on the trip to Skookioomie Falls.

"Either bundle up or freeze." Dorleen hugged her arms.

Nina drove along the road leading to the home's exit. "Have you always lived in Florida?" Of course, she knew the answer, but she wanted to hear Dorleen's response. Would she be honest?

Dorleen settled her brown leather purse on her lap. "No, I lived for a while in Maryland."

"Oh? Did you have family there?" Nina reached the exit and turned onto the main road.

"No family, just my friend, Cora. But the weather was too cold, just like here, so we chose to return to Florida and buy a resort."

So far, Dorleen's account matched Stephen's friend's report. "Ah, so your partner takes care of the business while you're here."

"Unfortunately, no." Dorleen's voice dropped. "She never reached Florida."

"What happened?" Nina injected surprise into her

voice.

"We had a terrible accident in Tennessee. Our car went off the road and into a lake. She—" Dorleen's voice broke. "Not something I like to talk about."

"I understand." Was Dorleen's reluctance due to grief or to guilt? Nina gave her a sideways glance, all she could risk while navigating through traffic, but Dorleen turned to the window. "Have you decided when to return home?"

"I hope to leave next week. Two more check presentations, and then I'm out of here."

"Presenting Ellie's bequests in person is a nice gesture." Nina slowed to negotiate a turn.

"I had no choice. My appearances were a condition of her will."

Dorleen's voice dripped sarcasm. Was the obligation such a burden? "I'm sure she would appreciate your following her wishes." Nina drove up a ramp and onto the freeway, accelerating to merge with traffic.

Dorleen straightened and gazed out the window again. "Where are we having lunch?"

"At the Benson Hotel, in downtown Seattle. I know you've been to our Richmond waterfront places with Roger, and I thought you'd enjoy a visit to the city."

"The Benson, you said?"

Allowing her a glance, Nina glimpsed alarm in the woman's eyes. "Yes, don't tell me you've eaten there and didn't like the food."

Dorleen fingered the clasp on her purse. "Uh, no, I've never been to the Benson."

While she concentrated on driving, Nina let the matter drop. At the hotel, she left the car with the parking lot attendant and then she and Dorleen entered the ten-story building. On the way to the restaurant, Nina kept an eye on Dorleen, but despite her alarm moments earlier, she showed no evidence of familiarity with the surroundings.

A few minutes later, seated across from Dorleen at a window table, Nina took a moment to enjoy the view. As usual, Puget Sound was a busy waterway, with container-loaded freighters, ferries, and private vessels of all sizes. Framing the scene were the majestic Olympic Mountains with their snow-capped peaks silhouetted against the sky. "Have you heard anything more about Roger's death?" Nina asked, after she studied the menu and, along with Dorleen, ordered the seafood salad special.

Dorleen frowned. "No, I haven't. Why should I?"

Nina sipped her water. "I thought you might have heard Marley gossip. Do you think his death was an accident?"

Dorleen opened her napkin and spread it on her lap. "The police called his fall accidental, so why should I think otherwise? But what do you know about his death? You seem to know so much about everyone." Her lips tightened.

Nina ignored the obvious dig. "I heard one of his ex-wives is handling his affairs." She then steered the conversation in directions she hoped would lead Dorleen to admit she'd been to the Hotel Benson. But, each time, the woman either sidestepped a question or gave only a noncommittal answer.

Their salads arrived. Nina sampled hers, savoring the tangy dressing, a perfect complement to the mixture of shrimp, crab, and salmon. Then, knowing she had only a limited time with Dorleen, she leaned forward. "You said you've never been to the Benson before, but—"

"Why do you keep harping on that subject?" Dorleen's eyes narrowed.

Nina took a deep breath. "Okay, I'll tell you why. I happen to know you have been here before."

Dorleen's jaw dropped. "What are you talking about?"

Nina sat back and spread her hands. "As you know, I'm helping my grandmother sort Ellie's belongings. I found a letter you wrote to Ellie, thanking her for an airplane ticket and confirming you'd meet her here at the Benson on January fifteenth."

Dorleen bit her lip "Okay, like the letter said, I was here."

The admission brought Nina satisfaction. "Why did you lie when I first inquired?"

"Because Ellie wanted to keep my visit a secret, and, even though she's dead, I honored her request."

"Why didn't she want anyone to know you came to the Northwest?"

Dorleen narrowed her eyes and leaned over the table. "If I tell you, will you drop the subject?"

At the sudden invasion of her personal space, Nina drew back. Still, she pasted on a smile. "Maybe."

Glaring, Dorleen slowly shook her head. "You are something else. But, okay, Ellie wrote to me about my dad keeping in touch with her over the years, and that when my parents died in a plane crash, of course the letters stopped."

"How did she know where to find you?"

"She hired a private investigator. Anyway, Ellie

and I corresponded. She asked me to visit her, and when I agreed, she sent me a ticket."

So far, Dorleen's explanation matched what Nina suspected. "Why didn't she invite you to Marley Manor? You could've been a guest there, like you are now. Why didn't she tell anyone about your visit?"

Dorleen sipped her water. "She wanted me to be a surprise to everyone. She planned to give a party, later, and introduce me to her friends. I figured meeting me in private ahead of time was to make sure she liked me before showing me off at Marley."

"That explanation sounds reasonable." Nina took a bite of the cornbread that accompanied her salad. Fresh and warm from the kitchen oven and slathered with butter, the morsel melted in her mouth. "Okay, you flew to SeaTac and met Ellie here at the Benson. When did you leave town?"

Dorleen spread butter on a roll. "A couple days later. Ellie said she'd be in touch about when I would return for the party, but then she died."

"Hmmm..." Nina tapped her chin with a forefinger.

"I know what you're thinking." Dorleen put down her knife, sat back, and folded her arms. "You think I flew here again, spied on Ellie at Marley Manor, attacked her, and drowned her in the lake." She pursed her lips and shook her head. "That idea is ridiculous."

Actually, Nina imagined that very scenario. "I do want to find out what happened that night, but I also wanted to get to know you."

Dorleen shrugged. "I can't imagine why. I'm leaving soon, and I don't plan to return."

Nina smiled. "I guessed as much. Anyway, I'm

glad we had this time together today."

With a snort, Darleen turned to gaze out the window.

On the ride home, Nina kept the conversation general, offering comments about the city and its environs.

Dorleen gave brief responses or remained silent.

Finally, Nina gave up. Still, she considered the outing a success, raising two important questions. Was Dorleen telling the truth about her innocence? Or was she a murderer determined to cover up her crime?

Chapter Twenty-Two

At home, Nina settled at the kitchen table with a cup of tea and her notes on the investigation. In the past few days, she learned a lot of information. Perhaps she made progress, after all. She added her new knowledge about Kimmie's mysterious friend Davey. After Roger's name, she wrote, *Accident or Murder?* Then she included comments about Harriet Hambly and Roger's argument and that, like Ellie, Roger took prescription drugs.

Surprisingly, she also learned something today from Dorleen. The woman admitted Ellie contacted her after her parents died in a plane crash and invited her to Seattle, as the letter in Ellie's box indicated. Plus, she offered a reason why her trip was kept secret. Nina frowned. Something about Dorleen's explanation didn't ring true, but she couldn't put her finger on the discrepancy.

Finally, she focused on the drug angle. Ellie's drugs came from Dr. Ravensbarger. Where had Roger obtained his medication? Had he been the doctor's patient, too? A shiver of excitement coursed down Nina's spine. If he had, that fact might be an important clue. Perhaps Jessica knew. Nina reached for the phone. Her grandmother answered after the first ring.

"Hi, honey. I thought you might stop by when you dropped off Dorleen. Joe and I looked forward to seeing you."

Nina took a moment to appreciate Jessica and Joe's interest in her visit. "I had a lot to do at home, but I wanted to ask a quick question. Do you know if Roger was Dr. Ravensbarger's patient?"

"Hmmm, I believe he was. I remember Ellie telling me she recommended Dr. R when Roger complained of stomach problems."

Nina's pulse quickened. "Are you're sure Roger saw the doctor?"

"No, but once when Roger joined us at dinner, he and Ellie compared notes on a medication they both took."

All right. Nina added the information to her notes. "Do you remember any details?"

"I'm sorry I don't, dear. But I'll give the matter some thought. Why are you asking?"

"A theory I'm working on." Nina shuffled her papers.

"Joe and I were just talking about you and your investigation."

"Oh, really?" Nina tensed.

"Yes, and we're worried about you. Do you really want to continue something that might be dangerous?"

"I appreciate your concern—both of you—but I'm in too far now to quit. I'll be careful."

"Well...all right, dear. But call us anytime you need help."

A smile touched Nina's lips. She really did appreciate Jessica's consideration, and, okay, Joe's, too. "I will, Gran. I promise." After ending the call, Nina made notes on their conversation. Roger and Ellie both took the same prescription for their stomach trouble.

Drugs, again.

Drugs led straight to Dr. Ravensbarger. Was he responsible for Ellie's death? If so, how could she prove he was the culprit?

****

Nina walked through a field of tall grass. A cold, heavy rain fell, and her feet sank into the wet ground. Where am I going? She had no answer, yet she continued on.

She came to a cliff. A man stood at the edge, his back to her, facing the dark, cloudy sky. Dread filled her. She wanted to turn and run away, but her feet stubbornly propelled her forward.

Just before she reached the man, she saw him turn. For a moment, she thought he was Stephen. Then she realized he was the man with no face. The man who haunted her. This time, instead of only a blank face, he had a nylon stocking over his head, allowing shadows to show through. If she were close enough, she might make out his features and discover his identity.

She crept toward him, step by measured step. Just when she thought she was close enough to see through the mask, he turned and jumped off the cliff. Nina ran the rest of the distance to the cliff. She paused a moment at the edge and then hurtled herself into space. She fell down, down, down, turning, spinning. Air rushed by, thundering in her ears.

With a scream tearing from her throat, Nina awoke. Her heart thudded, and her hands balled into fists. Another nightmare of the faceless man, yet for the first time, she sensed he did have a face after all. This dream was also the first time she jumped off the cliff after him. The terror of falling into space lingered, sending alternate waves of heat and cold washing over her. She sat up and hugged her arms. Her stomach churned. She swallowed hard against the urge to vomit.

Finally, she calmed enough to lie down and pull up the covers. Still, she remained awake, haunted by the dream and what it might mean.

****

On her break at the library the next day, Nina phoned Stephen and filled him in on her lunch with Dorleen.

"So, Dorleen admits to meeting Ellie. I'm impressed you convinced her to tell the truth."

"I finally had to confront her with the evidence." Nina sipped her tea. "But I'd like to know if she returned to town close to the time of Ellie's death. Would your friend Don in Florida grant us another favor and obtain copies of airline passenger lists?"

Stephen gave a low whistle. "I don't know if he can. Except to law enforcement, airline passenger records are confidential."

Nina heaved a sigh. "I was afraid of that restriction, but I did some research and found three ways she could have flown here from Florida that day, which would narrow his search."

"Okay, I'll ask Don if he can help."

Feeling a surge of excitement, Nina hung up. She was closer to solving the mystery of Ellie's death. With just a few more pieces to the puzzle in her possession, she would know exactly what happened that fateful night.

****

Friday afternoon after work, Nina drove to Stephen's house. Instead of eating out, they decided on a home-cooked meal. Baked salmon, rice pilaf, and coleslaw were on the menu. Stephen stood at the kitchen stove monitoring the salmon and rice while Nina added dressing to the slaw. Her thoughts drifted over the events of the day.

"I heard from Don." Stephen broke the silence.

She stopped mixing and looked up. "You did? So soon?"

"Yeah, he doesn't waste any time."

"Well?" Nina held her breath. So much depended on his answer.

"You got lucky. A Miami airport contact owed Don a favor." He held up a hand. "But if word gets out he hacked into the airlines' records, he could lose his job."

"I won't tell a soul." Nina solemnly shook her head.

"Don's email is in the folder." Stephen pointed toward the kitchen table. "Take a break and look at the passenger lists."

Nina flashed him a grateful smile. "Thanks. I'm almost finished, anyway." She gave the slaw a couple more stirs then sat at the table. Opening the file folder, she found a stack of computer printouts. "This is a lot of information."

"He sent the passenger lists for the three airlines you indicated, from the day Dorleen was supposed to initially arrive through two days after Ellie's death."

"Perfect." She scanned the names from the first airline's flight. Not finding Dorleen's name, she studied the second list. "Here she is, Dorleen Longman. Her name's on a returning flight two days later, just as she claimed."

Nina checked all the other lists without again finding Dorleen's name. She sat back and let her shoulders sag. "Dorleen appears to be telling the truth. She came here and left when she claimed, and she didn't return until after Ellie's death."

Stephen opened the cupboard, took out plates, and set them on the counter. "She could've flown to Portland, or some other place nearby, and then taken a bus the rest of the way. Or she might have rented a car."

"Yes, but discovering that plan would take a lot of checking." Nina stacked the papers together and replaced them in the folder.

"Although the research would take some time, I'm sure Don would help."

She made a dismissive gesture. "Don't bother right now. Let me think about the situation first." What should she do next? Had she obtained the desired information about Dorleen's air travel only to be faced with another dead end regarding Ellie's death?

****

When Nina went to Marley the following Monday, she encountered Harriet Hambly in the hallway carrying a load of empty cartons. "Can I help you, Harriet?"

Harriet flashed a grin over the top of the boxes. "Sure, Nina. Thanks."

Nina took several from the stack and followed Harriet to her apartment.

"Put your load over there." Harriet nodded toward a corner of the living room.

Nina placed the boxes then approached another pile with the lids taped shut. "What's going on?"

"I'm moving." Harriet added her load to Nina's.

Nina raised her eyebrows. "To another apartment here at Marley?"

Harriet stuck both hands on her hips and shook her head. "No, to California."

Surprise rippled through Nina. "Why? Don't you like living here anymore?"

"I decided now is the time for a change."

Time for a change? Or time to leave the scene of the crime you committed?

Harriet stepped to a wall covered with framed photographs. She removed one and handed it to Nina. "Take a look at this picture."

The photo showed Harriet in a kitchen with a tall man wearing a chef's hat. His arm hung around her shoulders.

"In case you don't recognize him, that's Monte Malone, the chef at Carleton's."

"Carleton's...okay..." Nina looked at Harriet and shrugged.

Harriet pursed her lips. "The five-star restaurant in New York. Haven't you been *anywhere*? I sent him one of my cookbooks. He used the recipes to feed many famous people—presidents, royalty, and movie stars. Oh, and speaking of movie stars, here I am with Salty Tremaine. He made all those comedies, you know." She grabbed another photo from the wall and thrust it at Nina. "He invited me to cook for one of his parties. Salty was my introduction to the glamorous world of Hollywood." Harriet showed Nina more pictures, all of her and a celebrity who knew her through her cookbooks.

"I don't like to brag." Harriet patted her hair. "But I have had a fascinating life."

"Yes, you have." Nina gestured toward the photos that now littered the table instead of the wall. "Before you leave, I'll give you the cookbook Ellie borrowed."

Harriet waved a hand. "I don't need the book. You keep it. Try some of the recipes."

What had changed Harriet's mind about repossessing the book? Still, Nina did not want to arouse her suspicion by questioning her sudden change of mind. "Thanks, Harriet. I'm not much of a cook, though, so I'll add the book to our Marley's library."

Two days later, during a phone conversation, Jessica mentioned that Dorleen had presented the last of Ellie's charity bequests and in a few days would return to Florida. Two suspects were about to leave the area. Nina needed to discover the killer's identity—and quickly. But how?

Chapter Twenty-Three

Nina spent the next several days searching for a way to flush out Ellie's murderer. She pored over all the notes she made during the past few weeks. She read everything she recorded about Kimmie and her friend, Davey, and everything she learned from Ellie's medical records and from the letters in her metal box. Next were the notes about Nurse Sheryl, Roger, and Dorleen, followed by the reports Don obtained—the background on Dorleen and the lists of airline passengers.

Despite no new information, Nina developed a plan for revealing the culprit, used in the mystery stories she liked to read. The idea always worked for the storybook sleuth, so why wouldn't it work for her? Okay, so the scheme was risky. She was desperate.

"I've had a breakthrough in solving the mystery of Ellie's death," she told her library committee that evening.

Lily looked up from stamping a book, her eyes wide behind her glasses. "You have?"

"We thought y'all gave up." Mabel put down the armload of books she shelved and came to stand near Nina.

Selma and Jessica, who labeled the shelves with category names, followed Mabel.

"Tell us." Selma patted her off-center topknot into place.

"Yes." Jessica's brow wrinkled. "We want to know."

"Take a seat, everyone." Nina gestured to the worktable. When they were settled, she folded her hands and leaned forward. "Remember when I went to the lake after the police were here to see if I could find something on my own?"

Everyone nodded and waited.

Nina lowered her voice. "Well, I did find something."

"You did?" Selma's eyes widened.

"You never said." Lily's lips formed a pout.

"I kept quiet because I wasn't sure what I found was important. Now, I know it is significant. I plan to search the area again, because I'm sure I didn't find all of…of *it*."

Mabel frowned. "What are y'all talkin' about?"

"I don't want to say, exactly." Nina spread her hands. "Not until I'm sure. Anyway, I'm revisiting the scene at the lake this Friday night."

Lily's eyes narrowed. "Why at night?"

"Because I want to recreate what I think happened." Nina's gaze took in the entire group. "The weather report predicts rain, just like the night Ellie died. Besides, if I go during the day, I might attract attention. I don't want anyone to know what I'm doing."

"Then why are you telling us?" Selma sat back and folded her arms.

Nina had an answer ready for that question. "Because I've kept you informed all along, I thought you'd like to know my latest plan." True—more or less.

Mabel shook her head. "Sounds dangerous."

"Don't go to the lake alone." Lily's brows lowered. "Like Mabel says, your plan's trouble."

"I agree." Selma's vigorous nod set her topknot dancing.

"I'm with them." Jessica swept an arm in an arc that included the others.

"I appreciate your concern, but I'll be fine." Nina flashed what she hoped was a reassuring smile and then pressed a forefinger to her lips. "But, remember, you must keep my plan a secret." After the committee meeting ended, Nina sought out Lorna, the resident she encountered in Nurse Sheryl's office and also her seat partner on the trip to Skookioomie Falls. Hopefully, with her penchant for gossip, Lorna would pass on Nina's plans to everyone she encountered. She found her in the basement recreation room working a jigsaw puzzle. Nina slipped into a chair beside her. "Hello, Lorna. How are you this evening?"

The woman's thin lips folded into a smile. "I'm doing pretty well, except for my feet. They hurt all the time."

"I'm sorry you're having problems."

"Sore feet are why I spend a lot of time sitting here." She pointed toward the half-worked puzzle. The box showed a picture of a covered bridge surrounded by large, leafy trees. "Do you like working puzzles?"

"I haven't puzzled much since I was a kid." After scanning the pieces, Nina selected one and placed it on the bridge's roof. The piece didn't fit.

"No, no, that part goes here, with the tree." Lorna took the piece and, despite her gnarly fingers, quickly found its home. She picked up two more and added them to the same area.

The tree took shape. "Wow, you're good." Nina sat back and smiled.

"You do enough of these puzzles, you develop an eye."

They chatted while working, and then Nina casually mentioned her plans for Friday evening.

Lorna's eyes glowed. "I hope you find some new clues."

"Me, too. Oh, and please keep my plans to yourself."

Lorna put a finger to her lips. "Don't worry, dear. I won't tell a soul."

Not wanting Lorna to know she hoped for just the opposite, Nina hid a smile.

****

The following day, Nina ate lunch with Stephen at Claire's Deli. The first part of the meal was spent discussing the upcoming issue of *The Richmond Review*.

Then, during a lull, Stephen put down his fork and leaned forward. "Moving on to this weekend, I'll pick you up on Friday at five."

Nina finished a bite of her spicy tuna sandwich and wrinkled her brow. "Pick me up?"

"To attend the Home Show at the Event Center. We set the date two weeks ago."

He gave her a steady look.

"Oh, I remember." She hadn't thought of the Home Show when she made plans for trapping Ellie's murderer. "I'm really sorry, but I can't go, after all."

Stephen frowned. "Why not?"

"Well, the truth is, I did forget about the show, and I arranged to be at Marley."

Stephen folded his arms. "Doing what, if I may ask?"

He could ask, but she wouldn't answer—not truthfully. He'd disapprove of her plan. "My library committee, you know." She waved a hand.

"Meet with them on Saturday night." Stephen picked up his coffee cup and sipped.

Nina shifted in her seat. "I can't."

"Why not?" He looked over the rim of the cup.

Should she cancel her plans for Friday night and accompany Stephen to the show? No. She'd worked hard to set the trap. If she backed out now, she'd be letting down Ellie. "Finding a time when we can all get together is difficult."

Stephen put down his cup. "I especially wanted you to help pick out furniture for the deck. Although I can knock down walls and remodel, I need assistance with decorating." He tilted his head." But you aren't really interested, are you?"

"Stephen, I keep reminding you the house is yours, not mine." She strove to keep her tone patient.

"I expect the house to be *ours* someday." His mouth turned down. "But maybe I'm kidding myself."

The coldness in his voice hurt. "Please don't jump to conclusions about our future just because I can't attend one home show."

He folded his arms. "Our problem is more than missing the show."

Nina's stomach tensed. "You're referring to my not wanting to see Dr. Young, aren't you?"

"Your reluctance is part of the problem. But I don't like what's happening between us lately."

"Well, neither do I." A few moments of tense

silence slid by. Her meal forgotten, Nina stared out the window at the people passing by on the sidewalk.

"We shouldn't discuss our problems here."

Stephen's comment drew her attention, and she turned to face him. "I don't want to talk about our disagreements, period. We just go 'round and 'round and never resolve anything."

"I don't want to fight, either." He set his jaw. "Look, neither of us is happy with the situation. Maybe we should take time off and give our relationship a rest."

Nina's heart skipped a beat. "Not see each other?"

"Yeah, for a week or so…or maybe longer…"

A knot formed at the nape of her neck. Absently, she rubbed the sore spot. He wanted out of the relationship. A week would turn into a month, a month into a year, and a year into forever. "A time out is a good idea."

His eyes widened. "You think?"

"Yes, for both of us. A week—or so—then we'll reassess." Holding her breath, she waited for his reply.

Several seconds passed, and then he said firmly, "Deal."

Her stomach in a knot, Nina stared at her plate. "I don't want to eat any more. I'll head back to work."

"I'll stay and have another cup of coffee."

Her hands shaking, Nina folded her napkin and put it on the table. She took her wallet from her purse.

Stephen put out a hand. "I'll get the check."

Shaking her head, she counted out the money for her half of the bill, plus a tip. "Goodbye, Stephen." Nina stood and with leaden steps headed for the restaurant's front door.

What would happen now? Was a time out really a good idea? Or was their relationship over?

Chapter Twenty-Four

Tears welled in Nina's eyes, blurring the landscape on her walk to Seaview Library. She pulled a handkerchief from her purse and blotted her eyes and cheeks. She couldn't break down now, not when she must return to work and face her staff as well as the public.

Somehow, she performed her duties the remainder of the day. At home, she listlessly picked at leftovers. None had any taste, and she had no desire for food, anyway. She mulled over what happened at lunch and came to the conclusion she could never be the person Stephen wanted, and he would never understand and accept her the way she was.

Separating now was better than later. Instead of relief, though, all she felt was a sad emptiness. Talking to Jessica might help, but Nina didn't want to bother her now that she was involved in her new romance with Joe McGarrity. Nina had other women friends, but no one she wanted to share this particular problem.

Dr. Young came to mind. Maybe she should have made a second appointment with the therapist. She was kind and understanding the night Nina visited her office.

The following day at work, she looked for text messages from Stephen. When none arrived, her spirits sagged. At home, she received no texts or calls. She could phone him. No, let him make the first move.

On Thursday, the storm the TV weatherman promised blew into town. The rain suited Nina's mood and was exactly what she wanted for her experiment at Marley. She put aside worries about her and Stephen's relationship and concentrated on making plans for Friday night.

On Friday morning while eating breakfast, Nina pulled out her notes and with dogged determination read them once again. The answer to Ellie's death was here somewhere—she just needed to find it. Moments later, the clue she hoped for stared her in the face, and her heart beat faster. The information was there all the time, but she missed seeing it. Now, she put together a scenario of how the murder occurred—and why. Yes, the scheme made perfect sense.

Her first impulse was to call Stephen and share her news. Then she reminded herself they were taking a so-called relationship break. She sat back and mulled over her choices. She could take the information to Detective Russell and let him handle the situation. But what if she were wrong? She still needed proof and would follow her plan to flush out the culprit.

By midmorning at the library, last-minute doubts again set in. By afternoon, she barely concentrated on her work. What if her plan failed? The murderer might not have heard about her upcoming visit to the lake. Or, the murderer might not care, dismissing Nina's investigation as harmless. A cloud of depression enveloped her. She was crazy. She was stupid. She was nothing more than a busybody.

Yet, after dinner, she methodically prepared to go to Marley Manor. She put on a lightweight rain jacket and pants and traded her low-heeled pumps for rainproof boots. After checking to make sure her cell phone was charged, she tucked it and a small flashlight into the jacket pockets.

The rain beat steadily on the windshield during the drive to Marley. Once there, Nina bypassed the entrance and instead searched for the dirt road leading to the woods on the lake's opposite shore. She found the road, turned onto it, drove a little farther, and then pulled off and parked. When she switched off the headlights, darkness quickly closed in. Nina sat for a moment, watching the rain trickle down the windshield. Did she really want to go through with this crazy scheme?

Straightening her shoulders, she stepped from the car and locked the door. Pulling up the collar of her jacket, she started out, making her way through the soggy underbrush toward the lake. If she gauged correctly, she would soon connect with the path leading to Marley.

After a couple wrong turns, she found the trail. In the distance, around a curve of the lake, the lights of Marley shone bravely through the rain. A single light burned on the roof of the boathouse and another at the end of the dock. Had only six weeks elapsed since Ellie met her death there? The time gone by seemed much longer.

Nina neared the Marley property, and the tall pine and fir trees thinned. Overhead, propelled by a stiff breeze, gray clouds scudded by. She left the path and hiked several yards into the sparse underbrush. Shielded by the bushes, she continued on toward the boathouse and the dock. She hoped the murderer would soon appear and put an end to this ordeal.

Thinking the person might be hiding inside, Nina studied the boathouse. The building was dark, except for the light on the roof, which beamed on the slanted ramp leading from the double doors to the lake. The doors were closed. The windows were opaque with reflected light, concealing anyone who might be on the inside looking out.

Underneath the dock, several canvas-covered boats huddled against the piling. Was the murderer hiding in one?

She crept as close to the boathouse as she dared then ducked behind a large rhododendron. Peering through the wet foliage, she shifted her gaze from the path, to the boathouse, to the dock, and back again.

The minutes crawled by. Nina strained her eyes until a headache threatened. Despite changing her position every few minutes, her calf muscles cramped, and pain spiraled up her spine.

Perhaps the murderer waited for Nina to show herself first. Maybe she must toss out more bait to bring about a conclusion. She straightened to make a move when she saw someone pushing a walker along the path. Who could that be? He—or she—wore an ankle-length coat with a hood that hid the person's face. Then the light from the boathouse shone on the walker, illuminating chrome legs and a basket between the handles.

A pink basket.

Shock rippled through Nina. Only one person at Marley had a walker with a pink basket—Lily Ciliano. What was Lily doing here? Was she crazy? Then she remembered Lily's warning when Nina told the library committee about tonight's plan. "Don't go to the lake alone."

Was Lily here to help Nina? How much help could she be, hampered by her walker? Whatever the reason for Lily's presence, Nina must remove her from harm's way. Plus, the woman could very well ruin her plan.

Before she stepped from behind the bush to reveal herself, she had another thought. What if Lily was Ellie's killer? Could she possibly be? She thought back to what she knew about Lily and Ellie's relationship. Not much. Lily was critical of Ellie and her reliance on Dr. Ravensbarger, but her censure would hardly justify murder.

Did the two have a history that preceded their days at Marley?

No, Lily was not a murderer. She was here tonight because of her misguided concern for Nina. She must be removed and quickly. Nina sprang from her hiding place and scrambled across the grass. "Lily!"

Lily stopped and turned.

Running to the path, Nina closed the gap between them. "What are you doing here?"

Mumbling, Lily hung her head.

Nina reached out a hand. "Come on, let's go home."

Lily raised her head.

In the light from the boathouse, instead of Lily's familiar features, Nina saw a face with evil eyes and a twisted mouth. A shiver snaked down her spine, and she jumped back. *Too late.*

With a mighty roar, the person lifted the walker and struck Nina. The metal legs hit her head and then landed with full force on a shoulder. Nina reeled backward. Pain spiraled down her neck and arm and into her back.

Still holding the walker her attacker lunged again. Nina threw up her hands to ward off the blow. The walker struck her left arm with a heavy thud. A bone cracked like a matchstick, and pain shot through her shoulders and back. Clutching her injured arm, she crumpled to her knees. "Stop, please, stop!"

Another assault met her pleas. Pain traveled along nerve endings to every part of her body. Before Nina could rise to her feet, another blow landed, this time on her head. "Help!" A spray of fireworks flashed before her eyes.

She must have lost consciousness for a while, because her next awareness was of being dragged by the feet across the ground. Bumping over stones and ruts jolted her awake. Where was her captor taking her? Her entire body, particularly her left arm, burned with pain. She wanted to scream but something filled her mouth.

She raised her head enough to glimpse her attacker. The figure now wore what looked like a wet suit. Form-fitting leggings and jacket outlined sturdy legs and a solid torso. A hood still hid the person's features.

Nina's captor dragged her into the lake.

Would she drown? Nina groped under water with her right hand and found a rock. She heaved the rock at the hooded head. The missile bounced harmlessly off the person's shoulder.

He—or she—whirled, eyes blazing behind a diver's mask. "Bitch!"

Water closed over Nina's legs. Her plastic rain suit was no protection against the icy chill. Soon water covered her stomach, her neck, and the back of her head. Water mingled with the rain on her cheeks, causing her to shudder. Her gag was yanked off. "Is t-this how you m-murdered Ellie?" she choked out.

"Ellie was easier," came the terse reply, and then the assailant's rubber-gloved hand covered Nina's face and pushed her into the water.

Holding her breath, Nina lashed out with her right arm and kicked her legs, thankful for all the athletic club workouts that made her strong. With all her might, she struggled to free herself from the hand that kept her face submerged.

Nina's head throbbed, and her lungs were ready to burst. Just then, the hum of a boat's motor drifted across the water. Who would be out on the lake on a night like this?

A commotion broke out above the water's surface. Voices shouted and water splashed.

With a last, desperate effort, she aimed another kick at her captor. The hands gripping her head suddenly fell away. Someone reached into the water, grasped Nina's arms, and pulled her to the surface. She opened her mouth to breathe in air—blessed air.

She vaguely was aware of being pulled into a rowboat. Relief flooded her. Lying on her back in the bow of the boat, she looked up and through watery eyes recognized Wally, wearing a sou'wester rain hat. What was he doing here? He'd come to find Lily. No, her attacker wasn't Lily.

"Does she need CPR?" Joe McGarrity peered over Wally's shoulder.

"N-no, I'm o-okay." Nina's chattering teeth made speech difficult. Plus, the rocking motion of the rowboat hurt her arm.

"Don't let the other one get away." Wally waved toward Joe.

"Not to worry." Joe shook his head. "I whacked him over the head with my oar and tied him to the boat so we can tow him in."

Nina closed her eyes and gave herself up to the motion of the boat gliding through the water. When the boat landed on the shore, Joe and Wally, their arms woven together to make a seat, carried her over the rocks to the sand. Jessica, holding open a blanket, waited to meet them.

"G-Gran, w-what are you doing h-here?" Nina cradled her injured arm, biting her lip against the pain.

Jessica wrapped the blanket around Nina and patted her shoulder. "You didn't really think we would let you confront a murderer all alone, did you? How badly are you hurt?"

"M-my left arm might be b-broken. Otherwise, I'm okay." She winced.

Two other figures dressed in raincoats and hats and holding umbrellas stood nearby.

"W-who are they?" Nina squinted into the darkness.

"Mabel and Selma." Jessica waved to the two women.

Nina groaned. "You all put yourselves in d-danger."

Mabel held up a cell phone. "Ah called nine-one-one, just like y'all said, Joe. The police're on their way."

Nina looked around, the movement again causing pain. "Where, where is—?"

"The guy who tried to drown you?" Wally pointed to a person lying on the ground, curled up like a comma. "Joe beaned him cold, and we towed him in. He's a little woozy but otherwise okay."

"Who is he?" Selma peered at the figure from under her umbrella.

"Don't get too close." Jessica held up a hand. "He's the murderer."

Joe nudged the body with a booted toe.

The person groaned and turned over.

"Let's see who you are, you devil!" Joe yanked off the facemask and shined his flashlight on the person's face.

The group issued a collective gasp.

"It's Dorleen!" Mabel's eyes widened.

Selma frowned. "I thought the murderer would be Dr. Ravensbarger."

"Me, too." Jessica nodded.

"No." Nina shook her head, causing another stab of pain. "This woman is not Dorleen." She scanned the group.

Everyone looked at her, mouths agape.

"Then who?" Wally stuck both hands on his hips.

"Cora." Nina pointed toward her assailant, wincing as pain rippled along her arm. "Cora Wilson."

Chapter Twenty-Five

The following afternoon, her left arm in a sling, Nina sat on the sofa in Jessica's apartment. In addition to her grandmother, Wally, Lily, Joe, Mabel, and Selma were also present. She had to smile. Trust Jessica to make the occasion a party. No sooner had everyone arrived than she served refreshments. The delicious aromas of French roast coffee, Earl Grey tea, and chocolate chip cookies filled the room.

Jessica, who sat next to Nina, adjusted the cushions behind her head. "I still can't believe what happened last night. Such a scheme."

Mabel rolled her eyes at Nina. "Y'all were so smart to figure out the real murderer."

"Tell us again." Selma selected a cookie from the plate on the coffee table.

Taking a deep breath, Nina repeated the report of Dorleen's and Cora Wilson's accident, in which Cora supposedly drowned. "But the drowning victim wasn't Cora. She was Dorleen."

Wally snapped his fingers. "I get the picture. Dorleen told Cora she was gonna be Ellie's heir. So, when Dorleen drowned, Cora decided to take her place and claim the inheritance."

Nina nodded. "The accident happened in the country. The small town coroner didn't question Cora's claim that she was Dorleen and Cora the dead person.

The two resembled one another, which made Cora's impersonation easier."

She plumped up the pillow supporting her broken arm. "When Ellie invited her here the first time, Cora used Dorleen's name to purchase her airline ticket. But when she returned with the plan to murder Ellie, so that she could gain the inheritance, she bought her ticket using her Cora Wilson identity. That way, no one could prove Dorleen was in the area when Ellie died."

"Did anything else about Dorleen make you suspicious?" Finished with her cookie, Selma touched a napkin to her lips.

Nina absently rubbed her broken arm. "The information Stephen's friend uncovered indicated Dorleen's parents died in a freak boating accident, but when Dorleen and I went to lunch, she said they were killed in a plane crash."

"A stupid mistake." Joe folded his arms and shook his head.

Jessica sipped her coffee. "I understand Dorleen was really Cora, and that she murdered Ellie. But what about Roger? She couldn't have killed him because she was with us when he fell."

Nina pressed her lips together. "My guess is, he somehow found out about the identity switch and blackmailed her. Knowing she had to get rid of him, she drugged his drinks at the falls."

Mabel nodded. "Then she hid his camera and made him think he lost it."

"She encouraged him to go back to the falls to look for the camera." Wally's eyebrows peaked.

Joe leaned forward and propped his elbows on his knees. "She didn't actually murder him but contributed to his death."

"She took a big gamble that paid off." With her right arm, Nina propped herself up far enough to reach her teacup. "But whether her actions can be proven remains to be seen."

Selma reached for another cookie. "The real Dorleen is the one I feel sorry for. She never inherited Ellie's money. What will happen to the money now?"

Wondering about the money also, Nina perked up her ears for an answer.

"Roger's share goes to his favorite ex-wife." Jessica picked up the teapot and refilled her cup. "According to Ellie's lawyer, Dorleen's bequest will now be divided among Ellie's charities."

"Nina, you're so smart to have figured out Cora's plot." Lily beamed at Nina.

"Still, I was completely fooled when I thought you were the person on the path." Nina shivered at the memory. "I could have sworn the walker with the pink basket was yours."

Lily's smile faded to a frown. "The nerve of that Cora, masquerading as me."

Nina nodded, sharing Lily's indignation. "She knew how concerned I was about leaving Ellie the night of her death. She figured I'd feel the same way about you and approach you to go home. Her plan worked."

"She was clever, all right." Wally scooted close to Lily and put an arm around her shoulder. "She turned that walker into a lethal weapon by filling the legs with lead shot."

"She's a vicious person." Mabel hugged her arms.

"Nina almost ended up like Ellie." Jessica patted Nina's knee.

Appreciation filled Nina as she gazed around the group. "But for all of you, I would have."

"We almost bumbled our rescue." Lily leaned against Wally's shoulder.

"How?" Nina straightened. "What exactly was your plan?"

With thumb and forefinger, Lily adjusted her eyeglasses. "I was stationed at Marley, near the back door, watching to see if anyone took that route to the lake."

"Mabel, Selma, and I were outside the front door." Jessica leaned forward and clasped her hands.

"Right." Mabel nodded. "We saw y'all's car, Nina. We expected you to pull into the parking lot, and when you drove past, we were mystified. We hurried to the road in time to see your car head around the lake, so we set off in that direction."

"Joe and I covered the lake side in my boat." Wally waved a hand toward Joe. "Ready to storm the shore if you needed help. We rowed rather than use the motor, so's not to make much noise."

"We went far enough out so we wouldn't be seen from shore." Joe leaned forward.

Wally frowned and shook his head. "Trouble was, we couldn't see the shore, either."

Joe nodded. "By the time we rowed to where we could see, you and Dorleen, er, Cora, were already in the water. Then, we cranked the motor, but the darn thing wouldn't start." He made a fist and pounded his palm.

"I told ya to test the motor beforehand." Lily pursed her lips.

"Yeah, shoulda listened." Wally patted Lily's arm.

"But we finally got the motor started and rescued you, Nina."

"Mabel, Selma, and I never saw where your car ended up." Jessica picked up the teapot and refilled Nina's cup. "We finally turned around and headed back to the boathouse. By the time we arrived, you and Cora were already in the water."

"Where do you suppose she put on that disguise?" Selma looked at the others. "Certainly not in her apartment."

"I never saw her leave by the back door." Lily shook her head. "She must've started out from the shed at the garden. She could've hidden the walker and her wet suit there beforehand. I still can't believe her nerve, pretending to be me." She pushed out her lower lip and folded her arms.

Nina sipped her tea, savoring the Earl Grey's fruity flavor. "But, Lily, if you had seen her, how would you have let the others know?"

"We had our cell phones." Lily pulled hers from a jacket pocket and held it up.

"The phones were Joe's idea." Jessica beamed at Joe.

Sighing, Lily shook her head. "But when I tried to call Mabel, to tell her I hadn't seen anybody, I reached her voicemail."

"Ah was tryin' to call Joe." Mabel ducked her head. "I wanted to tell him we'd lost sight of Nina. But ah must have memorized the number wrong, because ah got Tonio's Pizza instead."

"Well, I am so grateful for all of you." Warmth filled Nina as she swept her gaze around the room.

Smiling, Jessica gave Nina a hug. "We're thankful

for you, dear, for persevering and discovering the truth about Ellie's death."

"Yay, Nina!" Lily made a fist and pumped the air.

"Hurray for Nina!" The others chimed in.

Later, after everyone left, the doorbell rang.

Jessica rose to answer the summons. "I bet that's someone else inquiring about you."

A moment later, Nina heard the door open.

"Why, yes, she's here." Jessica's voice rang out. "Come on in."

Nina settled back against the sofa cushions, expecting to see one of her grandmother's friends, or perhaps the policeman who took her statement last night. When she saw Stephen follow Jessica into the living room, she felt her heart skip a beat.

"Look who's here." Jessica stood aside and gestured toward Stephen.

Stephen strode to the sofa, propped his hands on his hips, and slowly shook his head. "The minute I let you out of my sight, you get into trouble."

His teasing tone eased her tension. Still, his arrival brought tears to her eyes. She'd missed him so much.

Stephen pulled a chair close to the sofa and sat. Taking out his handkerchief, he dabbed at the tears. "Don't cry, honey. How are you feeling? Are you okay?"

"Still a bit shaken, but I'll recover." Nina mustered a smile. "I didn't expect to see you today. I suppose you heard last night's events on your scanner."

"No, I wasn't tuned in last night." He tucked away the handkerchief. "I didn't find out what happened here until this morning."

"Oh, right—you were at the Home Show. How was

the event?"

He lowered his gaze. "I didn't go."

"Why not?"

"I just didn't feel like attending." He shrugged and looked up again.

Nina noticed Jessica edging from the room. "Gran—"

"I just remembered I have laundry to put in the dryer." Jessica waved over her shoulder and disappeared.

Nina turned back to Stephen. "I'm sorry if what happened between us ruined the occasion."

"Not your fault. I could've gone on my own." He frowned and leaned close. "But why didn't you tell me the truth? You said you had a routine meeting with your library committee, and now I learn you set out to trap Ellie's murderer."

Nina struggled with guilt over not taking him into her confidence. "I didn't tell you because I knew you'd try to talk me out of my plan." She gave him a sideways look. "Wouldn't you?"

He straightened, and his eyes widened. "Huh! Wouldn't anybody in his right mind?"

She raised a hand. "Okay, but after some tense moments, everything turned out just fine. We found Ellie's murderer. Dorleen's partner, Cora Wilson, impersonated her so she could claim Dorleen's inheritance."

Stephen nodded. "I saw Joe on the way here, and he filled me in. What a story. He said you knew Dorleen was really Cora. How'd you figure out that fact?"

Nina explained the clues she discovered in the

information his friend sent and how they related to her suspicions.

"You're a darn good detective." Stephen grinned.

"Thanks." His praise warmed her heart.

He held up a forefinger. "But if you ever get involved in anything like this again, don't shut me out. I want to know what you're up to so I can help."

"I thought we were having a time-out in our relationship."

He frowned and shook his head. "The moment you walked out of the restaurant, I realized my mistake. But my pride wouldn't let me go after you. I hated every minute we were apart."

"Me, too." Memories of the loneliness she experienced without him filled her. She wished her pride hadn't kept her from calling.

Stephen took her hand. "I was wrong to push you to see Dr. Young. You were right—if you love someone, you accept them the way they are. But after Carly died, I fell apart, and a friend suggested I see a counselor. Not Becky, but a guy my friend knew. I took his advice and talking to a professional really helped."

Surprise filled her. "I never knew you saw a doctor. Why didn't you tell me?"

"I don't know." He shrugged. "I should've. But look, forget about Dr. Young."

Nina shook her head. "No, I won't forget."

His eyebrows peaked. "What do you mean?"

"You were right to encourage me. I've already seen her once, and I have a second appointment next Tuesday."

"No kidding?" His jaw dropped. "What made you change your mind? You've always been so against counseling."

"I know, but I went to see her anyway." The entire story behind the appointment could wait until another time. "I discovered I liked talking with her. She says she can help me with my nightmares."

Stephen nodded. "I'm confident she can. Remember, though, you don't have to consult her to please me."

"I'm not. I made the decision." Although glad the issue was resolved, she still worried about their relationship. "We have other differences too, Stephen. I'm not into house remodeling and decorating. I don't know if I ever can be."

"We'll hire a decorator. Differences are okay. If we were totally alike, we'd be boring. We have plenty of interests to share, not to mention great sex."

He flashed a teasing grin. After glancing around to make sure Jessica hadn't returned to overhear his remark, Nina laughed and batted her eyelashes. "Not to mention."

His eyes dark and serious, he studied her for a long moment. "I love you, Nina."

His words set her heart to pounding. "I love you, too, Stephen."

Stephen sat beside her on the sofa. He put his arms around her and pulled her close. Tipping up her chin, he closed his lips over hers in a warm and tender kiss. Happiness filled Nina, chasing away the loneliness she experienced during their separation. They were together again and had declared their love for one another. At this moment, what more could she ask for?

Chapter Twenty-Six

Two weeks later, on a Sunday afternoon, Nina stood in the middle of Marley Manor's new library and scanned the room. Everything was ready for the official opening, scheduled to begin at 1:00 p.m. All the books and magazines sat on the shelves, and the computer catalog was up and running. Comfortable chairs, tables, and reading lamps invited patrons to linger and enjoy the new facility. Bouquets of flowers sent by well-wishers added sweet fragrance and spots of bright color.

Jessica arrived carrying two foil-covered plates. "Where would you like me to put these cookies, dear?"

"Anywhere on the table." Nina nodded toward the lace cloth-covered table in middle of the room, with silver tea and coffee services at either end.

Jessica set down the plates and removed the foil.

Nina inhaled the nutty aroma that filled the air. "Mmmm, your pecan cookies smell wonderful."

"Fresh from the oven. But they look awfully lonely here all by themselves." She swept an arm toward the table. "Where are the rest of the refreshments?"

"Mabel and Selma are each bringing something, and so is Harriet Hambly."

"I figured Harriet would." Jessica straightened a stack of napkins.

"The kitchen is catering the rest. I'm sure we'll

have enough, but I need to check with the chef." Nina took a step toward the door.

Jessica propped her hands on her hips and gazed around the room. "What can I do while you're gone?"

"See if the flowers need additional water. Some of the bouquets arrived yesterday and need refreshing." She gestured toward the vases of flowers stationed around the room.

"Will do."

Before leaving, Nina went to the closet and took a wrapped package from her tote.

"What's that?" Jessica pointed toward the package.

"A book for Harriet, one that Ellie borrowed and never returned."

"Can you manage with your cast?"

"I'll be fine, thanks. If I had to break an arm, I'm glad it was my left instead of my right." Carrying the book under her right arm, Nina headed down the hall to Harriet's apartment.

Harriet answered the door dressed in an ankle-length plaid skirt, a black velveteen jacket, and a white blouse with a ruffled collar.

"Wow, aren't you fancy." Nina grinned and widened her eyes.

Harriet smiled. "I'll take that as a compliment. Did you come for my crumb cake? I'm just about ready to deliver the treat."

"I'm here on another matter. May I come in for a minute?" Nina looked over Harriet's shoulder toward the apartment's interior.

"Sure." Harriet stepped back and opened the door.

Once inside, Nina gazed around. All the walls were bare and the furniture moved to one side. Several large boxes with a moving company's logo stood in the middle of the floor. "Looks like you're all ready to go. When are you leaving?"

"The movers come tomorrow. I'm flying out the following day. What do you have there? Something for me?" Harriet gestured toward the package Nina held.

"This is for you, from Ellie." Nina held out the wrapped book.

Harriet stepped back and tilted her head. "Jessica already gave me the necklace from Ellie."

"I don't know what this is. The package was wrapped and addressed to you. We found it when we sorted through the last of her belongings." Nina held her breath, hoping Harriet would not detect her lie.

Harriet took the package and tore off the wrapping. "I can't imagine…" Her eyes widened. "Omigosh. Ellie's old school annual." Then she sobered and looked at Nina. "I suppose you're wondering why she wanted me to have this book."

Nina shrugged and kept her expression neutral. "So you would have something besides the necklace?"

Harriet's lips settled into a smile. "Yes, another memento. Thanks, Nina."

Relieved to have resolved that problem, Nina left Harriet's apartment and went downstairs to the kitchen. She had just finished talking to the chef about the refreshments when Kimmie arrived.

A lanky, teenaged boy accompanied her.

"Hello, Kimmie." Nina turned to her companion. "You must be Davey."

"Uh, yeah. But—" The boy's brow wrinkled, and he looked at Kimmie.

"This is Miss Foster, Davey." With a smile,

Kimmie gestured toward Nina. "She's the librarian at Seaview."

"Oh, right." Davey's lips broke into a grin. "Pleased to meetcha." He extended a hand.

As she accepted his handshake, Nina studied him. His blond hair showed dark brown roots, and his left ear sported a gold stud earring. He wore a navy blue parka over a white T-shirt, baggy black pants, and scuffed athletic shoes. His pleasant, youthful face was not the fierce or sullen countenance she associated with a criminal. "I'm glad to meet you, too, Davey. For a long time, you were our mystery man."

He shrugged. "Sorry, Ms. Foster, but I had to find the guy that beat up that woman."

"Davey did find him." Kimmie beamed and patted his shoulder.

"So I understand." Nina kept her gaze on Davey. "But I wouldn't mind hearing the story from you."

Davey looked toward Kimmie and raised his eyebrows.

Kimmie nodded. "Miss Foster's a friend."

Nina gestured toward the door. "Let's find a place to sit." She led the way to the reception area. When they settled into chairs tucked in a corner, she turned to Davey. "You said you found the man. What happened then?"

Davey nodded. "He was arrested on another charge and finally confessed to more crimes, including the one I was accused of."

"I'm glad the matter is straightened out. I also heard you talked to the police about seeing Cora Wilson in the boathouse the night Ellie died." The pieces of the puzzle came together, just as she'd predicted.

Davey leaned forward and clasped his hands. "I was in the rowboat waiting for Kimmie when someone came in wearing a long coat with a hood. I knew it wasn't Kimmie, a course, so I ducked down and kept quiet. When I looked again, I saw the person peel off the coat. It was a woman, and she wore a wet suit."

Nina leaned forward. "You're sure the woman was Cora?"

"Oh, yeah. I got a clear view of her face from the light outside the window. I already picked her out of a lineup."

Nina shifted her broken arm to a more comfortable position on her lap. "What happened then?"

He shrugged. "She stuffed her coat in a plastic bag and left."

"What did you do?"

"I got the hell, er, I left, too. I figured if she came back, she might discover me 'n Kimmie. I came up here to the kitchen. Chef let me wait for Kimmie in his office."

"Weren't you curious about what the person might be up to?"

"Well, yeah." He waved a hand. "But, hey, I had my own problems."

Nina nodded. "So, you didn't actually see Cora attack Ellie?"

Davey ran his fingers through his hair. "No, I didn't."

"What you did see at least puts Cora at the scene." Too bad, though, that he hadn't witnessed the crime.

Kimmie frowned. "Cora drowned Ellie? Then what did she do?"

Nina sat back and folded her arms, resting her cast

on top. "I think she took a boat from underneath the dock and rowed across the lake. She set the boat adrift and escaped into the woods. A drifting boat was found the day Ellie's body was discovered, but no one thought the two events might be connected."

"I hope she goes to prison." Kimmie twisted her fingers together. "I miss Ellie really bad."

Nina pointed toward Kimmie's wrist. "I see you're wearing the jewelry she gave you. I'm glad you have something to remember her by."

Kimmie held up an arm with the bee bracelet and then pushed back her shaggy hair to reveal the matching bee earrings. "Me, too. Thanks again for giving me the earring I lost, Ms. Foster."

"I didn't see any reason the police needed the jewelry." She turned again to Davey. "Are you with your parents now?"

"Naw, I'm in a foster home. Me 'n my parents don't get along. But I'm going back to school as soon as possible, and I'm hoping to get a job here, like Kimmie." He turned to her and smiled.

"Great." Nina nodded. "I look forward to seeing you both in the dining room when I come for dinner."

Nina watched them leave and then returned to the library. Her talk with Kimmie and Davey answered her questions about Davey's involvement. His testimony at Cora's trial would place her at the scene of the crime. Other evidence was recovered, too, now the police finally launched an investigation. Stephen learned from his source that they found traces of blood soaked into the wood around a nail underneath the dock. More spots were found in the drifting rowboat. The DNA matched that of Cora Wilson. Apparently, she cut herself on the nail when untying the rowboat to use for her getaway.

The bit of rubber Nina found in the lake proved to be from Cora's facemask. Nina's testimony would reveal what Cora said during their struggle. Surely, all the evidence would be enough to convict her of Ellie's murder. Whether or not she would be implicated in Roger's death remained to be seen.

Cora's arrest created new interest in the accident she and Dorleen had in Tennessee, and the case was reopened. Hopefully, the investigation would lead to the truth about Dorleen Longman's death.

When Nina reached the library, she saw the party was underway. Jessica poured tea at one end of the refreshment table while Selma served coffee at the other. Mabel and Lily presided over the punch bowl. Wally had Nigel in tow. Both wore red bow ties. Nigel accepted pats on the head and tidbits from the buffet.

Nina circulated the room, explaining the arrangement of the books and the computer catalog and checkout system. She spotted Lorna hobbling along on her cane and approached her. "Lorna, nice to see you. You must be feeling better."

Lorna nodded. "I am. But I feel terrible about what happened to you."

"I appreciate your concern, but I'm fine now. Well, except for my arm." She fingered the sling holding her cast.

"You told me not to tell anyone about your plans that night, but I might have slipped and the information was passed on to Dorleen. I mean, what's-her-name." She ducked her head.

Nina patted her shoulder. "Her name is Cora Wilson. But, don't worry. Everything turned out just fine...By the way, are you still seeing Dr. Ravensbarger?"

Lorna pursed her lips, creating a new set of wrinkles. "Not on your life. I'm fed up with him. I told my granddaughter about all his tests, and she said I ought to report him, because he might cheat Medicare."

Hearing Lorna ended her association with the doctor relieved Nina. "Ellie's records indicated he gave her a lot of tests, too. I've already reported the information."

"You have? Well, then, I will, too."

"If you learn he does the same with any of your friends, encourage them to file a complaint. Let's give investigators as much evidence as possible."

"Good idea." Lorna's eyes sparkled.

Nina accompanied Lorna to the buffet table, turning her over to Mabel and Lily. She continued greeting the guests, listening to their comments and answering questions. Then she spotted Stephen, who just arrived. They were spending the weekend together, as usual, but parted this morning while he stopped at the newspaper office and she came to Marley.

Catching her eye, he smiled and strode across the room.

He looked as handsome as ever in his navy slacks and light blue sports shirt, with the ever-present notebook and pen tucked in the breast pocket. Nina's heartbeat quickened.

When he reached her side, he put an arm around her shoulder. "How's the party?"

"Great. Everyone's impressed with the new library and having a good time."

"I see Joe is here."

Nina followed his nod to the buffet table where Joe and Wally sampled the hors d'oeuvres. "Joe helped set up the folding tables yesterday. He plans to move in."

Stephen's eyes widened. "With Jessica?"

Nina laughed. "No, not yet, anyway. He'll take over Harriet's apartment."

His eyebrows peaked. "How do you feel about his living here?"

"I'm glad for Gran, and for them both. I hope they'll be happy together."

"Me, too." He gave her shoulder a squeeze.

"Oh, I see Director Marshall. He asked to say a few words today." Nina waved to Will Marshall, a distinguished-looking man in his fifties, dressed in a gray suit and a red tie. She introduced him to Stephen and then, after calling everyone to attention, presented him to the others.

Will gave a short speech, thanking Nina and the committee for all their hard work. "I also have a surprise announcement." A smile lit his face. "Ellie left a generous bequest to Marley, to be used at our discretion. I'm sure she would want at least some of the money to be spent here." He gestured toward the surroundings. "The board of directors and I have granted the library a yearly stipend, to be used however you so desire."

Everyone clapped and cheered.

When the director finished speaking, Joe McGarrity stepped forward. "I have something to thank Ellie for, too. If not for her, I wouldn't have met all of you, including a very special lady." He turned toward Jessica and raised his punch glass. "Here's to Ellie. May she rest in peace."

"To Ellie!" chorused the crowd.

Stephen settled an arm around Nina's waist, drew her close, and whispered in her ear, "I'll add, here's to us."

"Yes, to us." Nina leaned her head against his shoulder, filled with love for this wonderful man who added so much to her life. Although the future still held challenges, today's happiness was all that mattered, and she vowed to enjoy each moment.

A word about the author...

A resident of the Pacific Northwest, Linda Hope Lee writes contemporary romance, romantic suspense, and mystery novels. She also enjoys watercolor painting, photography, collecting children's books and anything to do with wire-haired fox terriers.

Other Titles by the Author
Dark Memories
Finding Sara
Loving Rose
Marrying Molly
Murder Between the Pages, a Nina Foster Mystery
Under Gemini

Thank you for purchasing
this publication of The Wild Rose Press, Inc.

For questions or more information
contact us at
info@thewildrosepress.com.

The Wild Rose Press, Inc.
www.thewildrosepress.com